Old Clayborne Van Fleet could feel her gathering . . . somewhere . . .

Why couldn't she be still? He'd done everything possible. Could she not wait for him to die? It wouldn't be such a long wait after all.

He walked toward the french doors to close the drapes against winter drafts.

But the french doors flew open before he reached them.

Bludgeoning cold swirled into the room, carrying tiny snow crystals to sting him. And Clayborne Van Fleet knew that she was done with waiting.

Nothing and no one to hear the old man's screams but an empty house and two small red orbs that gleamed in the madness of swirling white on the balcony. . . .

Fawcett Crest Books
by Marlys Millhiser:

MICHAEL'S WIFE

NELLA WAITS

Nella Waits

by

Marlys Millhiser

A FAWCETT CREST BOOK

Fawcett Publications, Inc., Greenwich, Conn.

NELLA WAITS

THIS BOOK CONTAINS THE COMPLETE TEXT OF THE
ORIGINAL HARDCOVER EDITION

A Fawcett Crest Book reprinted by arrangement with G. P.
Putnam's Sons

Library of Congress Catalog Card Number: 74–79662

Alternate Selection of the Doubleday Bargain Book Club

Printed in the United States of America

First printing: December 1975

1 2 3 4 5 6 7 8 9 10

To Jane Fitz-Randolph

Acknowledgments

Donna and Ben Balsley for the Peruvian background. Arland, Bob and Ronald Enabnit for matters agricultural. Marcia Magill for editorial endurance. My parents and countless Iowans who aided in refreshing my memory of my native state.

Prologue

C layborne Van Fleet hunched at the massive desk and splashed bourbon into the bottom of a glass with a hand that could no longer still its trembling. The thick folded blanket around his shoulders slipped and he drew it back, then rearranged the front of his woolen robe to hold it together at the neck.

He sipped the liquor neat, an ounce of warmth before bed each night, to give him two ounces of sleep and a measure of freedom from description.

The fire in the grate played tricks with the shadows. The hiss and sputter of the overworked heating system made at least a small muted opening in the silence.

He checked again the list of duties for the housekeeper and her son and set it aside. Listening to grainy snow whirl against frostless panes, watching amber liquid glow in the lamplight, he wiggled his feet out of his shoes and placed them against the electric heater under the desk.

It was then that he sensed the stirring in the house. Felt the cold dread, never far away, permeate the blanket to wrap itself around his heart.

She'd been still for a month. Now what?

Could be just the imaginings of his mind. But he drained the bourbon quickly, holding the last drop on his tongue as if for comfort. Wiping the glass with the cloth on the tray, he turned it upside down as he had found it and reached for the cane that stood against the desk. In his haste he knocked it to the floor. He stretched sore joints to reach it, leaning over the arm of the chair. He used the curved end of the cane to jerk the cord of the heater from its socket in the floor, switched off the desk lamp. . . . If he could get to sleep before . . .

Clutching the blanket around him and carrying his shoes with the same hand, he hobbled to the door and into

7

the hall, where he automatically turned the thermostat back to normal. No furnace, no matter how large, could go on working that hard day and night.

Clayborne paused halfway up the circular staircase, remembering the fire in the library. Oh, well, let her see to it if there was trouble. She certainly wouldn't allow the house to burn, not now. He paused again at the head of the stairs, feeling the exertion of quickened efforts.

Only darkness at the other end of the upstairs hall. No glow from the tiny cracks around the locked door. Even the doves were silent tonight. But he could feel her gathering . . . somewhere . . .

"I've done all I can for the boy!" he shouted into the emptiness of the hall.

Why couldn't she be still? He'd done everything possible. Couldn't she wait for him to die? It couldn't be such a long wait after all.

He watched his stockinged feet and the cane move across the floor as he walked toward the French doors to close the drapes against winter drafts. That's all he saw now, floors. As age had bent his spine, he'd lost track of ceilings altogether.

But the French doors flew open before he reached them.

Bludgeoning cold swirled into the room, carrying tiny snow crystals to sting him. And Clayborne Van Fleet knew that she was done with waiting.

Nothing and no one to hear the old man's screams but an empty house and two small red orbs that gleamed in the madness of swirling white on the balcony. . . .

Nella Waits

1

*B*lack leafless branches curled and intertwined past second-story windows and double chimneys, forming only a spidery latticework in front of the house. The giant elms, meant to shield it from the highway, were dead.

A touch of chill January in the August sun.

Lynnette could only stare, her forehead and nose pressed against the bus' cool window.

Acres of cornfield surrounded the Van Fleet house. The fringe of ocean-gray-green tassles rippled first one way and then the other. Cornstalks rose so tall they dwarfed the fence posts, but even they could not hide the grotesque scene.

That's all that place needs, dead trees.

Old Clayborne had been dead for three years. Had they found his heir or did the Van Fleet house still stand empty? She wondered as the bus left the highway for the road to Roggins.

Even rows of corn had been her view for miles, made her vision blurry and head dizzy as they raced past with hypnotic frenzy. Lynnette fixed her eyes on the back of the empty seat in front of her. No matter how hard she pressed her feet against the floor, the gray towers of the Roggins, Iowa, Co-Op grain elevator drew closer. *I don't want to come back, Joey*, she whispered.

Elaine's farmhouse sat shabby and sullen in the heat. Her sister's car and the pickup were gone. The family would have gathered at the home farm now, around their mother.

Before she could look away . . . the tiny frame church swept by . . . where she and Joey had been married four years ago. He'd promised to get her out of Roggins. He had kept his promise.

They passed the cemetery where she'd buried Joey two years later . . . where they would bury her father tomorrow. A wrought-iron sign, arching over the entrance, announced its purpose in scrolly black letters . . . as if there could be any doubt.

Swinging right onto Main Street, the bus roared to a stop in front of Torgeson's filling station.

Why does the bus stop in Roggins? she wondered. *Nobody else does.*

It stopped just long enough to discharge Lynnette and her suitcases.

She stood on the humped sidewalk and stared dumbly at a weed growing through one of the cracks in the concrete.

Thick heat pressed in on her skin, forced her clothes and hair hard against her body. The stench of poisonous fumes from the bus scoured the mucous lining of her nose until her eyes watered.

It's only till after the funeral. She sat on a suitcase. It burned her legs.

Not one car parked in front of a store, not one person walking the blistering sidewalks. Roggins lay hushed under a damp malign heat that coaxed vegetation to steal in from the countryside, to push up through fissures between sidewalk and empty boarded store building, to tangle across vacant lots that dotted Main Street like missing teeth in an aging smile.

The inside of her knees were wet and Lynnette stretched out her legs. A fly with scratchy feet crawled on her thigh.

A deep rolling belch sounded behind her, rather like an imitation of a sick machine gun, startling in the hush that smothered Main Street. She turned to see Chris Gunderson shuffle across the street to his house.

Every little town had a Chris Gunderson. Roggins had several. He carried a narrow paper sack lovingly in the crook of his arm. A little something to keep him company until the pool hall opened. Unshaven, dusty, he wore dark green work clothes with a rumpled billed cap to match, his shirt long sleeved, the same uniform he wore year round. Lynnette had never seen Chris Gunderson work at anything.

A child ran out of the front door as he opened it and he lifted the sack to protect its contents. The young Gunderson paused to stare at her with pale Nordic eyes, a hall-mark of Roggins, and then turned back to search the weeds of the vacant lot next to his house.

The storefront on the other side of the vacant lot shielded the viewing parlor used by Minturn mortuaries servicing Roggins.

Joey lay in a coffin there the last time she was home, or what had been Joey . . . once fluffy black hair plastered to his head, heavy makeup that couldn't cover the damage to his face . . . the warped flooring had seemed to heave under her feet.

Mercifully a Cadillac moved up Main Street, heat lines wavering above the hood. It made a U-turn and stopped next to her suitcases. She picked them up, stuffed them into the backseat and crawled in beside her brother. If he'd met the bus in Minturn, where he had his law practice, he would have opened the door for her and put her luggage in the car himself.

Harold patted her shoulder with a ringed manicured hand. "Glad to see you home, little sister. Been a long time."

Lynnette struggled for an answer. The best she could manage was a choked, "How's Bertha?"

"Mother's holding up like a rock. The bad time will be after the funeral when everyone goes home." Harold turned up the air-conditioning and the car moved forward one block to a square concrete pier that stood in the center of the broad street and supported a stop sign. The Cadillac, the only moving thing for miles, came dutifully to a stop.

The faded wooden war memorial to her left. To her right at the end of the next block, her Aunt Vera's library. Lynnette looked away to her lap, where whitening fingers clutched her purse. *I hate this town!*

The second block of Main Street (there were only two) and directly in front of her now . . . the white ginger-bread house in perfect repair and paint . . . shaded lawn . . . birdbaths . . . picket fence . . . The clasp of her purse dug into her hand. The Stewarts' house sat in quiet cool respectability, a road's width apart from Roggins.

Harold leaned forward to stare at it. "I suppose you

still think of Joey sometimes."

"Sometimes!"

"Well, it's been two years, Lynn." The Cadillac turned back the way she'd come but on a graveled road, toward home and the Van Fleet house. "You should've gotten over it by now."

Harold drove slowly, one elbow resting on the armrest so that his hand could knead his chin, as if he were meditating some important decision. His stomach overflowed above his belt and Lynnette wondered if the steering wheel made calluses on it or if his shirts wore through where the wheel abraded them.

Harold was twenty years older than she, a college junior when she was born.

"Yup, glad to see you home," he repeated, his eyes skidding toward her behind dark-rimmed glasses as if he waited for a particular answer to this nonquestion.

The proper answer would have been that she was glad to be home. But she wasn't. "Why?"

"You're about all that Mom has left, Lynn," he said quietly.

"What do you mean? She has the family and she's related to half of Roggins. . . ."

"But Lynn, don't you see? Elaine and Leroy have each other and the kids. Margaret and I live in Minturn . . . and Mom would never leave Roggins. Besides, she doesn't get along well with Margaret. Aunt Vera is old and has to stay near the library."

But I'm the spinster-widow. The perfect answer to who's going to stay home on the farm and take care of Bertha. Harold, I'm only twenty-four . . . you can't bury me in Roggins.

"Mom and Dad would have taken you in after Joey died. But you had to go trucking back to Denver all by yourself. We've been worried about you clear out there. You should be back here." When she didn't comment, the flush deepened on his puffy face as it often did when things didn't go as he'd planned. Harold was a tidy planner.

The roof of the one-room schoolhouse showed above the cornstalks at the edge of the Olson farm. The Van

13

Fleet house loomed ahead on its hill at the end of the road. "Have they found Jay Van Fleet?"

"They think they might have this time, in Peru." Harold sounded impatient with the change of subject. "They found a man injured after that earthquake. He's in a hospital in Lima. The Benninghoffs are getting the house ready again but they won't have the electricity hooked up this time until they know this isn't another false lead."

"It would be odd to find out you'd inherited a fortune three years ago and didn't even know it." Jay Van Fleet had been the target of an exhaustive search.

Harold turned into the rutted lane of the Olson farm, flanked on either side by cornfields and then by the long fenced house yard. "Lynn . . ."

"Is the Van Fleet house still supposed to be haunted?"

"Of course. The Benninghoffs won't go near the main house at night." There was the sound of a sneer in his voice.

The lane circled behind the house and entered a farmyard filled with cars and pickup trucks. Harold drove up beside the gate.

"Well?"

She opened the door. "Well what?"

He snorted, the flush mottling. "*Are* you going to move back here?"

Lynnette looked toward the square box of a house where some old friends of her father's stood by the back door. Dressed in their Sunday striped overalls, some with suit jackets and all wearing hats, they looked hot and ill at ease as they shifted from one foot to another, kicked at the dirt with a toe or spit at the grass.

"Lynn?"

Her answer was to get out of the car and slam the door.

The men stopped talking as she came through the gate. They nodded in unison. Lynnette nodded back. When the screen door flapped closed behind her, she heard one of them whisper, " 'Bout time she got here."

She stood in the enclosed back porch and took a deep breath. Dishes covered the top of the chest freezer, the washing machine and the old metal sink. A huge mixing bowl full of weeping red jello afloat with browning ba-

nana slices . . . loaves of homemade bread . . . cakes
. . . pies . . . meat loaves. Some of the dishes were empty
and washed, all bore strips of adhesive tape with the name
of the owner so they could be returned when "it" was
over.

The smell of all that food in the airless room made
Lynnette swallow hard. The sounds of voices, occasional
laughter and the clink of dishes—the ritual gorging ses-
sion observed for funerals. . . .

Margaret, Harold's wife, bustled from the kitchen
carrying a cooked ham on a platter. "Why, Lynn, how
are you, dear? Mom will be so glad to have you home."
Her sister-in-law flashed her big teeth and found a space
on the freezer for the platter. She wiped her hands on her
organdy apron and kissed Lynnette's cheek. "My, but
you've gotten a tan this summer. Be careful, Lynn.
Makes the skin dry up."

Margaret's heavy perfume added one more unwelcome
smell to the room.

Harold grunted in with her suitcases and Lynnette
scurried into the kitchen but she heard Margaret's question, "Did you talk to her?"

"Tried to. Talking to her's like talking to a fence post."

That night Lynnette returned to Main Street, in the
backseat of Harold's Cadillac. He and Margaret sat in
front waiting for Bertha. Margaret filed her fingernails in
the dark. Harold stared at the mortuary, running his hand
over the bald spot on his head.

Night birds and crickets called, hushed and far away.
Fireflies darted among the dark fernlike weeds in the
vacant lot next to the mortuary.

A man laughed in the pool hall down the street.

Lynnette hadn't wanted to "view" her father, had
wanted to remember the live Olaf, even if he had been
senile and silly, the gentle old man whose blank eyes could
grow tender over a kitten or a grandchild. . . .

More laughter and a catcall from the pool hall. Chris
Gunderson spilled out onto the sidewalk in a puddle of
smoke-yellow light, picked himself up and wove past
them to his house.

The screen door of the mortuary squeaked and her mother stood on the sidewalk under the streetlight talking to Aunt Vera, her father's sister.

". . . 'course she will." Bertha sounded exhausted. She was geared more for expending energy than emotion. "Ain't no sense in her going back there when she's got a perfectly good home here." Her white hair glowed under the spider web of "invisible" hairnet in the lamplight.

"Do you think there might be a man in Denver?"

"Huh! What man would want a skinny old brown thing like her? And secondhand at that. She'll stay here where she belongs."

Harold dropped them off at the farmhouse and Bertha disappeared into the ground-floor bedroom. After fifty-two years of marriage, she would sleep alone tonight.

Lynnette dragged herself up the stairs. Heat filtered down from the attic and up through the floor to hover stagnant, choking, thick with the smell of dust, old wallpaper and stale urine. She imagined she could still see the shadowy ghost of the dark-blue metal chamber pot that had sat in the hall for so many years. Until Bertha had relented and had a bathroom installed in the pantry.

She sat on the edge of the bed and tried to will her weary mind to action. What was she to do? She had nothing left in Denver but her clothes and a month's rent due on her apartment. *And a few happy memories?*

Finally Lynnette fell back onto her lumpy mattress and slept without covers in the airless heat.

Joey and her father visited her dreams and old Clayborne Van Fleet. . . .

She awoke after midnight, tousled and sticky wet, to stand by the window, trying to breathe air in through the screen. The leaves on the box-elder tree hung limp in the moonlight.

Out of a habit she'd acquired in childhood, Lynnette stared up the hill to the Van Fleet mansion. Where no one cared to venture after dark. So deserted that even the electricity wasn't connected.

There was a light in a room on the second floor.

2

*A*ncient evergreens, grown fat with time and rich Iowa soil, towered above the cemetery, lower branches spreading across older graves, tilting upright monuments and cutting off sunlight to thin dank grass.

If Roggins was deteriorating, its cemetery was growing.

The limousine turned right at the Van Fleet vault and stopped behind the hearse. Lynnette looked back at the vault, her thoughts on the light in the empty mansion on the hill and the elusive heir, Jay Van Fleet.

Olaf Olson took his place next to his parents. Reverend Birmingham performed the graveside service quickly to spare them from the heat. Then everyone gathered around Bertha.

Lynnette slipped across the road to Joey's grave. . . .

A thorny rosebush had been planted on one side of the headstone. A robin swooped to land, saw her and flew off, its feet barely touching the gray marble.

He's not here. He never was here. Joey is nowhere.

Still she waited . . . for some feeling of grief . . . regret . . . anything. But all she felt was the hot sun and the presence of the woman who came to stand beside her.

"You had to take him away." Rachael Stewart rubbed one white-gloved hand over the other, standing lovely and petite beside the grave of her only child. She'd played the organ at Olaf's funeral.

Lynnette looked into eyes the color and shape of Joey's. "He took me away, Mrs. Stewart."

"And now you both are back. . . ."

"I don't plan to stay."

"I think I'm glad to hear that . . . *Mrs*. Stewart."

All afternoon Lynnette helped Margaret carry food and lemonade to familiar faces above plates balanced on knees. She relieved her sister, Elaine, at the kitchen sink while sweat dribbled between her breasts and her feet

17

swelled in her shoes. The wake continued. All it lacked was booze.

By 4:30 she could stand no more and retreated quietly upstairs. As she peeled off her clammy dress, sounds filtered up through the air register in the floor.

The clinking of dishes, heavy footsteps and her Aunt Vera's voice . . . "Yes, but he couldn't have gone on the way he was. Bertha couldn't have handled him much longer. She's lucky to have Lynnette now."

Lynnette grimaced and changed into lightweight slacks and tennis shoes. She could remember, at her wedding shower, overhearing Aunt Vera telling someone behind a closed door that it would be a blessing for her parents to have her married. "Bertha will have her hands full with Olaf. Lynnette was a change-of-life baby. She's been nothing but trouble. . . ." Aunt Vera's tune had changed.

Opening the window in the hallway, she pushed out the screen and slid through to the back-porch roof, hesitating at the edge of the shingles. The trick was to keep her toe from catching in the eaves trough and to clear the narrow sidewalk. Could she still do it? She bit her lip and grinned.

Lynnette jumped, landed on her feet with her knees bent and lost her balance, bouncing back hard on her rear. Giggling, she ran out of the house yard and threaded her way between cars.

Safe in the barn, she leaned against the door. Her giggles turned into full laughter but hot tears stung her cheeks.

She was not alone. Tears, laughter, near hysteria dried up in one gulp. She turned toward the man in the stall to her right.

Roger Jenson propped against a pitchfork, his only movement the barely perceptible stroking of his dark chin.

Some of her earliest memories were of this boy from across the road. Playmates, fellow misfits, classmates. A cool but comfortable comradeship, until she'd sensed the change in him . . . the danger she couldn't describe. But to a teen-ager in Roggins, even danger had its appeal.

"You cut your hair," he said finally.

18

She nodded, wondering why he should be the first to notice, why after four years they hadn't bothered to exchange hellos.

"I didn't know anyone was out here." Lynnette rubbed her bottom and checked the back of her slacks.

"What'd you do, jump the roof again?"

"Yes. My landing isn't what it used to be."

He chuckled, that mock-evil chuckle she'd often teased him about, and continued cleaning out the stall.

She'd wanted to be alone.

A tomcat growled a warning and began backing down the crude ladder that hung from the hayloft. Halfway down, he turned and jumped into a pile of hay, causing dust to swirl in the sunrays slanting in through the thick cobwebs that crawled over the windowpanes.

She climbed onto the edge of the wooden manger and leaned against a bare wall to watch Roger work. "Does Bertha still keep livestock?"

"An old milk cow and a handful of chickens. She lets me keep my prize boar in this stall. Better keep away from him. He's nasty."

"Aren't they all?"

Roger's look was long and level through incredible lashes. "Yeah, but he's good," he whispered, "real good." He won and she looked away first. "Sired about half the porkers in the county last spring."

Be interesting to know what all you sired last spring.

He piled dirtied straw by the stall door. Carefully opening the lower half of the door, he kicked the straw out, keeping one hand on the latch. An infuriated guttural roar came from outside.

"Shut up, you bastard!" Roger slammed the door and spread fresh straw on the floor.

Wiry, quick, efficient—he seemed smaller and lighter than he really was. Joey once remarked, "That guy's all hormones and doesn't even know it." And she'd answered, "He knows it." Joey had given her a careful look but let it drop.

The sharp odor of fly spray mingled with that of old manure and dusty hay and the sweet smell of dried alfalfa.

"You weren't at the funeral this morning."

"I figured somebody's got to look after the living while everybody else's looking after the dead." He crawled onto the manger to lean against the partition wall, facing her and lit two cigarettes. "Figure you can use one of these about now."

"I'd gladly trade it in for a pitcher of scotch."

"Don't carry any of that with me, but I got some cold beer at home."

"Myrtle lets you keep beer in the house?"

"My house. I'll keep anything there I want to. My old man left everything to me."

"I didn't know that."

"Neither did I until I turned twenty-one. But I let her live there as long as she behaves herself."

"Behaves herself? Myrtle Jenson? When has your mother done anything else?"

There were new lines about his eyes and mouth that made him look older. "When she starts in on the mind-your-morals crap—it's habit, you know—I just put my head over to one side and squint my eyes and say, 'Now, Myrt . . .' She gets right back into line."

"Oh come on, Roger . . ." *Don't relax with him, you fool.*

"Honest. Do you know, Lynn, it's making a human being out of that woman? I'm even beginning to like her a little. Okay, laugh, but I'll tell you something, smart ass. Last Mother's Day? I took her breakfast in bed."

"Oh, Roger, I don't believe a word of this. Did she eat it?"

"Every bite," he said with a trace of his lopsided smile. "After she got over the shock. Even asked for seconds."

"What's gotten into you? Was it Vietnam?"

He blew smoke rings that drifted toward her on the dusty air. "Could be. Taught me life's too short for crap anyway. It's a wonder we never set fire to this place. Had some great times out here . . . you, me and Hymie."

"How is Hymie?"

"The same." He shrugged. Hymie Benninghoff was the caretaker of the Van Fleet estate.

There was a clopping of hooves on concrete and the

cow lumbered through a side door and began eating the meal in her manger, her tail whipping flies from her haunches.

"Does Hymie still think there's a ghost up there?"

"Sure he does. He figures she's waiting for her bastard to come back. Wish he would. I'd like to buy some of those fields I'm working for him."

Lynnette recalled the summer old Clayborne produced a nephew and stunned Roggins. The story that his sister, Nella, had died abroad had been accepted. But evidently Nella had given birth to a son shortly before her death and Clayborne had the child raised in the East. It was still hard to believe that the Van Fleets could postpone such a scandal for that long. At twenty-one, Jay Van Fleet visited Iowa for the first and last time. The town had never stopped talking about it.

"Remember, Lynn, when we snuck up to meet Hymie and get a peek at the nephew? And old Clayborne came running down on us with a stick?"

Clayborne's ancient face had been a mottled bluish color. He'd expressed his rage in weird sounds reminiscent of the squeal and snort of a pig. Lynnette's only impression of the nephew had been one of tall blondness and a startled expression. Later there were newspaper photographs of Jay Van Fleet that gave away nothing of what lay behind the face.

Roger stood on the edge of the manger and jumped the alley. "I'll milk her tonight. Bertha's busy." He dropped to the floor beside the cow and grabbed a three-legged stool. "I figure you're going to get this job soon."

"I'm not staying, Roger. I'm getting out."

The milk buzzed as it hit the bottom of the pail. Roger turned to look at her without missing a stroke and said quietly, "You haven't got the guts to get yourself out of a paper bag with a blowtorch in your hand."

"I got out once before."

"No, Cinderella. Prince Charming Stewart took you out. Led you by the hand. You didn't have to do nothing but follow. That's about all you're good for—following."

She slid off the manger and started for the door without speaking. She knew better than to bait Roger Jenson. But he was away from the cow, out of the stall, and between Lynnette and the door before she could reach it.

"And old Bertha's just waiting to lead you into happy spinsterhood, with bread dough under your fingernails and cow shit on your shoes. Soon everybody will forget Mrs. Joey Stewart ever happened. They'll think of you as Lynnette Sue Olson, same as you always was." He clutched her arm and chuckled low, "The nice little spinster who takes such good care of her mother, sings in church every Sunday and helps out at the ice-cream social. And I'm going to enjoy just being around to see it."

His laughter followed her out of the barn and stuck in her head even after she reached the house.

*L*ynnette sat in a dead elm and listened to the quiet.

No swish of birds' wings. No lazy insects droning through shafts of sunlight.

She cleared her throat and exchanged stares with the windows of the giant house across the concrete bib of its driveway. She had the compulsion to introduce herself. . . .

Creviced limestone, strangled with ivy, looked cold and shadowy under an August sun that left her damp and listless. The white of the front door stood out against deep green ivy and multipaned windows peered over trimmed shrubbery. Hymie Benninghoff's mower had left ridges of grass clippings on the lawns that smelled like dried tea leaves.

This was her second visit since the funeral two days before. She'd come to see Hymie but had missed him both times. She'd always had a fascination for the Van Fleet house and anything was better than being around Bertha.

There had been no time to tell her mother that she was leaving, for Bertha had retreated into a private mourning Lynnette couldn't bring herself to disturb. And then, of course, there was no money to leave on. . . .

A faint uneasiness intruded upon her thoughts. Her depression and her imagination were making something sinister of the quiet of this unhappy place. That was all.

But the house seemed to crouch among its shrubs and barren trees, as if it waited, as if it could move suddenly off its foundations and transport itself, ivy and all, across the drive. . . . *Something's going to happen!*

Lynnette had been about to heave herself off the limb and run when she sensed the withdrawal of the quiet. She settled back and grinned. Really, how could a grown woman be so . . . It was just that she'd been raised on stories about this place.

A halfhearted whistling, the clicking of shoes on the pavement. A bird warbled tentatively behind her.

She expected to see Hymie and was again preparing to leave her perch when she stopped so quickly she almost fell from the tree.

She saw instead the heir to the Van Fleet estate, shuffling up the drive with a tired gait as if he'd walked all the way from Peru.

Not the dashing, elegantly tailored man in a sports car she'd pictured, but a pale man in worn Levi's with a duffel bag over his shoulder. His blond crew cut had grown out, his sideburns were long and thick. But he was still the Jay Van Fleet from the newspaper photographs . . . and she was trespassing.

It was hard to hide in a tree without leaves.

But he didn't take his eyes from the house as he stopped in front of her, dropped the duffel bag and sat on it. One hand kneaded the back of his neck as he considered his inheritance. His jacket was tied by its arms around his waist and she could see strips of white through his T-shirt. He sat there long enough for her leg to go to sleep.

Finally he spoke in a half-strangled whisper, "Okay, house. Here I am. Now what?"

Her giggle was out before she could clamp her teeth on it.

With her hand across her mouth, she watched him stiffen, rise slowly and turn to look first at her dangling feet, then his eyes moved casually, deliberately up her body to her face.

Lynnette looked down into the empty stare of a shock victim. The expression she'd seen on a neighbor's face once after a tornado. She'd felt a prickly chill then too.

Jay Van Fleet's mouth grinned, but his eyes did nothing. "You building a nest? Or just flying through?"

"I was . . . wandering around. I thought you were still in the hospital . . . and . . ." She smiled feeling too silly to go on.

His grin deepened. A touch of it crept into the colorless eyes meant to be blue. He reached up to help her down, wincing as he caught her weight, his fingers stabbing painfully into her rib cage.

"You live around here?" Their positions were reversed now and he looked down at her.

24

"My folks own a farm near here. I'm back for my father's funeral."

"Oh . . . sorry." He stared past her at the naked elms. "What's with the trees?"

"Dutch elm disease."

His sigh was heavy as he turned back to the waiting house. "Doesn't anything get born around here?"

Hymie and his mother had kept the house ready for this day. The windows gleamed. All but one, the last on the right on the second floor. A pane was broken and a white dove flew to sit in the hole, turning its head from side to side to peer at them with reddish-pink eyes.

The quiet advanced again, gradually enveloping them, silencing a lonely bird singing behind them.

"Aren't you going in?" she asked finally, in an attempt to break the disturbing quiet and the spell of the house.

He watched the dove without speaking, his hands on his hips.

"Do you want me to go in with you? I've always wanted to see the inside anyway."

He shook his head slowly. "You . . . don't want to go in that place."

"Why not?"

"Because I don't want to go in that place."

"Are you afraid of doves or do you think your mother will come clanking out of the woodwork?"

He studied her intently. "You are not a lot of help, do you know that?"

"Oh, come on, you don't believe it?" Lynnette realized with a start that they were whispering.

Jay faced the house, hesitated and then picked up a pebble from the grass near the drive. He threw it gently, perhaps because of his injuries, and it landed just below the window with the broken pane and fell to the shrubbery beneath. The dove didn't move.

He gave Lynnette a curious sideways glance. "I've been wiped out by an earthquake. What can a house do?"

Picking up his duffel bag, he lifted it carefully over his shoulder. "You seem to know who I am. What's your name?"

25

"Lynnette . . . Stewart."

"Okay, Lynnette. You first."

She half expected the door to be locked and to creak when opened. But it moved smoothly at the turn of the knob.

The quiet inside was even deeper than that outside. . . .

Wood paneling, dark and heavy, covered the front hall from floor to ceiling, blending with the stairway and slender banister that circled up the wall to the right. A grandfather clock sat silent on a shadowy corner . . . time-darkened cane chairs and umbrella stand. . . .

They stood on a floor of black marble.

Jay flicked a light switch and stared at the chandelier in the ceiling.

"The electricity isn't connected. You weren't expected so soon."

"Great." He looked to the top of the staircase as if expecting someone to come down and greet him.

Wondering why anyone would lavish so much money on gloom, Lynnette moved to the faded pictures of the Presidents of the United States marching in vertical rows up the stairs.

"Of course, I did see a light on the second floor a few nights ago." Her voice sounded different in the quiet hall.

"Just who do you represent, the scare patrol?"

She followed him down a narrow hallway with faded yellow wallpaper and closed doors. A long house but not relatively wide. The semicircular room at the end of the hall was on the back of the house. Drapes covered its curved outer wall.

As Jay pulled the cord, the drapes opened and sun streamed into the room. The entire wall was window, cut into square panes. The carpet had once been white.

They looked across the flagstone patio to the sweep of lawn. The trees here were not elms and this side of the house did not appear so desolate. Some distance from them gaped the hole of an empty swimming pool. In the direction of the gatehouse, sun gleamed blindingly off a corrugated toolshed.

"I can see up here from my bedroom window." She pointed out to him the Olson farm at the bottom of the hill. "This place is too quiet. I feel like screaming."

"Well, don't." He gave her the full effect of his vacant stare. "Not unless you want to see a grown man in little pieces on the rug."

"Are you really nervous? You remind me more of someone in shock."

Jay looked at her hair, then her eyes. "And you remind me of . . ."

"Root beer." Joey had once told her that her eyes were the color of root beer.

"No, root beer's too dark. But I seem to remember my uncle's one sensible habit."

Lynnette followed him into a room that filled the house from front hall to sunroom. Paneling enveloped this room too, where there were no windows or bookshelves. Jay Van Fleet rummaged through the drawers of a desk the size of a bed.

"You remind me of . . . bourbon." He pulled out a bottle and glass. Pouring a little, he handed the glass to her and then tipped the bottle to his lips.

"I believe. You *are* nervous."

"Medicine." He slumped onto one of the four couches and put his feet up on a coffee table. "I'm to have complete rest and quiet."

"You came to the right place. Roggins hasn't made a noise in years. And this house is as quiet as a . . ."

"Don't say it."

She sipped her drink and wandered about the room, examining book titles, spinning the globe. Behind the desk four tall flags stood on pedestals, a United States flag, an Iowa flag, and two she didn't recognize. "The Van Fleets must have been a patriotic lot. Presidents on the stairs, flags in the library."

"You seem to know more about them than I do."

"There aren't many secrets in Roggins. What do you know about the family?"

"That Clayborne died a bachelor at a very ripe age and that as the bastard son of his spinster sister, I'm the last of the herd and inherit this. Don't know any dirty old man around town who looks a lot like me, do you?" He leered as he put the cap on the bottle.

28

"Unless he 'fesses up' you'll have a rough time finding your father. You'll see your eyes and coloring on over half the people of Roggins."

"I'll probably manage without him. Drink up and we'll take on the second floor while we're bottle-brave."

They were whispering again as they reached the head of the stairs. Jay had picked up his duffel bag in the hall and he dropped it on the bed in the master bedroom, which had two bathrooms, black marble for the master, pink marble for the mistress, gaudy brass taps and small oval mirrors. Lynnette emerged from the pink marble bath to find her host sitting cross-legged on the bed, his head propped on his hands.

She sat in a chair and waited for the tour to continue, the only sound the soft cooing of doves in a distant room.

He cleared his throat carefully. "How'd he die?"

"Who?"

"My uncle."

"Clayborne? He . . . jumped off the balcony." She motioned toward the French doors.

"That's what the lawyer said in his letter." His eyes narrowed and he shook his head. "Ninety-one-year-old men don't commit suicide."

"Was he that old? Well . . . maybe he stumbled and fell."

"Then why did they call it suicide?"

"Because he . . . look, you should get the facts from the lawyer, Henson. I was in Denver and just know what people say."

He got off the bed to stand beside her chair, his look and his stance with his hands on his hips making her uncomfortable. "What do people say?"

"They say . . . he took his shoes off."

"His shoes off . . . ?"

"His shoes were up on the balcony and he was down in the snow. His leg was broken and . . . if you're going to accidentally fall off a balcony, you don't take your shoes off."

"He died of a broken leg?"

"No. Do we have to talk about this?"

"Yes."

29

"He froze to death." She slid out of the chair. "He lay in the snow all night with a broken leg and froze to death. Hymie didn't find him till morning. Now, aren't you glad you asked?"

She moved quickly to the door. "Look, it's been nice meeting you, thank you for the tour, but I think I'll leave. You're getting as creepy as your house. . . ."

"No, wait."

Lynnette turned back to an enormous smile that exposed a perfect set of teeth. The smile was meant to charm and with a ski-slope tan around it and sunglasses to hide the impersonal expression in the eyes above it, it would be devastating. But as it was, it looked so phony she had to laugh.

His smile shrank. "What's so funny?"

"You. Okay, I'll show you where people say it happened." She led him through the French doors onto the balcony. How did this house stay so cool in an Iowa August? she wondered, as they followed the balcony past additional French doors, draped closed, to the other end of the house. "As far as I can tell—from my mother's description that she garnered over the Roggins hot line and your lawyer, Henson, his shoes were somewhere in this area and he was down there."

He looked over the wooden balustrade and then ran a finger over its white unbroken surface. "Well, I suppose if you're crazy enough you could leap out of your troubles even at ninety-one . . . but why take your shoes off?" He didn't sound convinced. Jay glanced sideways at the French doors opposite, his lips set in a grim straight line covering the beautiful teeth. The drapes were drawn, their linings stained. The panes of the doors were clouded and dirty.

They could hear doves cooing inside the room.

"I got the impression from Mr. Henson that your uncle was eccentric but that his mind was sound to the end."

"No, he's been bananas as long as I can remember."

"That's funny. No one around here was aware of it."

Jay shrugged. "The first time I saw him—I was ten— he traveled on a train halfway across the country and stayed one day."

"Did you live in an orphanage?"

"No, private homes, private schools, Connecticut, New York, Georgia, Florida, he paid other people to love me." This time the practiced smile was a pitch for sympathy. He'd make a good con man, she thought, if it weren't that his eyes were saying, "I don't like attachments."

"So he stayed one day and you knew at ten that he was crazy?"

"Yeah. He spent the whole day telling me I should write a letter a week, about myself, how I was feeling, what I was doing . . ."

"Maybe he cared more than you thought."

"He didn't care." He held the door for her as they returned to the dark of the master bedroom. "I was supposed to address the envelopes to him. But write the letters to her."

Lynnette shivered in the sudden cool of the house and moved into the hallway and then to the stairs. "Her?"

"My mother." The whispery, throaty quality of his voice echoed in the stillness.

"Nella? She was dead . . . wasn't she?"

Jay took her elbow and guided her down the stairs. "She died the day I was born." He flashed her a mock ghoulish smile but again the colorless eyes disagreed, suggesting instead an unmasked fear.

Jay Van Fleet sat on the front step of his house, his back to it.

He should walk to the gatehouse and find the Benninghoff woman and her dull-witted son. He should see about the electricity, call the lawyer, find something to eat. He should rummage in his bag for a pain pill.

Instead he unlaced his boots, drew them off and then removed his socks, letting the sun and air soothe his sore feet. What he really should do is walk away from this place and disappear . . . but then, he asked himself, how could he disappear from himself?

He pulled the last cigarette from its crushed pack and lit it with his last match. Inhaling shallowly, out of respect for his battered rib cage, he squinted at the dead tree where the girl had sat, her hair mussed so that the sun gleamed through it, sparking the amber to gold at the ends. A picture of litheness and youth, careless innocent laughter he could still hear . . . and then with surprise he'd recognized the wary woman peering through the little girl eyes.

He hoped she'd return to Denver soon.

Hunger burned the lining of his stomach and made the cigarette taste sour. The quiet was so deep he could hear the sounds inside his head, like after the church had come down on him and he'd known he was dead.

He'd lain there under all manner of things . . . not particularly frightened because he'd known death would be like this . . . no feeling of contact with the mass of rubble . . . immobile but weightless. . . . He hoped the others had died as painlessly.

The panic came with the return of feeling and the realization that he still breathed because it hurt so much and that the darkness above his face was not rubble but a small misshapen circle of night sky with a star in it. The church had caved in on them in the morning. . . .

Then the earth quivered and the church settled, dust and plaster sifted down to his face and he couldn't turn his head or muster the strength to spit the dust out. . . . He knew then that there'd been an earthquake . . . and he felt better knowing why the church had fallen . . . and he lost consciousness again. . . .

A dog yapped above him, one of those scrawny village dogs, and above it a lighter daytime sky. . . . The tawny dog circled the hole, sniffing and barking whenever Jay would moan. A claustrophobic fear that the animal would fall down the hole onto his face and he would suffocate produced cold moisture on his forehead.

The day and his conscious awareness of it would come and go but the dog seemed always to be there. He longed for a quick death, and when the pain in his body numbed, he tried to compose his mind for it. But the more numb his body, the more active his brain became, devising small horrors, playing on his abhorrence of being enclosed, immobile, trapped. Another tremor might close in the hole, cut him off from that precious circle of light and air. He might lay there for days . . . dying slowly, horribly.

Jay didn't believe the human voices. His mind was devising another trick. Even when a face appeared in the hole, he didn't believe it. The comforting voices in Spanish were not real.

He must have made a sound, for a soothing voice spoke to him.

It was dawn when they lifted him from the rubble. He could neither move nor speak. The dog was gone. The village was gone. But two forms lay covered on the ground. The priest? Harry? The girl? The baby?

Cold flowed from the house at his back, chilling his spine despite the fact that the rest of him was sticky with heat, intruding upon his memories.

Damn his uncle for making him come back here . . . to the home of his fear.

He scratched uselessly at the tape that bound his middle and stood barefoot on the hot pavement, turning to face the house.

He'd learned in an otherwise interesting life two things

33

that he could have done without. Clayborne had taught him the meaning of fear and Harry had taught him the meaning of loneliness.

The dead trees reflected back from the windows, their black jagged reflections cut up by panes. The dove no longer sat in the hole.

Jay had watched, with a casual curiosity, fear and loneliness at work on others. And then he'd spent a summer here. Slightly amused by the old man's tales. Until the house went to work on him. And he fled, two weeks before he'd meant to. Promising himself and his uncle he'd never come back.

But the damage was done. His ability to fear went with him, lying dormant but full grown inside him until Vietnam. He'd have lived through that experience much better had he not first visited the Van Fleet house.

He'd recognized the look and smell and taste of fear the moment he'd landed. Even before his first patrol.

And then a few years later . . . Harry. His first and last friend. He'd had many friends, the kind he could cheerfully turn his back on when it was time to go. But he'd let Harry talk him into that harebrained partnership. From then on, when he was alone, he was alone with Harry. A comfortably unclinging friendship that left a searing hole when the church collapsed on Harry.

Jay felt sick. The pain in his chest had killed the hunger.

He started down the drive to the gatehouse.

If that damned house would just behave itself for a few months, until he got his health back and collected the money, he'd set a match to it before he left.

A white dove cooed soothingly from the broken window.

*B*lade-edged leaves slapped her face as Lynnette picked her way through cornstalks and stumbled between ridges of clotted earth. She walked in a forest of moving green where shade and sun changed places with each rustle of breeze.

A single thread of a spider's web caught her across the throat. Except in early morning when they were beaded with dew, it was impossible to see these threaded highways among the cornstalks.

Sweat and dust itched along her bare arms as she climbed the fence. Heat had reclaimed her the moment she'd left the cool of the Van Fleet house.

She crossed the road without looking back. Jay Van Fleet wasn't what her mind had built him up to be. He was handsome and a little mysterious, but so seedy looking and so phony, so obviously self-centered. Half-consciously, for some months now, she'd waited for someone to stir her out of mourning for Joey. But no one had.

Jay Van Fleet hadn't either.

Her chances of meeting someone in Roggins, Iowa, were remote. Anybody who was anybody had left after high school. Bertha just had to lend her the money for back rent and bus fare.

Lynnette had sold the car and used what insurance money Joey left to finish her college degree. Only to find that Denver didn't need high school English teachers. It seemed no one did.

The only job she could find was that of secretary-receptionist in a small engineering firm. And she lied to get that, forgot to mention her degree for fear her employer would decide she was too intelligent to handle simple tasks, that she would soon become bored and find another job. Jobs of any kind were scarce.

She was given the position on the basis of her appearance. As her young employer told her with a grin, "You can always teach a pretty woman to type, but you can't teach a good typist to be pretty."

Lynnette could have qualified for low-income housing with her meager wages but was too proud to apply. Instead she shared a tiny studio apartment with a stewardess who was often away. She endured poverty gladly to keep her place in the sun.

And then, after six months, her employer called her in and her little world fell around her for the second time.

"Believe me, Mrs. Stewart, this is nothing personal. But we're forced to reduce staff because of the recession. You understand. We're letting the gals go first because the men have families to feed."

Who will feed me? she asked herself, staring at his bolo tie.

"I'll be happy to give you a glowing recommendation. . . ."

Lynnette cleaned out her desk and left within the hour. She'd spent a month in a hopeless search for another job when Elaine called. Their father had wandered into the machine shed and collapsed. When Bertha had found him, he was dead. Lynnette was needed at home at once.

It had taken almost her last nickel to get here.

The Olson mailbox stood beside the entrance to the lane. She extracted a sales catalog and a handful of letters, most of them sympathy cards by their shapes.

Corn forests rustled and flapped softly as she started down the lane. Lynnette could remember pretending that they were crowds of people, the lane a wide red carpet that led to the golden throne of a prince. And she, the Princess Belinda, walked with stately dignity between the crowds of admirers.

But a disrespectful voice in her head would jeer, tell her she was just dumb old Lynnette Sue Olson, wearing yellowed lace curtains that were torn, walking down a dirt lane between cornfields. And the voice would tell her to keep an eye out for dumb old Roger and Hymie who were likely to be hiding in the corn to ambush her with dirt clods.

She grinned at the thought of the child that had been

and threw the catalog into the air. Why had Clayborne wanted his nephew to write homey letters to a dead mother? Had Jay written any? He'd probably made up the story on the spot, just to get her reaction.

The next day was Sunday so Elaine came to haul them off to church. Lynnette rode in the back seat with "the children" and realized how quickly they were outgrowing that description. Her niece, Alice, was eleven and Dennis must be sixteen by now.

She sat, sticking to one of the front pews, between her mother and sister and stared at the metal plaque beside the stained-glass window. She knew it by heart. "In Memory of Nella Louise Van Fleet." She thought of Nella's son, alone in the cold house on the hill.

Her father's and Joey's caskets had rested in the exact spot where she'd knelt with Joey and become his wife. . . .

Joey's mother sat on the organ bench, prim and composed, her lovely hair piled high by a Minturn hairdresser. Rachael Stewart watched the minister with sophisticated blank attention. Suddenly, without moving her head, she let her eyes drop to meet Lynnette's. The message that passed from Rachael to Lynnette in that brief glance was unmistakable, icy cold, and most unchristian.

And across the aisle, Joseph Stewart, Sr. . . . looking too much like his son . . .

There seemed to be no safe place to look so she stared at her hands. Her head ached.

When they stood to sing, Bertha had to tilt to share the hymnal with her. At seventy, her mother had shrunk little from her original six feet and weighed close to two hundred pounds.

Most of the tiny congregation was female. When Rachael's organ hit the high tones of hymns composed for God knew what kind of vocal cords, the screeching made Lynnette's teeth grate.

Reverend Birmingham intoned clichés in his rich modulated voice. From the careful wave in his hair and whiteness of his uncallused hands to his manner of speech and dress, city stuck out all over him. He exhorted them to donate for the new altar, to feel sorry for the hungry and to volunteer for the next ice-cream social.

After a morbid visit to the cemetery they went to Elaine's for dinner. The shabby farmhouse was rich with the smell of roasting pork from the overheated kitchen.

"Jay Van Fleet's moved into the big house," Leroy announced the minute they sat down. "Myrtle Jenson called before you got here." He grinned slyly at his mother-in-law. "She said she thought you'd want to know."

"Well, I already know. That woman don't have to tell me nothing. Lynnette met him yesterday."

"Pass Lynn the horseradish," Elaine ordered. "That's what you said on the way to church, but you didn't tell us what he was like or what kind of a car he was driving."

"He was walking. Probably thumbed it. He doesn't look too well . . . health-wise. His chest is all bandaged and he's very pale."

"He walked? With all that money?"

"Maybe he hasn't got it yet."

Bertha peered importantly over her spectacles. "Invited Lynnette into the house and showed her around. She told me all about it."

"You went into the house with him alone? And let him show you his chest?" Leroy's shock was only half real, his round face made rounder by the food stuffed into his cheeks.

Alice's eyes went wide and soft. "Was he handsome, Aunt Lynn?" she asked, wrinkling her nose to keep her glasses up.

Lynnette squeezed her niece's pudgy hand. "In a way."

"What way?"

"Well, he's quite tall and has good shoulders."

"What color is his hair?" Alice was all Olson—from the pale blond hair to the pale blue eyes behind thick lenses. In another year Lynnette would be looking up at her, too.

"Kind of a dusty blond, ash blond, I guess."

Lynnette spent the next half hour describing Jay Van Fleet and his house until the talk turned to Olaf and the hog market.

After dinner she found herself at the steamy sink with Elaine while the rest of the family retreated to the living room to nap or read the paper.

Hot, tired and too full of food, Lynnette felt drugged. And she knew the moment Elaine took them home, there would be a repeat of the morning chores and then more heavy food and dishes to wash. A whole day filled to the choking point with things that she didn't want to do.

"I wish you'd think about the social." Elaine used a forearm to brush hair off her sticky forehead. "I'm on the committee and we could work together. It's a good way to meet people."

"You mean there's someone in Roggins I haven't met?"

"Well . . . you haven't seen them for a long time. It's fun, Lynn."

"No way. I'm not the 'social' type. Thanks anyway." Damn Roger Jenson.

Elaine changed the dishwater and the topic of conversation. "Mom and Leroy get along if they don't see too much of each other." She bent to search Lynnette's face. "But they couldn't . . . well . . . they just wouldn't get along in the same house." She used the back of her wrist to push her glasses up on her nose and left a streak of soapsuds on her cheek.

"The only sensible thing is for Bertha to sell the farm and get a little house in town. She doesn't need a farm and a big house. Besides, she could keep better tabs on the local gossip if she were in town."

"I don't know, Lynn . . ." Elaine glanced over her shoulder to the living room. "I don't think she'd leave the farm . . . and the two of you could make out for a while. The kids and I would come and help. . . ."

"Why me?"

"Because there's no one else."

Her sister's damp round face flushed with concern and tenderness. With eleven years between them, Elaine had often seemed more like a mother than a sister.

"It's not fair, Elaine."

"What's not fair?" Dennis stood behind them jangling a set of car keys. He was small for his age and darker than Lynnette. He wouldn't fit in this family either.

Elaine frowned. "Where are you going?"

"Anywhere." He tossed his head to get the hair out of his eyes, winked at Lynnette and left.

Elaine waddled to the window, too much elephantine leg showing under a short orange dress and the insides of her knees slapping together, preventing swollen ankles from ever meeting. She'd never rebelled in a family where a light appetite was mercilessly ridiculed.

Lynnette joined her sister and they watched Dennis crawl into the cab of the pickup and gun it out onto the highway.

"He gets more like you every day, Lynn. He worries me."

As Lynnette strained behind the rusty push mower the next morning, a car turned into the lane.

Bertha looked up from the garden. "That'll be the lawyer. I'd better put the coffee pot on."

"What's he coming for?"

But her mother slammed the screen door without answering. Just as Lawyer Henson's tired Ford stopped in front of the gate, Harold's car pulled into the lane.

Fussing, dusty Mr. Henson looked small as he shook hands with a florid bulging Harold.

"What's up? The reading of the will?" She tried to stamp out an ember of hope. Wouldn't it be funny if her father had left her a little money that she could use to escape her mother?

"We *are* here to discuss financial matters."

"And you should be in on this, Lynn."

Bertha and Lynnette shelled peas during the discussion in the kitchen. Idle hands drove Bertha frantic. She managed the peas, the discussion, the rolled lefse smeared with butter and brown sugar—effortlessly.

To get right down to business over coffee in Roggins was unthinkable so the talk turned to Jay Van Fleet, Lynnette's visit on Saturday and Mr. Henson's on Sunday.

"There's no doubt that this is the real Jay and heir. I'd know him anywhere. But we did run into a little trouble. Clayborne had left a letter with his will to be presented to his nephew when he died." Next to Bertha and Myrtle Jenson across the road, Lawyer Henson was the biggest gossip for miles.

"Well, I gave it to him yesterday. And do you know what it said?" He paused for effect. At the hint of approaching drama even Bertha's hands were stilled halfway through the choking of a pod.

"Clayborne wrote that it was his wish the Jay live in the house as a token to the memory of his mother, Nella. And that if he chooses not to, the inheritance should go to Mrs. Benninghoff and her son."

Harold snorted and slammed his cup to the table. "That won't hold, Henson. You can fight that."

"I intend to. But that letter plus the internal revenue people are going to hold up the settlement of the estate for at least six months, probably a year. And young Van Fleet isn't excited about living there any longer than necessary."

"I should think not. The place is too big for one man and the Benninghoff woman has an awful time getting anybody to clean it. That worthless boy of hers isn't much help either. Must cost a fortune just to heat that barn." Bertha scratched her head and shook her apron full of empty pods into a paper sack. "Why would the old fool go and do a thing like that anyway?"

Lawyer Henson stirred thick cream into his coffee with a time-speckled hand. "He was very attached to the house. Perhaps he was reluctant to see it pass out of the family. Although who would want to buy a mansion in the middle of the Iowa countryside, I don't know."

"Big waste of space, if you ask me," Bertha grumbled. "'Tore down all them perfectly good barns just to build it."

"What barns?" Harold asked.

"That was before your time. I wasn't even born when Clayborne's father moved in from the East and bought up stone barns. Lots of them around then, limestone from the pits this side of Minturn." Bertha paused to drop her upper plate and clean off the gum with her tongue, then scrunched her mouth together to seat the false teeth into place.

"Well, he buys them up, has them torn down. Paid an

awful price for 'em. Farmers made out real good. Old Van Fleet has the stones made into a house. Could have had brand new blocks for a fourth the price. But no, he wanted the house to look old."

Lynnette spoke for the first time, "Then the Van Fleet house isn't as old as it looks?"

"Ain't as old as this one. That's what comes from having too much money. Anyway, he moves his young wife in there and they don't talk to nobody. That was his retirement home. Left the business in New York to Clayborne."

"Yes, that was quite a scandal, as I hear it." Mr. Henson pushed his cup aside and began arranging papers on the table. "Cecil being so much older than his wife. She was his second wife, you know, not Clay's mother. But Nella was born here." He cleaned his bifocals carefully. "Now, Harold, I want you to look at these figures. They do come out about like I thought when I spoke to you the other day. Your mother will need a loan until things are settled."

Lynnette looked up slowly. "A loan?"

"Everything's tied up, Lynn, until the tax people have looked it over. Even the joint checking account is frozen." Harold turned to Bertha. "I wish you'd had everything put in your name when Dad started going, like I asked you to."

Bertha stared absently into her cup and then reached down the front of her dress for her handkerchief. "Just never got around to it, Harold. Guess I didn't want to admit how bad he was until he was so bad I didn't have time to do anything but look after him and the place."

"Anyway, I'm going to lend you gals enough money to operate on until the estate's settled."

Lynnette knew the blood was draining from her face by the sudden look of concern on the men's faces. "But Harold . . ."

"Now, don't worry. You and Mom will be just fine. I'll see to that. It's kind of like young Van Fleet's problem on a smaller scale."

"How long before . . ."

"Six months to a year. Probably more like a year and

then there'll be enough for you two to be comfortable. There's some dispute over the boundaries of the south forty and that . . . Lynn, what's the matter?"

She'd let her head drop to her arms so they wouldn't see her struggling with tears.

Lynnette raised her head in time to see Mr. Henson's embarrassment. "I was going to borrow money from Bertha to get back to Denver."

A dangerous flush moved up Harold's face. "Denver! I thought we'd settled that."

"I don't want to hear no nonsense about Denver, Missy!" Bertha turned to Mr. Henson. "Now, isn't that gratitude? I ask you. And me spending my last penny to get her things shipped back here."

Bertha grabbed a handful of pea pods and set to work with expert fury. "And I paid your rent, too. Took all the cash I had on hand. What do you mean not paying your debts? Olsons always pay their debts, Missy Olson. I taught you better."

"It's *Mrs. Stewart.*"

"Well, who's feeding you? The Olsons or the Stewarts? And don't go looking for favors in that direction. From what I hear, Rachael Stewart has a three-cornered fit at just the mention of you."

"Now, ladies . . ." Mr. Henson shifted papers uncomfortably.

But Lynnette ignored him. "How did you know about the rent, Bertha?"

"Your landlord sent a bill, that's how."

"He sent the bill to you?"

"No, he sent it to you. But you didn't open it . . ."

"So you did. I didn't even see it."

"You brought it in from the mailbox. You'd have seen it if you'd bothered to look."

"You opened my mail . . ."

"I thought you'd be glad to have your debts paid up and your stuff with you. He threatened to give it to the Salvation Army."

Lynnette stood, the empty pods in her lap spilling to the floor. She walked out onto the back porch and leaned against the screen door.

43

"Denver, she says. Poor Olaf must be turning in his grave." Bertha launched into the speech Lynnette knew by heart. "After all I've done for her. Practically died bearing her and about killed myself raising her. She was into everything—cupboards, pots, face cream. Nothing but trouble.

"And when she got older she couldn't do anything right. Mess up every job I gave her. Not like Elaine. Wouldn't eat, wouldn't sit still in church. Then she gets uppity and starts calling me Bertha instead of Mother . . . racing around in cars with that Roger and nitwit Hymie. Sneaking out of the house at all hours. I've had my troubles with her, I can tell you. . . ."

"Now, Mom. You can't treat her like a child anymore, she's . . ."

"I'll treat her like I feel, Harold Olson, and you stay out of it."

Lynnette closed the screen door quietly and walked past the pump, the fruit cellar, the wash house, the old outhouse . . . "Damn!"

She walked quickly up the lane, no admiring dream crowd or prince on a golden throne this time.

"Damn and double damn and . . ." She paused at the end of the lane to search for a word that could convey her feelings.

Lynnette turned toward the Van Fleet house. "Shit!"

7

*A*s Lynnette climbed the board fence that separated corn-fields and lawn, she noticed the shimmer of water. Two long hoses ran from the house to the swimming pool, and Jay Van Fleet lounged on one of several reclining deck chairs. His skin wasn't much darker than the bandages encircling his rib cage above the dark blue swimming trunks.

Enormous sunglasses hid his eyes, and as she came up beside him she wasn't sure if he was awake.

He didn't move or turn his head. "Who goes there?"

She bent over him and answered in the spookiest whisper she could muster, "The ghooost of Nella Van Fleeeet."

Dazzling teeth emerged, and before she could jump back his hand shot out and grabbed her forearm. "I'd say from the feel . . . that it's really the little widow who likes to sit in trees."

"Trespassing again."

"Yep. Guess I'm going to have to do something about that." Jay released her and turned stiffly to a bucket of ice beside the chair. He pulled out two bottles of beer, opened them and handed her one. "There . . . your punishment. Be brave and take it like a man."

She slid into the chair at an angle to his.

"What's the matter? Afraid I'll take it back?"

"No, but we widows have to be careful. How did you know?"

"That you were a widow? The plow boy—what's his name?—Jenson."

"Roger. I might have known." Lynnette concentrated on not thinking about what else Roger might have said.

She'd been right about Jay Van Fleet. Even without the tan and with those sunglasses hiding his expression, he was formidably pleasant to the eye. "Would you do me a favor? Take off your glasses so that I can tell when you're lying through your beautiful teeth?"

His forehead wrinkled and his lips tightened as he pondered her request.

"You fighting me?"

He pushed the sunglasses up over his hair, and she relaxed under his impersonal gaze.

"Why did you come here, Mrs. Stewart?" he asked bluntly.

Why had she come and how to phrase her answer? She was aware of the house lurking behind him, the chill gray limestone blocks that had once been barns, the sun's glare on the windowpanes and the unexpected white of the balcony's balustrade.

"I guess I was looking for solace . . . in the company of a fellow prisoner." Her finger made streaks in the moisture on the bottle as she told how fate had again imprisoned her in Roggins and of Lawyer Henson's remarks on Jay's situation. Her eyes burned with angry tears that couldn't surface.

Jay Van Fleet started to laugh, then decided against it, clutching at the bandages on his chest. "Hell, you don't need money to get out of here. Just get on the highway and stick out your thumb. You'd be in Colorado in two days."

"That's easy for a man, but . . ."

"There are girls doing it every day."

"With my luck, I'd get raped."

He pulled the sunglasses down to cover his eyes again and smiled. "You might at that."

"I would have considered it a few years ago if I hadn't married Joey and left. But now . . ." She had a disconcerting double view of herself in his sunglasses. "I'm older. I've been through too much to trust the world that far. Are you going to sit here as lord of the manor until you can inherit?"

"I don't know what else I can do. It's not too bad . . . there's a fund for the house and personal expenses that I can draw on till things are settled. And that's more money than I've ever had at one time." But he didn't sound happy with his situation.

"You're going to get bored. . . ."

"Yeah, I've seen Roggins. Anything doing in Minturn?"

"It's not exactly filled with wine, women and song."

"The song I can do without." He drained the brown bottle and reached into the bucket for another. "The wine I can buy. But the women . . . might have a problem there. . . ."

She ignored the invitation in his smile. "You're a geologist, aren't you?"

"I thought so, when I got out of college. But after Vietnam, I didn't know what I was. Worked in the oil fields in Venezuela. Then I quit and took off free-lancing with a partner."

"Free-lance geologist?"

"Yeah. Look at rocks and countryside for a good place to drill holes, sell the information to the highest bidder. Good way to lose your shirt, but you move around a lot." He ran his hand through sun-streaked hair that covered his ears. "Guess I'm more of a mover-arounder than a geologist."

A motor revved suddenly, sputtered, choked and died.

"Do you have company?"

"That's just Hymie fixing the old Bentley we found in the garage. He a friend of yours?"

"Oh, yes. I've known Hymie all my life. Think I'll go over and say hello. I haven't seen him since . . ."

"What's his problem anyway?"

Lynnette stood looking down at her host. A drop of sweat slid over his Adam's apple and caught in the well beneath it. "Hymie? He's not too bright. A little backward . . . retarded, I guess."

"He's not retarded around an engine. And he's a *big* son of a bitch." Jay removed his sunglasses to chew on one of the ear pieces. "You're not afraid of him?"

"No. And you needn't be either. He's big but harmless."

"Nobody's harmless, little widow," he whispered. "Nobody." He released the catch on the lounge so that it lay flat, gave her a scornful look and closed his eyes in a gesture of dismissal.

She decided he really was a bastard and left him, throwing a "Thanks for the beer" over her shoulder.

Jay Van Fleet had probably had little cause to get close

47

to people, she reasoned as she walked toward the house. Born without a family and kicked from place to place— such a life would have made him withdrawn, distrustful, sometimes rude. She'd been defensive herself and Roger Jenson was twice as rude as Jay with half the cause. Still, she could feel the resentment growing.

A dove watched her from the balcony, ruffling its feathers as she walked beneath. Mrs. Benninghoff waved at her from a kitchen window.

The garage was attached to the kitchen end of the house and had stalls for four cars. Hymie bent over the fender of the Bentley on the drive, whistling tunelessly.

She could remember how he'd been teased as a child. And now he'd grown into a brute of a man with overlong arms. From behind it would be easy to fear him.

But when he turned and saw her, the loose mouth and silly face made her giggle. "Hi, Hymie."

He laid a hand on her shoulder and it felt like one of the limbs on the dead elm above them had fallen on her. The loose jaw tightened and the resulting smile looked normal. "How come you haven't been up to see me before this, dumb old Lynnette Sue?"

"I have been, several times. You weren't around." The Bentley, a steel gray, had real running boards under the doors. "Does this crate work?"

"Works beautiful. Always did." Hymie hid his grin by ducking under the hood. "Had to mess things up some so's I could fix it again so's you-know-who'd think it'd been sittin' unused for a long time."

The sun was high and hot, shining through bare still branches, leaving strangely contorted shadows on the dark green grass under the elms. She leaned against the Bentley, her eyes tracing the lines between the limestone blocks of the Van Fleet house. "Hymie, do you ever go into the main house at night?"

"Not me. Not at night." He scratched the curly brown fuzz that covered his head. "Why?"

"I saw a light up here the night before my father's funeral."

Hymie's eyes moved to the house behind her. "Couldn't have. No electricity then. Nobody here."

48

"Well, I did see a light. How do you know someone wasn't camping out in the house that night, with a lantern or something? A transient maybe?"

Hymie's expression grew calculating, he looked almost intelligent. "She . . . don't need light, Lynn."

"Don't start that . . . I don't want to hear about your old ghost. Your stories have worked on me so that I'm almost afraid of that house myself. And I don't believe in ghosts."

"Sure you do. Else you wouldn't mind hearing about it. Everybody believes in secret or the word 'ghost' wouldn't mean anything. Come on, let's find some shade. I want to hear about Colorado." His speech was slow, like his movements, his voice pitched unexpectedly high, adding to the incongruity that was Hymie.

They walked toward the gatehouse and sat in the shade of an ash, swatting mosquitoes and shooing flies. Hymie was always hungry for news of the outside world. She poured her own hunger for the sunny West, the Rocky Mountain, into her conversation, ending up with her job, the people she'd worked with, her roommate and then unemployment and imprisonment in Roggins.

"Your new lord and master said I should hitchhike West. But I'm afraid to, Hymie, and then not have money for a place to stay or a job when I get there. Of course, if I get desperate enough I just might . . ."

"No." He took a swipe at a bee who seemed attracted by the bright colors of her blouse. "No, some jerk might . . . If you want to go that bad, I'll give you the money." The big ugly face with the crooked nose, the slack jaw, a smear of grease, seemed to waver as the leaves above them moved slightly.

"Oh Hymie, I couldn't . . ."

"I'll lend you it then. I got money. Think on it." He unfolded clumsily and stood, extending a giant hand down to help her up.

"I'll have to think . . . you're an awfully good friend, Hymie."

"Wonder," he said as they walked toward the Bentley.
"Wonder what?"

49

"Wonder if dumb old Lynnette Sue can still do a helicopter . . ."

"Oh no! I'm too big. I . . ."

But before she could run, he grabbed her around the middle in a bone-crunching grip and hoisted her over his head. Giving a monstrous roar, which sounded something like a bear and nothing like a helicopter, he balanced her on one extended hand forcing her to tighten her muscles and straighten out to relieve the pressure of his hand on her abdomen and to keep a giddy balance.

This was an old game. One she'd never been too fond of and one he'd used to show off his gargantuan strength to Roger Jenson.

The ground was too far away, her balance too precarious. She'd outgrown the coordination that used to keep her straight and aloft as Hymie's propeller. "No, Hymie. Put me down!"

But he reached up with his other hand and pushed her, while the hand under her pivoted as far as it could and then bounced her up to pivot back so that the process could be repeated.

And then there was another face below her, pale, tight with horror. "Put her down, you son of a bitch!"

Hymie let her fall for a fraction of a second until he could clasp both hands around her middle and lower her gently to the ground. "Sorry, Mr. Van Fleet. We was just . . ." He looked helplessly at Lynnette who clung to him for balance until the blood stopped beating at her eardrums.

"It's just a game Hymie likes to play . . ." She tucked herself back into her bra automatically, then was embarrassed to realize she'd done it in front of two men.

Jay was clearly unamused by Hymie's antics and the brown bottle in his hand quivered. "Sounded more like he was killing you. No more of that. Understand, Hymie?"

"Yes, Sir." Hymie looked properly hangdog.

Mrs. Benninghoff rushed out of the small courtyard just off the kitchen and hurried toward them. "Oh, Mr. Van Fleet, I'm so sorry. I've told Hymie he's too big for such things. Those two grew up together and they always got into mischief. Please don't be angry. Hymie

I'm ashamed of you." She brushed back wisps of hair that refused to stay in the bun at the back of her head. "But she's always been good for my poor Hymie . . ."

"I just don't want it to happen again." Jay looked suspiciously from Hymie to Lynnette and caught her giving her tormentor a jab with her elbow. "I asked Mrs. Benninghoff to fix some extra lunch if you'd like to stay," he said, then turned and walked off around the back of the house.

Lynnette stared after him. "Did he mean me?"

8

L ynnette sat in the alcove of the breakfast room on the padded-leather bench against the wall and watched Jay Van Fleet through sparkling windowpanes as he walked toward the house from the pool area, where he'd donned a short-sleeved sweatshirt and sandals.

Through an open door, she could see a polished dining-room table with rounded corners and the back of a captain's chair. Above the table hung an ugly glass chandelier with dangling doodads and fake candles.

Mrs. Benninghoff elbowed through swinging doors with a plate of corn on the cob. "After all the years of keeping you kids out of the house and here I am serving you lunch." She winked. "The young Mr. Van Fleet seems friendlier than his uncle, doesn't he?"

"I don't see how he could be anything but." Old Clayborne had been a recluse who'd refused admittance to anyone but the Benninghoffs, occasional cleaning help, Lawyer Henson, and for one brief summer, his nephew.

Jay held the door for Mrs. Benninghoff as she returned to the kitchen. Lynnette slid around the corner of the boothlike arrangement with her back to the windows, so that he could sit where she had.

His con-man smile . . . "Thanks for warming the seat. The sun never seems to heat up this pile of rocks." He ate at a leisurely pace, without speaking or looking at her, and she tried to keep dripping butter off the linen tablecloth.

Finally she could stand the suspense no longer. "Okay, let's have it."

He looked up with wide-eyed surprise, chewed a mouthful of corn and swished off his teeth with a swig of beer. "Have what?"

"Why did you ask me to lunch?" *Why do I get so irritated with you?*

"You are one suspicious woman, you know that?" He

wiped melted butter off his lips and considered her a moment. "What's between you and Hymie?"

"Nothing, we're just friends, like I told you."

"Do you always let your friends throw you around like that?"

"I didn't want him to, but sometimes he gets out of control."

"How far out of control?"

"I've never seen him get violent or hurt anyone. But if you go around calling him a son of a bitch too often, he'll have a perfect right to take a swing at you. And with Hymie that could be fatal."

Jay poured her a cup of coffee. He was a strange combination of good manners and insulting rudeness. "Seems like a weird sort of friend."

"We lived far enough from town that Roger Jenson and Hymie were the only playmates I had. We were born the same year and just naturally got together."

He finished off the platter of sweet corn and started on the sandwiches. Mrs. Benninghoff's cooking and the enforced respite from his travels would be good for him. He looked less gaunt than when she'd first met him.

Finally he poured himself some coffee and lit a cigarette. He played with the matchbook, tapping and turning it on the table. "How'd your husband die?"

"Car accident. Why?"

"Just curious. In Colorado?"

"Yes."

"And you still want to go back there?"

"Yes. It's a nice place to live. Have you ever been there?"

"I did some time at the School of Mines in Golden." He leaned back against the wall and looked at her sideways. "I'll lend you the money to go back to Colorado."

"Don't tempt me." She set her cup down too quickly and sloshed coffee into the saucer. This was the second time a solution to her problem had been offered in an hour, and she had trouble believing in them. "I don't have any collateral." She tried to keep her tone light to hide her confusion.

"Now you're tempting me." He stubbed his cigarette

and slid out of the seat. "No interest and no strings . . . if you'll just go."

"Why should you lend me money?" She moved around and stood, looking up at him.

"Maybe . . . maybe it's pity for a fellow prisoner. Or maybe . . ." He reached out to touch her hair lightly. "It's that pretty little farm girls make life too complicated."

Lynnette was still trying to sort out her feelings when the sound of a car coming up the drive brought them all out the door to the courtyard.

A gleaming station wagon stopped by the front door and when Lynnette recognized the man getting out, she grinned. "You're in for it now."

"Who is it?" Jay asked.

"Reverend Birmingham. Your grandfather built the Methodist church in Roggins and the family kept it going. About thirty years ago your uncle cut himself off from almost all his contacts in Roggins, including the church." She gave him a meaningful look. "The Van Fleet fortune has been sorely missed. Roggins is a Lutheran town."

Mrs. Benninghoff had gone ahead of them to greet the minister. Lynnette stood back with Hymie as the housekeeper introduced Jay to Charles Birmingham. They shook hands, sizing each other up. They were about the same height, and the older man was obviously surprised at the appearance of the younger. Jay did not look like a man of wealth in his rumpled swimming trunks, faded sweatshirt and sandals. He presented quite a contrast to the almost overgroomed minister, who must have been warm in his suit coat and tie.

"I just stopped by to welcome you to Roggins and invite you to the Sunday services at our church."

Jay looked over his shoulder at Lynnette and then at the house and down the drive. "Oh, well, I . . . don't know . . . Churches are . . . heavy stuff . . . kind of . . ."

"We Methodists aren't the fire-and-brimstone types, Mr. Van Fleet." His broad smile was charitable.

"Got a thing about churches." Jay folded his arms and then unfolded them to scratch at his bandages. He shifted from one foot to the other. "Had one fall on me . . ."

Mrs. Benninghoff cleared her throat and offered to bring coffee to the library if the Reverend would like a cup. He accepted quickly and turned back to Jay. "Fell on you? . . . Oh, the earthquake, I see . . . That's good, very good." He chuckled and walked over to Lynnette. "I see you've already met some Rogginites. How are you, Lynnette, Hymie? I trust your mother is recovering from her grief under your kind care, my dear?"

Before she could answer he turned back to Jay. "It was very pleasant indeed to see that gate standing open on the drive, Mr. Van Fleet, and I must confess that it gave me hopes of being able to see the inside of this fine house. Your uncle had an unfortunate aversion to visitors. In the six years I've lived in Roggins, I've never set foot in it."

Jay nodded, shrugged and motioned him toward the door and then gestured for Lynnette and Hymie to follow. When they didn't move, he repeated the gesture behind the minister's back, mouthing a silent "please."

"I think he doesn't want to be left alone with our overwhelming Reverend Birmingham, Hymie."

Hymie grunted and followed her into the house.

She stepped once again onto the black marble of the hall. The sticky moisture on her skin felt as if it were beading into ice crystals as it met the chill. She decided that it wasn't really as cold as it seemed . . . just the change from the heavy heat outside.

"Truly a remarkable air-conditioning system for a house this size—and so noiseless. Is it central?"

"Very." Jay smiled and opened the door across from the stairway. "This is the living room."

White mounds silhouetted against dark carpet . . . furniture covered by dust sheets. White knickknack shelves and alabaster figurines relieved the grim paneling. The uncovered piano had gathered a fine layer of dust and a spider had webbed the pedals together.

Reverend Birmingham peered under the dust sheets and into glass-fronted cabinets. "You don't use this room," he murmured the obvious.

"It's a lot of house."

"You'll just have to marry and fill it with children."

"Yeah . . . uh . . . this is the dining room." Jay quickly opened a connecting door and stood back for them to enter.

As Lynnette passed him he whispered, "Wipe that smirk off your face."

"Irish Chippendale! Magnificent." The Reverend moved from buffet to table.

Scenes, depicting the American Revolution and done in woodblock wallpaper, extended from floor to ceiling. Armies of men—understandably ill at ease in mercilessly tight breeches, flags unfurled above them, prancing horses, stiff-sailed ships in the background.

Hymie said nothing, but followed Lynnette around like a sheep dog.

Mrs. Benninghoff served coffee in the library and stayed to point out items of interest. As she carried the tray back to the kitchen, the rest of them filed through the hall and up the stairs.

The Reverend looked about the master bedroom, showing even more interest than before. "This was your uncle's room, wasn't it?"

"Yes." Jay drew a pair of jeans over his swimming trunks.

Reverend Birmingham moved to a corner bookcase beside the fireplace and began to examine titles.

Lynnette grew restless, waiting by the open door. She noticed a faint but disagreeable odor that hadn't been apparent downstairs.

At last he turned from the bookcase, his forehead creased. "Your uncle seemed to have a rather strange interest in parapsychology and transmigration, didn't he?"

Jay, in the process of tucking his sweatshirt into his pants, stopped with one hand in a compromising position and stared at his visitor. "I . . . wouldn't know. Never really knew my uncle." But as everyone else moved into the hall, he stayed where he was, his eyes on the bookcase.

Finally he joined them and then stopped, sniffing. "There's that smell again. Maybe one of those birds kicked off. We'd better get that window fixed, Hymie."

He and Hymie had a long silent staring contest that Lynnette found curious.

Reverend Birmingham opened one of the doors that lined each side of the hall. Lynnette left Jay and Hymie staring at each other and joined him. The windowless hall had been dark but the curtains were open in this bedroom. She stood blinking in the bright light while he again peeked under dust covers. A dove cooed somewhere near. And then another.

"Funny." He hunched his shoulders and arched disciplined eyebrows, giving the impression of gleeful fright. "The innocent call of a dove seems quite eerie in a big silent house, doesn't it?"

He laughed at her expression. "The real problem, you know, is the stories one hears of this place . . . quite normal for a small town . . . but one is preconditioned." He smiled soothingly and patted her shoulder.

There were four bedrooms on each side of the hall, all shrouded with dust sheets. A narrow door opened to the attic stairs.

The doves grew silent, the air fouler as they neared the door at the end of the hall. Jay and Hymie caught up with them as they reached it.

"Uh . . . Reverend? That door's locked. Hymie, here, seems to have lost the key. It's just another bedroom . . ."

But Reverend Birmingham had already opened it.

Lynnette expected disturbed doves to flutter about, but there was no movement in the room. The shredded gauze of curtain at the broken window lay still against it.

The minister pushed at the door and it moved quietly back against the wall, exposing a room as large as the master bedroom. A room covered with dust . . . hanging, motionless cobwebs . . . peeling wallpaper . . . bird droppings and feathers.

She felt the two men close behind her, heard one of them gasp. But no one stepped over the threshold. The stench formed an invisible barrier.

Reverend Birmingham took out a handkerchief and held it over his nose. Lynnette cupped both hands around her own nose and mouth. They smelled faintly of salt and butter and felt cold against her face.

"Was this your mother's room?"

"Yeah . . . first time I've seen it. Hymie, when did you unlock it?"

"Didn't, no key."

"Why, in heaven's name, was it left in such a shocking state?"

"My uncle locked it up and wouldn't let anyone in. Mrs. Benninghoff says she hasn't been in here for thirty years."

"Well, someone has." And the minister pointed to the clear imprint of a shoe in the dust, followed by others not so clear and crisscrossed with a pattern of bird tracks.

There was a general crush at the door and Lynnette found herself propelled into the room as the others entered and then passed her.

No one had bothered to cover the furniture in Nella Van Fleet's room. Dust and grime muted and merged all the colors into gray and brown.

On the floor a sparrow lay on a thick 78-rpm record, its legs pointing stiffly at the ceiling. The doves had either taken refuge under the bed or left through the hole in the window. A small black credenza sat just inside the room, an ugly thing with tarnished gold scrollwork down its sides.

"Know him?"

Lynnette turned to see the three men looking down at the floor on the other side of the bed. Jay had pulled his shirt up over his nose and mouth, exposing the tape on his midriff.

As Lynnette moved around the end of the bed, Hymie grabbed her with uncharacteristic quickness and held her tight against his chest, a big hand covering her face. But not before she'd glimpsed the gaping mouth, and bulging eyes, that seemed to have no lids.

"Chris Gunderson," someone said.

9

*T*he uniformed man at the bottom of the staircase glanced nonchalantly over his shoulder as Nella moved behind him. He pursed his lips as if to whistle but produced only a hissing sound, while he studied the walls and rubbed the palm of one hand against his pant leg.

When Nella passed him, he cleared his throat and fingered the weapon in the holster at his belt.

Uniformed legs appeared rounding the curve in the stairs. He whirled and unsnapped the narrow leather strap of the holster all in an instant.

"Something wrong?"

"No." He was leaning casually against the banister now. "Why?"

"You looked a little jumpy. Everything all right down here?"

"Fine. Just fine. How's it going up there?"

"About done. They'll be bringing him down shortly. Hold your nose when they do." He watched the other man's face closely. "This is quite a house, isn't it?"

"It's very nice."

Nella moved out of the entry hall and toward the library. She did not care for these strangers in her son's house. Her room upstairs was fairly choking with them. Voices from the library indicated that there were even more there.

But the urge to warm herself on just the sight of him was too great and she entered.

He sat in the golden glow of sunlight by a window, her golden boy grown so tall and fine. The soft light hair she longed to fondle, the pale eyes wide and intent upon the man beside the fireplace, the strength of his jaw line . . . Couldn't he feel her love, her pride, across the room? How could he not?

But the picture was spoiled by the girl on the floor, leaning against his chair, shapely slender legs beneath a scandalously short skirt, her skin so bronzed by sun it almost matched her hair and eyes.

"Just exactly what time . . ." The man by the fireplace paused as she moved up behind him. He turned to look right at her but then turned back to the girl. "What time of the night did you see this light?"

The girl answered in a soft frightened voice, and Nella did not care for the way Jay leaned forward to catch her words. She'd been here too often of late, this girl.

That stupid servant, Hymie, appeared to follow Nella with his eyes. It seemed only a moment ago that he'd been a fat slobbery baby crawling around on the kitchen floor while his mother prepared Clay's meals.

Time was different now than it was before, different and erratic. How could Hymie have grown in a moment and yet it seemed an eternity since she'd been separated from her own child?

Clay was in the kitchen once and she'd followed him, her hatred trying to reach him. The crawling baby had looked directly at her and smiled, drool dripping from his lower lip.

Nella thought she'd been seen, had made contact with their world at last, but no one else noticed her and the baby soon lost interest.

Hymie knew she was in the room now though, could sense her general direction, she was sure. So few servants left to look after her son and his house. She must be careful with the servants.

She moved closer to Jay's chair and he stood and walked away to the fireplace. To get away from her? She hadn't meant to disturb him. Or better to see the girl?

Jay stood head and shoulders above the man who began to question Hymie. Her beautiful son, even with the silly shabby clothes and hair, every precious inch so straight and well formed. No one would take him away from her again. But grown men marry and leave live mothers? Why not a dead one? She must not let this happen.

She felt her hate direct itself toward the girl on the floor.

Some of the men moved about the room, some sat and

listened, one took notes. Not all of them wore uniforms.

Nella knew she could draw strength from this room full of people, but she did not dare. She could not risk frightening her child away.

It would take time to reach him. But if she could reach Clay for hate, she could reach Jay for love. In the meantime, she was growing weak.

Nella moved out of the library to seek the dove.

10

*W*hy can't we buy them in cans like other people?" Alice complained from the porch of the washhouse where she sat snapping pole beans.

Lynnette stood inside at the long canning table setting glass jars into the wire holders of a blue cooker. *I'm with you, Alice.*

"You just be glad you don't live in the city where there's no good dirt to plant your own and you don't have to eat that tasteless stuff they put in cans." Bertha, tongs in her hand, watched over yet another cooker.

Elaine, carrying two buckets of water from the pump, sidled past the girl on the porch and managed to pry open the screen door with her elbow. "Wonder what Chris Gunderson was doing at the Van Fleet place and what Mary Jane is going to do now with all those kids to look after."

"They'll do without, same as they always done. Drunken bum never provided for his family anyway."

Lynnette rubbed her aching back muscles and looked at the water and growing pile of snapped beans in the dishpan on the porch. More water to wash more beans to put in more jars to . . .

"Can't think why she didn't tell no one he'd been gone for a week." Elaine dumped washed beans from the colander into Lynnette's dishpan.

"Probably figured he was on a bender and glad to be rid of him for a while."

Lynnette scratched her leg where a drop of perspiration had trickled down the inside of her knee and eyed the long rows of jars cooling on the table. This did it!

She'd accept Hymie's offer to help her even though she felt like a rat taking money from him. But she was reluctant to become indebted to Jay Van Fleet.

Thunder grumbled distantly, adding an exclamation to her own silent but growing anger.

Through the row of fly-spotted windows over the canning table, she could see a dark cloud bank on the other side of the sunlight. The contrast of sun on approaching rain clouds lent an eerie light to the small world that lay breathlessly waiting. . . .

"Fill those jars, Missy, and stop daydreaming. You're about as much help as Alice."

Lynnette bent over the jars yawning in front of her, but she was seeing herself getting off the bus in Denver, breathing in the dry air that would banish the Iowa stickiness from her skin.

She'd tell Bertha as soon as Elaine and Alice left and catch the bus in the morning. She had little to pack. Most of her things were still enroute from Denver, but she didn't mind. She was reaching for freedom and "things" seemed unimportant.

And she smiled for the first time since she'd witnessed the horror of Nella's putrid bedroom.

She'd blotted most of that from her mind, but all week little irrelevant details would jump out in unsuspecting moments . . . the smell of grease on Hymie's overalls as he'd forced her face against him . . . Jay Van Fleet's frozen expression as they'd waited in the library for the authorities from Minturn . . . Reverend Birmingham praying with his eyes open for Chris Gunderson . . . the policeman, who questioned her about the light in the window . . . the way Hymie and Jay avoided looking at each other . . . the little sparrow with the stiff legs.

After a thorough but short inquiry, it was decided that Chris Gunderson had died a natural death. Heart failure. But the question of why he'd been in that house at all went unanswered.

"More like scared to death," Hymie had muttered knowingly.

By the time the threatening clouds lay over the farm, blotting the sunlight, the beans were "done up." Lynnette waved as Elaine and Alice drove off and then stood in the empty farmyard watching the heavy cloud stretch and writhe above her. Lightning flashed down behind the barn but no rain, no breeze to move the muggy, charged air.

"Get in here and help get these beans to the fruit cellar before it rains!"

In the washhouse Bertha knelt, putting jars into boxes. She pushed back a damp coil of white hair and paused to look at her daughter. "What you think about when you just stand around doing nothing is what I'd like to know."

Lynnette sighed as she knelt beside her mother and drew an empty box toward her.

Bertha grunted out with her box. "I'll take these on ahead. You hurry and fill that one. Three or four trips ought to do it."

Thunder shook the washhouse floor. Lynnette hurried to fill her box and carried it out to the cement steps of the cavelike fruit cellar. Only a small bare bulb in the center of the arched roof lighted the hole. Lynnette almost tripped over her mother, who sat motionless on the bottom step, her box still on her lap.

"Bertha, is something wrong?" She just managed to squeeze in beside her and set her own box on the dirt floor at her feet.

Her mother sat rigid, turning only her head to Lynnette, her eyes filling.

"Are you sick?" *Don't be. How would I ever get you up these stairs?*

Bertha shook her head and looked back at the cellar. Lynnette followed her gaze and drew in a quick, dank breath.

The walls and ceiling were brick-lined, wooden shelves covering the sides and back. Mason jars filled every inch of shelf space and even the board platform sitting on the earthen floor along one side. Canned tomatoes, pork, chickens, peas, pickles, preserves, fruit, corn . . . and an entire shelf, three jars deep, that ran the length of the cellar, filled with canned string beans from previous years. Potatoes and crab apples rotted in great piles on the floor.

"Oh, Bertha . . ." Lynnette lifted the box from her mother's lap and laid it on top of her own.

Lightning lit the steps and Bertha's white hair with the funny streaks of yellow at the crown. She turned to speak but then rose and left the cellar.

64

Lynnette stayed behind, trying to understand what she saw, remembering the days when the family and two hired men and weekend company would clean out the cellar by spring.

A lonely drop of rain hit the back of her neck. Lynnette switched off the light and went up the steps, bending to close the big doors in the ground.

Bertha stood at the fence beside the gate, the hem of her skirt uneven because of the way she stood.

Lynnette walked up behind her. "It's starting to rain. Come on in the house."

"Such a waste . . . all that food . . . I'm getting as bad as Olaf . . ." There was an odd croak in her mother's voice.

Rain spotted the sidewalk near the gate. Hard warm pellets touched her face. "Please, let's talk about it in the house."

"I knew there was plenty in that cellar. It's just habit . . ."

"I know . . ."

"No, you don't know, Missy!" Bertha turned and there were raindrops on her spectacles. "Getting old is a dirty trick and you don't know about that yet."

Lightning cracked quite close. Wind and thunder seemed to rush in together. "Please, let's talk about it in the house." Lynnette could feel her hair plastering itself against her forehead, could smell the incredibly rich odors of wet earth.

"Two freezers packed full, a big garden crying to be put up . . . one old woman and a slip of a girl who don't eat nothing to use it all . . ." Water dripped off her nose. "A dirty trick!" she shouted above the wind that made the branches overhead whip and dance.

Lynnette dragged at her mother's arm. A wet maple leaf slapped into her face. "Maybe Elaine and her family could use some of it."

"They can't use the stuff from their own garden. I taught Elaine how to grow a good garden." The wind left and the storm settled into a steady, soaking drizzle. "Work is all I know . . . all I'm good for . . . now there's nobody to work for. You'll be clearing out of here the

65

first chance you get . . . I can tell by just watching you . . ." She lowered her voice and her gaze was so direct, so hopeless, Lynnette couldn't look away. "That's what you're planning, isn't it?"

The rain on Lynnette's cheeks felt warm like tears. "Yes . . ."

Her mother walked slowly toward the house, seemingly shrunken and aged during the storm.

"Bertha?"

But Bertha didn't stop and Lynnette followed her into the enclosed back porch where they stood dripping onto the concrete floor.

Lynnette looked away and knotted her fists. "I'll stay . . . for a while . . . till you get adjusted . . . just for a while, okay?"

Her mother dipped into the front of her dress for a soggy handkerchief "I'm too old to adjust."

"You have to. You can still plant a garden. Just make it smaller. Adjust in little ways . . . I'll try to help. And couldn't Mary Gunderson use some of that food? With eight kids and no husband she's going to need help."

Bertha straightened and wrung out her apron over the drain in the floor. "Do you think she'd take it?"

"People gave you food when your husband died."

"Wouldn't be like charity or nothing . . ." A flicker of excitement appeared in the red-rimmed eyes. "And she could have that big ham in the freezer." A suggestion of a smile . . . "We'll get Leroy to load it all in his pickup." She took off her heavy black shoes then peeled off her rolled stockings. "You'd best get out of them clothes, Missy, before you catch your death. And don't forget to milk the cow."

Lynnette pressed her face against the screen door. *No. I won't forget to milk the cow.*

11

*L*eroy's truck broke an axle and Elaine called the morning they were to deliver the food to Mary Jane Gunderson to say it couldn't be fixed in time. So Lynnette called Hymie and he arrived with his pickup. While he loaded the truck, she raided the freezers and persuaded Bertha to part with some additional hamburger, sausage and two dressed chickens.

"I don't like you riding with that goofy-looking ape. How he gets a license, I don't know." Bertha peered anxiously over her spectacles as she wrapped fresh eggs in newspapers.

"Hymie's not that retarded and I've ridden with him many times."

Her mother had taken a real interest in organizing the food, appeared to have forgotten her useless feeling. But as Lynnette drove off with Hymie, she turned to see Bertha once again sagging against the fence.

Roger Jenson, on a snorting green tractor, pulled out of his drive and onto the road just ahead of them. Hymie slowed and instead of passing, laid on the horn.

Roger wore a fatigue shirt with the muted camouflage pattern over blue jeans. He didn't turn around but gave them the finger over his shoulder. Hymie grinned and leaned across Lynnette to return the gesture as they passed.

"So when are you going to take my money and run for Denver?"

A butterfly mashed against the windshield and she watched the yellow juice splay in the wind. "I'm not going, Hymie . . . not for a while."

Soft brown eyes studied her and looked back to the road. "Big Bertha?"

"I promised in a weak moment to stay a little longer. I don't know what to do. I can't leave her now, but the longer I stay, the more she'll get to depend on my being here."

"How long's a little longer?"

"Who knows? I doubt I can help her adjust but . . . I'm promising myself to get out before winter."

"The money'll wait . . . when you're ready. Look who's coming."

The steel-gray Bentley came up fast, its top down, and passed them with a glint of sunlight and toot of its horn. The passenger, her long bright hair horizontal in the wind, sat very close to Jay Van Fleet.

Hymie watched the Bentley in the outside mirror. "That old crate moves."

"Who's that with him?"

"Some sweet thing he picked up in Minturn. His mother can bug him at night, but she can't hold him in the day. He's around long enough to sleep and eat breakfast."

"Do you really believe a mother who's been dead for thirty years would—"

"I believe it, but I can't say why. Don't understand women alive, let alone dead." He slapped at a mosquito. "All I know's old Mr. Clayborne fought her for thirty years. He lost."

"Fought a dead woman? Hymie, did he ever tell you that?"

"Never had to. I feel things. You don't think it was his idea that her boy had to live in the house."

"Don't try to tell me she wrote that letter."

"No, he did. She made him. Only way she could get Jay to come home was to have him inherit. Old Mr. Clayborne had to die."

"You think this ghost of yours killed Clayborne? And Chris Gunderson too, I suppose."

"That's what I think. Problem is I don't know why Gunderson was there." He slowed the truck and leaned over the wheel. "Wonder what'll happen to Jay Van Fleet, alone there. Nella can't hold him long . . . he's full grown. Got his own ideas."

Lynnette shivered in the heat. "Hymie, I hope you don't talk this crazy to everyone."

"Just stay away from Jay Van Fleet," he said in that

funny high voice as he stepped hard on the accelerator. "Don't want to have to worry about you, too."

She'd angered him and felt the rebuff in his stiffness. The only thing they'd ever argued about seriously was Nella Van Fleet.

Roggins slept at midmorning. Joey's father, tall and lean, stepped out of his newspaper office and walked a few doors down to the drugstore. Otherwise Main Street was bare.

Hymie parked in front of the Gunderson house, across the street from Ollie Torgeson's gas station. The door stood open and a bicycle lay across the front steps.

Mary Jane sat on the porch wearing a shapeless flowered garment, which couldn't hide her enormous overweight.

"I'd better go talk to her first, Hymie, she doesn't know all this is coming."

Mary Jane was braiding her hair in the one braid she always wore coiled on top of her head. She stepped around the bicycle to meet Lynnette.

"Lynn Olson? Is that you? I hardly know you anymore, you're getting so grown up and sophisticated." Her smile didn't fit a newly bereaved widow.

"Stewart."

"Oh, I'm sorry. I keep forgetting you've been married and widowed already. And me working for the Stewarts, too. Think I'd remember, wouldn't you?"

She coiled the thick braid on top of her head and fished in her pocket for some bobby pins.

"Want some coffee? Got the pot on. Hymie, come on in," she yelled in the direction of the curb.

They sat in the kitchen and ate the remnants of the offerings from Chris Gunderson's funeral. Lynnette would have bet that, though worn, the kitchen was as clean as Bertha's.

"I'm sorry about Chris . . ."

"Oh, don't fret about that, Lynn. Probably worse for you two finding him that way."

Lynnette had a brief mental glimpse of the staring mottled thing on the floor of Nella Van Fleet's bedroom and felt the convulsive shudder one feels when all the senses work to reject something, and she put it away from her carefully.

"This'll sound hard, but he was getting to be more of a handful than all the kids, not that he was home much. I feel a little sad but a lot easier, if you know what I mean . . . probably like you felt when your dad died." She munched down a date bar and reached for another. Subtlety was not Mary Jane's thing and somehow Lynnette liked her for it.

"Do you have any idea why he was at the Van Fleet house?"

"Probably looking for booze money. The kids and I took to hiding what money we made. Maybe looking for something he could sell. Poor Chris was going downhill fast."

"Are you overstocked with food from the funeral?"

"No, we've worked through most of it. Why?"

"Well . . . my mother has two freezers and a locker in town stocked to the brim, and she couldn't get this year's garden into the cellar. She wondered if you could use some of it with your big family."

"Well, I never thought Bertha Olson had it in her." The loose flesh on Mary Jane's arm jiggled as she slapped the table. "Can you beat that?"

Hymie grinned into his coffee.

A boy, about seven or eight, slid noiselessly across the chipped linoleum, grabbed the last date bar and ran.

"Roddy, you save room for lunch!" But Roddy had disappeared out the back door. "Oh, well, nothing spoils his appetite. Takes after me."

"We'll understand if you don't want to take the food, but the pickup's full and some of it shouldn't sit out in the sun . . ."

"Take it? Of course I'll take it. Just can't get over your mother thinking of a thing like that."

Lynnette helped Mary Jane stack jars of canned food on dusty shelving in the basement as Hymie carried boxes down the stairs. They'd filled the refrigerator with meat, eggs, cream, milk and fresh vegetables.

"I'll cook that ham tonight. This'll sure help, Lynn. Thank Bertha."

"How will you manage now, without Chris?"

"Oh, he hadn't worked for years. My three oldest have part-time jobs, and I clean at your mother-in-law's and at the parsonage. Wonder if Mrs. Benninghoff still needs help up at the Van Fleet place."

"I know she does, but would you want to work there?"

"It wouldn't bother me none." She stood back and viewed the full shelves. "Seems like Christmas. And I don't believe in the ghost like Chris did. He wouldn't even let me work up there, you know."

"He believed in Nella's ghost?"

"Sure he did." Mary Jane switched off the light at the head of the stairs and closed the door to the basement.

Roddy Gunderson sat at the table scraping crumbs from the date-bar pan with a knife. He eyed Lynnette suspiciously out of the corners of his eyes, his lips pressed tightly. His appetite might take after his mother's but he looked like a younger, less dissipated Chris Gunderson.

"Came home one night, years ago, saying he'd seen her . . . or something. He'd snuck into the place through the fields. He was scared to death . . . course he got to seeing all sorts of things when he was drunk, which was most of the time." Mary Jane opened the door to the refrigerator to stare at the contents.

When she turned back to Lynnette, she frowned. "Funny he should go back up there, come to think of it. Always said he'd never get near that house again."

12

*H*ymie parked the pickup by the gatehouse and leaned forward to peer at the Van Fleet house through the windshield.

Grass needs cutting. Ivy around the door needs trimming. Broken window where the dove's looking back at me not fixed yet. Just walk in and fix it, he says. Don't see him offering to do it.

A miller moth crawled up the windshield. Hymie could feel its fear. It slipped and fell to the dashboard. He picked it up gently. Wings and feet feathered at his palm.

Hymie heaved himself out of the truck and released the moth, watched it weave toward the house, waited expectantly . . .

About ten feet from the house the moth stopped its erratic flight. It hovered a moment, seemed almost to bob on the air and then turned to fly back, straight and certain, barely missing Hymie's head in its haste.

Some crawling things and mosquitoes moved right on to the house, but most bugs turned away before they reached it. Interesting.

He looked again to the window of Nella's room. What would she do now with a grown man for a son? *She's murdered to get him here. Will she murder to keep him? Who can stop her? Could Nella be jealous? Mothers are funny things. . . .*

Hymie spit at a tree root and decided he'd better keep little Lynn Stewart away from Nella.

As he walked toward the house he could feel the change in the atmosphere at the place in the air where the bugs stopped.

His mother had his lunch waiting in the kitchen. She talked and prepared lunch for Jay and the sweet thing from Minturn, turning quick worried glances on him as he ate. "Mr. Van Fleet wants the ivy cut around the front door and the chemicals changed in the pool. Hymie, eat all that jello. I read where it's good for the skin and nails. They're going to lunch at the pool. She seems like a nice girl, but kind of silly, I was wondering if he'd take a fancy to Lynnette. She looks so lost since her husband died. Don't you think?"

Hymie belched and stretched his muscles.

She didn't wait for an answer, but picked up a tray and started for the door. He found a toothpick and lifted the other tray.

She went ahead of him across the lawn and he noticed again the widow's hump forming from her shoulders. Always the black dresses. Once, when younger, he'd wished she'd wear bright pretty clothes. She worked too hard. Now there was Nella's son to stuff with food and fuss over. The more work and worry, the happier she was. Women were funny, but mothers the funniest of the lot.

The fat white dove with the red eyes moved out of the way of his farm boots. Hymie had taken a dislike to doves. There were about nine or ten of them roosting on an overhead branch, pretending they were unnoticeable.

His mother fawned over Jay Van Fleet . . . and so did the girl from Minturn. Her wet cornsilk hair covered her back better than her swim suit covered her chest. What would it feel like to be that drop of water running from the top of her suit down the wet-sand color of her skin to her navel?

He watched the girl shudder as she met his eyes, and he rolled the toothpick over to the other side of his mouth. She'd be about as easy to crush as that moth he'd held a while ago.

Jay lifted his sunglasses and Hymie recognized a fellow watcher in the squinted eyes, the lack of expression. He understood that suspicion and curiosity lay behind the careful blankness and he smelled fear beneath the grimy combination of sweat and suntan lotion. Interesting to watch this man, but he didn't like the feeling of being watched.

White skin showed where the tape had held Jay's ribs together, and puckerish scrapes still trying to heal.

The sounds of flirting laughter and tinkling ice filled his head as he walked back across the lawn. He spit into the pfitzer beneath Nella's room, where he'd found Clayborne Van Fleet frozen in the snow.

Then Hymie headed for his hiding place.

A light shone in the snug gatehouse as Jay Van Fleet drove the Bentley up the drive that evening. It wasn't the first time something inside him had itched to knock at the Benninghoff's door and ask if he could sleep on their floor. The thought of the slow dumb smirk that would spread across Hymie's face made him drive past. Jay knew he'd be tempted to put his fist through that smirk. The result would be the creaming of Jay Van Fleet.

After the Bentley had been put to bed he stood on the paved apron and watched the clouds cover the white slice of moon. They slid swiftly, silently, their edges made fuzzy by the dull moonlight behind them.

Jay's awareness of the light was sudden. It drained away a good chunk of the treasured intoxication he'd managed to bring home from Minturn. He looked up to the second-story window, knowing—without knowing— the source of that light.

He watched it for a moment, swearing in a harsh whisper, and then he ran, his ribs protesting as his shoes jarred on the pavement. The front door seemed to fly open at his touch.

Pausing only to flick the light switch, he slid precariously on the polished blackness of marble. Jay had an instant and ludicrous impression of disapproval from the sedate cane chairs and silent grandfather clock at the foot of the stairs.

By the time he reached the cold of the second floor, his injured ribs seemed to pierce his intestines and he was stone sober.

He fell against the wall by the light switch, a helpless rage choking off the running stream of curses.

Frigid darkness smothered the upstairs hall. He closed his mouth against it.

No light showed under the tight-fitting door at the end.

He groped for the light switch with a moist hand. The

74

door stood open . . . wide open. It had been closed when he left . . . hadn't it?

He moved his tongue over his teeth and started down the hall. His feet rustled at the carpet, nudged at the quiet.

He knew there were no longer any bulbs in Nella's room, but he pressed the switch. Nothing happened. His shadow on the floor, with the light behind him, seemed to waver, grow and then shrink. The illumination pierced only a little of the blackness. The sound of his own breathing reverberated from the walls.

Remnants of Chris Gunderson assaulted his nose and the smell of old dirt . . .

"What the goddamned hell do you want!" His scream echoed around him.

The only answer—a rustling and the soft cooing of doves.

One of them fluttered into the light on the carpet. It ruffled its feathers and pouched out its chest, watching him with red-bead eyes.

Jay pulled the door shut and turned back down the hall. "Goddamned fuckin' house . . . screwed-up, son-of-a-bitchin' pile of moldy rocks!" He stomped down the curving stairs, across the black marble, through the downstairs hall to the library. "¡Carajo!" He left lights blazing behind him. "¡Puta!"

In the library he turned on every ceiling light, wall sconce and lamp and then lit the wood Hymie had left in the fireplace. He pulled out the bottom drawer of Clayborne's desk so viciously that the bottles clanked sharply. "Esta casa . . . Esta casa de mierda, ya me llego . . ." Jay kept the drawer stocked much better than his uncle had. He wondered whether he used it out of sentiment or as some kind of ironic joke on himself.

Selecting a bottle of Chivas Regal—why drink bourbon on an expense account?—he carried it by its neck to the fire. In between healthy slugs of scotch, he swore at the flames. Two drunks in one night was going to make a blue hell of tomorrow.

Gradually the combined warmth of fire and liquor stilled the anger.

Harry's leering face wavered in the flames and that of the solemn priest . . . the stricken expression of the girl . . . the unformed features of the sleeping infant.

Jay carried the bottle with him out of the house.

Crossing the drive, he sat against the roughened trunk of a dead tree and faced the house.

The only lights in that house were those he'd left on himself.

The stories of his potty uncle and Hymie Benninghoff had set things rolling. They both wanted to keep people out.

Gunderson died of a sick drunken heart.

His uncle died of exposure. He took his shoes off and left them on the balcony because he'd gone bananas.

Hymie was trying to drive him out so that he and Mrs. Benninghoff would have the place to themselves, forever.

The doves were there because the window was broken.

Bugs didn't like the place because it was so cold.

And it was so cold because . . .

Jay took a deep drink from the bottle and lit a cigarette. The scotch no longer burned his throat and the thick night heat was better, warmer than the fire. It felt good to sweat a little . . . that girl had been warm and sweating too . . . and smooth. Jay hoped he hadn't left her pregnant. Nothing like a bastard spreading bastards . . . probably took pills or something.

At one point the face of the little widow had come to him. For some reason that vision had spurred him to exploits that surprised him and apparently delighted . . . he'd forgotten her name.

What was it about the widow Stewart that stuck in his head? She'd better get to Denver soon. He'd offer her more than enough money to get there. Buy her a car to get there. Jay gestured with the bottle and cool liquid dribbled onto his fingers.

She was the same color all over . . . amber . . . weird, really, and too thin.

When he felt sufficiently numb, he staggered back to the house. But he tossed for hours in Clayborne's bed, the chilled silence in the room accentuating the buried loneliness of a lifetime.

His thoughts turned to things that surfaced in the depth of night when his will was weakened by lack of sleep and distracting activity. The smug comfortable relationship of Mrs. Benninghoff and her son in their secure cottage by the gate. The easy familiarity between Lynnette and Hymie. He experienced an equal measure of envy and disdain but couldn't help wondering what it would be like.

Jay had never known a woman he'd feel free to throw around, as Hymie had Lynnette, unless he'd slept with her first, pretended to commit himself. The fact that it was pretense usually spoiled any hankering to see that particular woman again.

Just before he slept, Jay Van Fleet dreamed that something touched his hair and something cold brushed his cheek, that the rumpled covers straightened out and pulled up to his chin. . . .

13

*L*ynnette reached under the hen for the warm egg and received a painful peck for her troubles. "You, I wouldn't *mind* eating."

The speckled hen jumped from her box and stalked out of the hen house, defeated but proud.

Counting the eggs in the wicker basket, Lynnette decided someone was shirking. Couldn't blame the poor things. All that work for nothing. *Just like me.*

She plowed through the group of disgruntled chickens in the henyard. "Have fun, ladies."

Roger Jenson, on his sputtering tractor, mowed hay in a nearby field. He wore a straw hat with the brim rolled up at the sides like a TV cowboy.

It was September and the heat had dried. Sunflowers cast yellow brilliance on the low weeds by the corrugated machine shed.

She squeezed through the opening left by one of the sliding doors. A rat the size of a tomcat watched her from under the giant rusting combine.

The old Oliver her father had been so proud of sat dusty and rejected on flattened tires. Olaf had once hauled her up on that tractor seat to hold her on his lap and explain why sometimes, on a farm, pets were butchered and eaten, why Snowflake—her special calf—was gone forever. She'd refused to eat any meat but chicken for months. Her father's hair had been gray even then.

Lynnette had passed the machine shed often since July but hadn't entered it until now. There was no sign on the dirt floor of the place where Olaf had lay dying.

Leaving the shed, she passed the stock truck, its axles resting on concrete blocks, one door hanging open from its hinges.

She circled behind the hog sheds to keep out of sight from the house. Bertha would have more work for her to do. Once these sheds had been busy with young life. Now weeds fought each other for control of the pens outside. Board fences that had separated sows and their litters from neighboring families sagged and peeled.

A procession of hired men had helped Bertha keep the farm going as Olaf's condition worsened, his brain denied more and more of its life-giving blood by arteries clogged with the residue of a lifetime of good plain farm food. But they soon found themselves spending more time playing orderly to the aging giant than being farmhands and moved on.

Lynnette raced across the space between the hog sheds and the barn. Roger's boar lay snorting in his sleep in a patch of mud beside the water trough. Flies crawled over him and his ears twitched.

She skirted the boar's pen and walked into the pasture. Stretching out with her hands behind her head, she watched frothy clouds form and reform then fray apart as though as torn as her own emotions.

Sun, always her ally against depression, gradually warmed her skin and clothes and hair . . . the gentle ache in her body . . . the ache for Joey that would still come at odd moments.

The grass around her rustled and Roger Jenson stood above her. Sweat had streaked the field dust on his face. Pinpricks of light dotted his skin through the holes in the straw hat. "Bertha's been calling for you."

"I know." She sat up and brushed her cheeks with the back of her hand.

He removed his hat and used his handkerchief to wipe off the inside of the band. "What's eating you? As if I don't know."

"Why don't you just go away?"

"Good idea." But he replaced the hat and sat beside her. "If I don't, I might be tempted to lay you right here in the pasture. Bertha'd come over the slope and raise the sky about six feet and . . ."

"Roger, don't you ever think of anything else?" *Look who's talking.*

"Not unless I'm working. Then even, my mind wanders sometimes. Plow some crazy furrows that way." He lit a cigarette.

"Roger, I'd like to be alone."

"Crying alone's no good." He lit another cigarette and handed it to her. "Hymie said he offered you money to get away. How come you're still here?"

"I couldn't leave Bertha just then. But I'm going to."

He lowered silky lashes and chuckled. "No way."

Lynnette swung at him but hit the brim of his hat instead, knocking it off his head. He flicked the cigarette into the creek, wrestled her back on the grass and pinned her arms above her head, all with a broad grin and absolutely no effort.

"Look. Don't get sore at me. I'm not keeping you here. But no matter what you do, the Olson family'll think of something to keep you from leaving. Face it, it's fate. Not Roger Jenson."

She lay limp beneath him. He kissed the end of her nose, the dark stubble on his chin rasping her skin.

The sound of a car pulling in to the farmyard made them both relax. He stood and helped her up. "Tell you what. Since you're leaving so soon, let's go to a movie in Minturn tomorrow night . . . celebrate your leaving town." He retrieved her egg basket and his hat. They walked toward the barn.

"Not unless Hymie goes too."

Roger stopped, his dark eyes searching her face. "Sure. Why not?"

When they rounded the barn, Harold's Cadillac stood by the gate, a U-Haul trailer attached to it. Bertha, Margaret and Harold talked beside it.

"Where have you been? I've been calling and calling," Bertha said. "That cow's about to bust an udder."

Lynnette took the egg basket from Roger and handed it to her mother. "What's in the trailer?"

"Your things finally arrived at the depot and we brought them out," Harold told her. "Rog, would you help me carry this stuff upstairs?"

"Sure." He lifted out a box. "Looks like you plan to stay awhile after all," he whispered as he passed her.

Lynnette watched them carry her belongings into the house. There was something final about the arrival of these things. When Roger lifted Joey's black skis from a partially destroyed wrapper, she turned away.

"These yours?"

"No, Joey's." She watched a purple martin swoop through a swarm of mosquitoes. "Mine should be in there somewhere."

Bertha turned back from the gate. "You never told me you rode on them skinny sticks. That's dangerous. You hurry and milk that cow now. Could thank them for bringing all this. Harold left work early and everything."

"Thanks a lot!"

Roger was waiting by the empty trailer after she'd milked the cow and put the milk through the separator. "You've got cow shit on your shoes."

"Go to hell."

"Okay. But not till I take you out tomorrow night. I'll call Hymie."

"Lynn?" Margaret stepped out of the back door. "Can you come in and help?" She started toward them.

"Tomorrow night, around seven." Roger walked off.

Margaret examined her fingernails and tried to pull her upper lip down over her front teeth. "Well, you two seem to be hitting it off again."

"Margaret, don't."

"Don't what?"

"Just don't."

Lynnette was at the counter, up to her elbows in slimy mashed potatoes when a car came down the lane. They all gathered on the screened front porch.

"Who in the world is that?"

"I've never seen a car like that."

Lynnette was the last one to recross the kitchen and go out the back door as the steel-gray Bentley pulled up to the gate.

14

"**M**r. Van Fleet, I'm so thrilled to finally meet you." Margaret leaned over the door of the Bentley on the driver's side patting her teased hairdo. With the canvas top back Jay was open to assault. "We were so happy to hear you'd been found and notified of your good fortune. And that earthquake must have been a terrible experience."

Harold ran a finger over the Bentley's fender. "Where did you find this beautiful antique? It has to be worth a fortune."

"In the garage." Jay, unable to get out of the car, could not have expected such a crowd. The tilt of his eyebrows above the sunglasses suggested disbelief. Lynnette, amused, stood by the gate, offering no assistance.

"It's Nella's car." Bertha looked at it as if it were awaiting the command to attack. "And I never thought I'd see it sittin' here!" Her face had turned gray under the white of her hair.

"Really? Is this your mother's car?" Margaret pulled at the back of her skirt.

"Of course it is. Think I'd forget? Almost ran me down right by my own mailbox." Bertha stomped toward the house, not even glancing at Lynnette as she passed.

"Mom? Excuse her please, Mr. Van Fleet. She's old and recently a widow. We never know how she's going to take things." Margaret's smile was deprecating and Lynnette could have hit her. Bertha never did anything she didn't fully intend to do and could outthink Margaret with no effort.

"I'm afraid you'll have to excuse us too, Mr. Van Fleet. We know who you are but we forgot to introduce ourselves. That was my mother, Mrs. Olson, this is my wife, Margaret, and I'm Harold Olson." He put out his hand forcing Jay to struggle around the right-hand steering wheel to shake it. "I'm a lawyer with a practice in Minturn. Won't you come in and tell us what we can do for you? I'm sure my mother . . ."

"I came to talk to Mrs. Stewart and I can do that right here."

"Mrs. Stewart? She doesn't live here." Harold looked disappointed behind the dark-rimmed glasses. "She has a house in town. The big Victorian frame at the west end of Main Street."

Jay pointed to Lynnette, his mouth twitching ever so slightly. "I meant *that* Mrs. Stewart."

Lynnette moved forward. "I'm just Harold's sister. One of the other planets that revolve around him. Also chief charwoman. Would you excuse us please, Harold, Margaret?"

"Well, if that's all . . . he wants . . ." Harold escorted his wife through the gate. They paused at the back door but Lynnette and Jay watched them until they entered the house.

"You can get out. I'll keep them from eating you." She nodded toward the faces crowded at the kitchen window.

"I'm beginning to see why Colorado looks so good to you." They stood facing the barn, their backs to the house. "Do you suppose they can lip read?"

"I'm sure of it. What did you want to see me about?"

"Just wanted to know if you'd like to come up for a swim. We'll be draining the pool soon. Mrs. Benninghoff could fix us something to eat after . . ."

"Say no more. I'll get my suit."

As she came into the kitchen, Margaret said, "Mom's agreed we should ask Mr. Van Fleet in for dinner, Lynn . . ."

"No, we're going out. You go ahead." Lynnette started for the stairs.

"What about your own supper, Missy?"

"I'll eat later with him. Hurry up, your food will get cold." She slipped up the stairs and changed out of her blue jeans into a dress with matching coat. There was no time for a bath and she hoped the pool would wash off the smell of cow. Rummaging through the unpacked boxes, she found a swimsuit and raced downstairs and into the bathroom.

No one was seated at the table and they crowded around the door.

"You are not going out with him, Missy Sue! Rich men only take out girls like you for one reason. I won't have it." Bertha squinted reddened eyes and pursed her lips until her nose wrinkled. "And once you've lost it there's no getting it back."

"Lost what?" Lynnette brushed up her hair to fluff it and then stopped, the brush still on her head. "You mean . . ."

"You know what I mean."

She started the brush in motion again but couldn't help staring at her mother. "Bertha, I was married for two years."

"I don't want to hear about it. I just don't want you going out with him. That's final."

"I am twenty-four years old. I will go out with whom I please. Your dinner is getting cold."

"What's that thing hanging out of your purse?"

"My swimsuit."

"Why, that wouldn't cover—"

"Bye now. Don't wait up. I'll be late." She had to squeeze through the crush at the bathroom door.

Jay had just settled her in the Bentley when Bertha yelled from the kitchen window. "You be home by nine thirty, hear?"

Before starting the engine, Jay laid his head on his arm against the steering wheel, the slow smile exposing more and more teeth. "Nine thirty?"

"Mr. Van Fleet, if you get me home before two tomorrow morning, I will poison your pool. Got that?"

"Right." He laughed and turned the Bentley around in the farmyard with all the roaring, screeching and crunching of gears he could get out of it.

Their gay mood lasted through the changing into suits, even in the cold house.

But once in the water they sobered and swam in silence.

Twilight darkened the water. An early cricket rattled somewhere nearby. Jay began diving for debris on the bottom, bringing it up and flinging it out.

She dived to help him and found it hard to distinguish debris from peeling paint in the decreasing light. The water felt cooler at the bottom.

Lynnette came up grasping nothing. Whatever she'd grabbed had slipped away before she surfaced. She treaded water looking for it and then dove again, keeping her eyes on a dark patch of something sinking slowly to the bottom. For a long warm slinky moment her leg slid down Jay's as he was coming up. She released the air in her lungs before she'd meant to and forgot all about the dark patch.

When she broke the surface, still empty-handed, he was waiting for her. "That was nice."

"I wasn't watching where I was going."

Jay continued to dive, slinging wet silver-blond hair out of his eyes each time he surfaced. The skin that had been wrapped in bandages was still a lighter color than the rest. He was breathing hard when he swam over to grab onto the concrete next to her.

Three gray and white doves flapped above them and disappeared over the house.

"Damn birds. We fixed the window and now they're roosting in the attics. Cleaned the room, too. You'll never guess who helped."

"Hymie?"

"Gunderson's widow."

"Mary Jane? You shouldn't have asked her to do that room."

"Told her she didn't have to. She took one look at all that dirt and waded in. She and Mrs. Benninghoff worked in there for two days."

The chandelier in the dining room spread light and shadow across the lawn. Through the window they could see the housekeeper moving about the table.

"I'd heard that Mrs. Benninghoff doesn't stay after dark."

"She doesn't. Leaves dinner on a warmer and does the dishes in the morning. You must rate with her."

Lynnette pushed off with her feet against the side to swim toward the ladder but found her legs suddenly entangled with Jay's. She went under. His hands on her waist turned her around and brought her up sputtering. "Jay . . ."

"When are you leaving for Denver?"

"You're certainly anxious to get rid of me." She pushed away from him and ended up closer.

"I sure am."

She was chilled and his body felt warm through the holes that laced the front of her suit.

"I sure am." His lips were cool as they touched her forehead and then her nose, passed up her mouth and moved down to her throat. They slid up to her lips and she shuddered as they submerged, the length of his body forcing her down, a sudden warmth spreading inside her. They rolled over and surfaced.

"I've . . . heard of a breathless . . . kiss but . . . you almost drowned me"

"Funny. I could have sworn you were enjoying it."

She reached the ladder and hauled herself up, but not before she received a stinging slap on the bottom. "Sometimes men . . ."

"Yeah, I know. Life's hell, isn't it?" The beautiful smile was followed by bitter laughter.

Mrs. Benninghoff had turned off the chandelier and lit candles by the time they'd changed. She even stayed to serve them a puffy omelet with spinach salad, hot rolls and a slender bottle of wine.

The grandeur of the dining room; the quiet presence of the housekeeper; the fact that neither of them were dressed for the elaborately simple preparations; the distortions of shapes, shadows and colors created by the unsteady light of candle flame; and the way her host had retreated into himself since she'd rebuffed him at the pool—all these combined to make it a strained dinner for Lynnette.

She sensed that she had hurt Jay Van Fleet. It surprised her that anyone could hurt so detached a man, and it worked on her until she felt she'd been cruel.

She tried to reach him. "If you're going to live in a house like this, you'll have to shop for some fancier clothes."

He remained silent as he poured the pale wine.

"You really saved my life tonight," she tried again. "I get so bored and lonely on the farm . . . and trapped. My mother doesn't drive and so there's no car. We have to rely on my sister to take us shopping."

The colorless eyes were watching her now, more washed-out than ever in candlelight. For just a moment his expression reminded her of the look on Bertha's face as she'd stood in the rain.

"Look, I am trying to apologize." *For what? I didn't practically drown him or slap him on the fanny.*

"Why should you be lonely? You're surrounded by family and friends."

"More like suffocated." A cold draft crept from somewhere to coil around her ankles. Lynnette shivered and felt more depressed.

Mrs. Benninghoff returned to clear their plates and Hymie stood in the door of the breakfast room behind a cart bearing dessert and coffee, anger in the set of his shoulders and lips. He didn't meet her eyes. He helped his mother serve the sponge cake with a thick hot sauce.

"The dinner was wonderful, Mrs. Benninghoff."

"Thank you, Lynn. We'll be going now, Mr. Van Fleet. Just leave everything here and I'll clean it up in the morning."

"What's the matter with him?" Jay said when they'd left.

"He's angry with me . . . for being with you." The horses on the wallpaper pranced in the flickering light.

"Jealous?"

"No, it's not you. It's your mother."

The quick squinted glance, the tight lips, the spoon held at an unnatural angle . . . a drop of the sticky licorice-flavored sauce fell to the table. "My mother . . ."

"This will sound silly . . . but Hymie believes that she, or her spirit or whatever, lives in this house. That she wants you near her because you're her son, I guess. And that she might hurt me. He's worried."

"Why should she hurt you?" His question was unnecessarily sharp.

"Who knows? Hymie's full of wild ideas. You just have

to understand him. Maybe he thinks Nella wouldn't want any feminine competition or . . ."

"Let's move into the library and light a fire." Jay rose quickly and blew out the candles. They retreated to pillows on the floor in front of the fireplace. He poured cognac.

"You don't seem to fit all this," she said, trying to avoid the subject that seemed to disturb him.

"You're telling me! Think I'll grow into it?"

"If you're going to be a rich playboy, you'll have to go see old movies. There aren't many around here to study." They grew silent, even the fire seemed to burn quietly, almost as if the quiet of the house was weighted like the water in the pool, forcing sounds in on themselves.

"Tell me about your life . . . what it was like growing up without a family." Anything to start the conversation, anything to stop the quiet.

To her surprise, he began talking, more to the fire than to her, stretched out on the floor with his chest on a cushion, his cheek resting on his hand.

He talked for a long time and his story was so different from her own that she forgot the chill at her back that the fire failed to warm.

Moved from home to home, family to family, then from school to school, at the apparent whim of an Eastern lawyer—Jay could have formed few deep relationships. Here was the man of thirty discussing without emotion spending his holidays in the deserted dormitories of boarding schools while his classmates went to their families, a pet dog and a turtle that were not allowed to move on with him, running away repeatedly and being "hunted down" by the police.

Lynnette listened without interrupting, feeling the loneliness of such a life, seeing the stoic yet rebellious little boy collecting smooth pebbles and then rocks, hiding them under his bunk in a boarding school and having them confiscated because the maid couldn't clean under the bed.

Something at the back of her mind reminded her of the phony Jay, the con-man smile, and warned her that this was a play for sympathy, a possible prelude to something more substantial than the pass at the pool. She could see why he'd built the false front, why he'd had to learn to use charm to get what he wanted.

Yet she couldn't help becoming involved in his story.

"The University of Miami was my first coeducational experience. I spent two years studying females and then I went to the University of Michigan to study geology. Old Clayborne paid for anything that would keep me out of Iowa." Jay added a split log to the dying fire.

"You did come one summer. I remember seeing you."

"And after that to the School of Mines in Colorado for graduate study."

"And then to South America?"

"No, I got drafted."

She waited for him to continue and when he remained silent she said, "You were able to see some of the world then."

"Mostly smoke and mud."

"Vietnam?"

Jay nodded, his lips forming a tight line. He was not going to discuss Vietnam.

"Were you really in a church when the earthquake hit Peru?"

"Yeah. And afterward I spent a long time under it."

"Did you run in for shelter or were you praying there wouldn't be an earthquake?"

"No. I think I was about to get married."

"You think?"

"It was a strange situation. If I'd been in the States"—the big smile exposed the perfect teeth, the direct look dared her to look away—"I'd have been at the wrong end of a loaded shotgun."

"Oh . . ."

"I told this priest I wasn't meant to marry. I'm a walking disaster area. He wouldn't take my word for it and the church fell in." He shook his head comically, but he looked almost as pale as when she'd first met him.

"And this partner you mentioned. Is he still in Peru?"

Her question wiped the smile from his face. "Harry? Yeah, he's still there." Stretching his arms out in front

89

of him, he yawned in an attempt at nonchalance. "Still under the church."

"Isn't there any subject I can bring up with you that isn't a no-no?"

"There is one." Rising stiffly, he walked in and out of shadows to the desk. As he pulled out a drawer there was a rustling sound in the hallway. The door stood open. She could see nothing but darkness.

He returned carrying a picture album, part of a white envelope protruding from its pages. "When are you leaving for Denver?"

"Soon."

"Good." Jay settled beside her, the album on his lap, and removed the envelope. "This ought to get you there in style. You don't have to pay it back. Just go as soon as you can."

The envelope bulged with twenty-dollar bills. "Jay . . . I can't take this. It's special of you to want to do this for me but . . ."

"I'm not going to look you up in a few years and ask for repayment. I'll put it in writing if you want."

"I don't mean that . . . it's just that I don't need it anymore. I've found a way to get there." Lynnette handed the envelope back, again sensing that she'd hurt him, but his face showed no sign of it. "Thanks so much anyway."

"You're sure?"

"I'm sure. What's in the album?"

"Pictures." He put the envelope on a low table, stared at it and moved a lamp to the floor in front of them. "Found it in Nella's room."

"Ah hah! In a secret panel beside the fireplace . . ."

"No. In a top dresser drawer."

On the first page was a picture of a baby engulfed in a lacy christening dress, propped on a dark tapestry that had been draped over a chair. The graceful, faded handwriting beneath it read, *Nella Louise Van Fleet*. Posed portraits with various solemn adults followed as the baby grew into a little girl.

"This is the one I wanted you to see." Jay paused at a large picture taken on the lawn at the back of the Van Fleet house. *Nella's eighth birthday party*. His hand covered the rest of the writing. "Guess who these people are?"

"How would I know?" But she moved the lamp closer and bent over it.

A handsome young couple posed on a white metal love seat. An older bald man sat in a chair next to them, his hand on the shoulder of a girl sitting on the grass in front of him. The girl wore a large bow at the back of her head. She dominated the picture because she alone had not posed all the expression out of her face. She looked vital, intensely curious and quite capable of mischief.

Three other children, one about two or three; and none of them as well dressed as the rest of the group, completed the picture. The house behind them appeared more homey than now and not at all sinister.

"This one has got to be Nella. The other children don't seem to belong there. The young couple are her parents?"

"No." Jay pointed to the young man in the love seat. "That's old Clayborne."

"I can't believe he was ever that good looking." He sat tall and straight, his legs crossed, his dark hair waved back from his face, a thin mustache above his mouth. "My earliest memories of him are of an ancient bent man."

"This is his stepmother, my mother's mother." He pointed to the other occupant of the love seat. She appeared younger than her stepson. Jay's finger moved to the older man in the chair behind Nella. "And that's her husband, Cecil, my grandfather." He still held his hand over most of the writing on the page. "You were right about Nella. Do you know who the other kids are?"

"Servant's children maybe? Invited for the party? They're dressed so differently." Two girls sat cross-legged beside Nella, one very young, the other about Nella's age. A tall boy sat on the end of the row. "That one's very pretty if you don't notice the clothes," she said of the older girl.

Jay lifted his hand from the page. "It's your mother."

"Bertha? Can't be." But the second row of names

read—*Olaf (12 years), Vera (3 years), Bertha (8 years), and Nella (8 years).*

"I don't know of many Berthas around here but the name Olaf was common in my father's generation. I wonder if that boy is my father." The only familiar thing about him was his hairline.

"Did he live around here then?"

"He was born in the house I'm . . . staying in now and so was his younger sister, Vera. She's still alive, runs the library in Roggins. It must be them. And Bertha was born at the farm across the road, where Roger Jenson lives. I can't remember my folks ever talking about Nella. It's hard to believe. This Bertha's hair looks darker than mine. I thought all the Olson's were blond except me and my nephew."

"She wasn't born an Olson."

"That's true. But this makes her the same age as your mother. I'd understood Nella was much younger. How old was Nella when she died?"

"Forty. Seems kind of old for a woman to be messing around begetting a bastard, doesn't it?"

"Not necessarily. Women can mess around just as long as men can."

"Yeah? How old are you?"

"Twenty-four . . . Let's look at the album."

Lynnette stared at the three children beside Nella. Obviously her aging relatives had been young once. Someday a young Olson might stare at her own youthful pictures in amazement. Odd that a common thing like aging should be so hard to conceive.

"I wonder if Nella was driving the Bentley when it almost creamed your mother at her mailbox."

"It was her car, at least according to Bertha."

Jay began turning pages and they watched Nella grow from hair ribbons to dark lipstick and no eyebrows. It became apparent when Nella's mother stopped adding the pictures and her daughter began. Men appeared in greater numbers, alone or with Nella, most of them posed in exotic settings labeled Bern, Madrid, Lima, Barbados, etc.

"None of those men look like you. But she really traveled, didn't she? And first class."

The snapshots stopped suddenly. Several photos were loose in the back of the book and had been taken much later. Nella, at the Van Fleet house in those photos, barely resembled herself. The lithe, vivacious playgirl had sobered and thickened, her hair had darkened. Her eyes had lost their mischievous sparkle.

"I wonder why she never married."

"Probably, like me, she found it more fun to play around."

"Yes, but look where it got her."

"She'd have grown older anyway." But he studied these last pictures carefully.

"That's what my family wants to do with me. Bring me back here for good, trap me in nothingness and spinsterhood."

He put the snapshots back into the album and checked his watch. "You can be trapped anywhere, little widow."

"I'd better be getting home now. I've enjoyed the evening." Lynnette glanced over her shoulder, thinking she'd heard that rustly swishing sound in the hallway.

"It's only midnight."

"At least it's not nine thirty." She started to rise and giggled. "I'm going to need help. My feet are asleep."

Jay pulled her up by the shoulders and, as she placed her weight on leaden feet, her ankles ached with weakness.

"Try jumping around." A hint of Nella's mischievous gleam crept into his eyes.

"Oh, I can't. They're more dead than asleep."

His hands moved from her shoulders to her back and she fell against him, not bothering to ward off his lips. He stood slightly shorter than Joey but he was thicker. It was delicious to be enveloped that way.

"What's with you anyway? All night you've been looking at me like you wanted me to haul you off to the bedroom, and whenever I touched you, you'd jump away like a goosed kangaroo."

"I know. It's just one of those days. I think I can stand

93

now." She moved away reluctantly. "It has nothing to do with you, really."

"What does it have to do with?"

Lynnette stooped to retrieve her purse and thought a moment. "I think it's completely dependent on my menstrual cycle." She softened the outrageous statement with a shaky laugh.

"Can't be good for you to reject it like that, give you cancer or something." He helped her into her coat. "Just one more for the road." She was flat against him again, soaking in the warmth of his skin and breath. The longing to belong again . . .

It was then that the cold moved up from the floor around her bare ankles to her back, over her shoulders and into her face as she staggered away from him. It entered her mouth, filling it, choking her lungs. A sound, like air screaming past a racing car, grew and hissed into her ears, burning them deep inside. . . .

15

*T*he screaming air tried to smother her. It crawled down her throat. She found it hard to breathe.

Her body writhed with heaving spasms that could not reach her clogged throat as her esophagus attempted to rid itself of the strange foreign matter.

Lynnette didn't realize she was on the floor until Jay bent above her. He made swimming motions with his arms as if he were trying to reach her through water. His lips moved, but she could hear only the screaming air in her head.

She could feel her own fingernails clawing at the skin of her throat but was unable to control them.

Hymie's shaggy head wavered above her. She felt herself being lifted. None of his body heat penetrated the cold surrounding her.

The room rushed by at crazy angles, upside down. Lynnette knew Hymie was running but couldn't feel the jostling. In the hallway the faded flowers on the yellow wallpaper seemed to writhe and twist as she did.

The staircase in the entry hall swept by and they were outside.

She caught a glimpse of darkness with stars in it before blackness weighted her down. *I'm going to die.*

The wild writhing of her body slowed and then ceased.

But the choking pressure was suddenly torn from her. Burning air returned forcibly to her throat and lungs. The screaming stopped. The blackness lifted.

Stars.

Hymie lowered himself to the ground, still holding her. Sweat dripped from the end of his nose.

Jay stood beside them looking back at the house.

Hymie rocked his body as Lynnette cried and gasped. His heavy hand kneaded her back.

"How did you know what to do . . . to come here?" Jay asked weakly.

"Bugs stop here. It's all right now, Lynn." Hymie rolled her back against his chest making soothing noises. But when she looked up, he too was staring at the house.

Jay knelt beside them. "You were out in the hall all the time?"

"Yep."

"You knew something was going to happen . . ."

"Afraid it would. I feel things."

Lynnette sat up. "What was it . . . the screaming? . . ."

"I didn't hear any screaming. You didn't make a sound. I thought you were having a fit . . . or a seizure. But I couldn't reach you . . . I . . . but Hymie could. I don't get it." Jay's hand shook as he touched her cheek. "I couldn't reach you. It was like . . . like the air between us went thick."

"Did you see anything?"

"Just you . . . sort of . . . strangling, I guess." He ran his fingers through his hair then rubbed the back of his neck. "But there was something there." His voice dropped. "Something I couldn't see."

"Something like what?" Hymie asked. Lynnette could feel his body shudder beneath hers.

"Just thick air . . . cold thick air."

"But what was it? What happened?" She tried to regulate her heartbeat, but everything seemed out of rhythm. The effect was sickening, frightening.

"We all know what it was." Moist beads stood out on the parts of Hymie's face that were not in shadow. "We all know *who* it was."

Lynnette moved to the grass between them and they watched the house, hunched together like three children afraid of the dark.

The house lay bathed in moonlight and shadow, dark stones, creeping ivy.

Light from the open door glimmered on the ancient silver Bentley in the drive. Elms stretched inky fingers toward the house . . . the sudden soft cooing of a dove roosting somewhere on the roof.

"But why?" Jay whispered. "I've read some of those books old Clayborne had about the supernatural or whatever. There's nothing like this. They're just corny—

96

anecdotes about ghosts walking through walls and throwing things around and crying ladies in dark halls, really corny stuff." Jay looked away. "But nothing like this."

"That's because they're dreamed up by people who want it to happen to them. This"—Hymie spit into the grass—"is the real thing."

"Do you two really believe that that was Nella?"

Jay shrugged. "I had it half figured that Hymie was rigging the whole business. But nobody could rig that."

"Stay away from him, Lynn, and if you can't do that, stay out of that house. She's dangerous. She killed Mr. Clayborne and Gunderson and she just tried to kill you."

It was ridiculous. But Lynnette was grateful for the warm touch of the men on either side of her as they clung together against a common enemy.

There was another explanation, surely. Where had she seen a similar happening? Where?

The boy in grade school who had an epileptic seizure? She hadn't known its name then, but he had writhed on the floor as she had tonight. The teacher had rushed to him and forced a fat pencil between his teeth, but there was already blood on his tongue. Gordon something. The family had not stayed in Roggins long. *Am I epileptic?* His eyes had rolled back until only the whites . . .

Bertha had often complained that she was too active, always into things, couldn't sit still in church. Were hyperactive children prone to epilepsy when they reached adulthood?

No. Gordon wasn't what her memory was signaling.

The man in the restaurant who'd choked on a piece of meat. She and Joey had seen him clawing at his throat when he fell to the floor.

A man at a nearby table had pulled the offending food from the victim's throat. An ambulance had screamed outside. . . .

But could you choke hours after eating? Still it made more sense than the ghost of Nella Van Fleet.

The grass blades felt damp and prickly against her bare legs. There was a chill hint of impending winter in the air.

"But why should it be safe here?" Jay broke into Lynnette's thoughts and the quiet of the night.

"Bugs stop here." Hymie nodded sagely. "Won't go past here," he added as if that answered the question.

"Are you sure she can't reach beyond here?"

Hymie didn't take his eyes off the house. "I've felt her other places . . . a few times."

"How could she travel here after she died? What does she want?"

"She wants you. She made sure you had to come back to the house to get the money . . . had to live in it."

"How can you know any of this, Benninghoff?"

"For a long time I thought maybe she just wanted to hound Mr. Clayborne. But then he died and that letter showed up with the will. Mr. Clayborne hated you. He wouldn't have left you sitting so good if he could've helped it."

"Hymie, Jay was the only heir left."

Hymie ignored her. "You making time with Lynn is a threat to Nella's getting her baby back. A pretty young woman is liable to take you away from your mother. Be careful, Van Fleet. Nella's waited thirty long years. Are you taking Lynn home or am I?"

"I'll take her."

"I left my purse in the library."

Hymie started toward the house. "You stay there, I'll get it."

"Wait here, I'll bring the car to"—Jay shrugged helplessly—"to where the bugs stop."

Hymie leaned toward Jay once Jay sat in the car. "Better sleep at the gatehouse tonight. I don't think she'd hurt you, but I don't *know* it."

"Thanks." Jay sounded very much like he meant it.

The Bentley looked large on the outside but inside, it seemed cramped.

"Jay, I can't believe that was your mother tonight. Maybe I did have a seizure of some kind or choked on something."

"Then why couldn't I reach you?"

"I can't explain it. But Hymie's a little . . . slow. You can't take everything he says for fact. I don't believe in ghosts, do you?"

"No." He turned out of the lane onto the highway.

"But they scare the hell out of me anyway."

"You know, other than a slight headache, I don't feel like any of it happened. Do you suppose we dreamed it?"

"You can explain it away, any way you like, little widow. But I have to live there."

Harold's Cadillac was still parked by the gate and lights were on in the house when they drove into the farmyard.

"Suppose they're waiting up for you? It is after nine thirty."

"Looks like it, damn it!" She opened her door quickly. "I must rush in and explain that I haven't lost my virginity."

"I didn't know widows still had any of that to lose."

"Neither did I. Thank you for the first part of the evening at least, and Jay . . . be careful."

He smiled wanly. "None of it happened, remember?" He drove the Bentley out of the farmyard in a much more subdued manner than before.

Margaret met her at the back door. "It's after one o'clock. Harold was getting ready to come look for you." Her sister-in-law's eyes took in the rumpled hair, the stained dress, and came back to rest on the scratches on Lynnette's throat.

Lynnette felt a sudden weariness. Anger combined with the effects of a hard swim, liquor, and the chilling attack to bring her slight headache to full force. She moved to the kitchen where Bertha sat propped at the table and Harold dozed in a chair.

"I've had enough!" Lynnette's voice hissed alarmingly like her mother's, and the room seemed to move out of focus, the oil burner and Harold seemed to tilt.

"Enough of what, is what I'd like to know." Bertha too took in her appearance.

"How dare you wait up . . . treat me like a . . ."

"Like what you are." Bertha crossed the kitchen and again Lynnette blinked as the floor tilted. "Don't worry. This won't happen again." Bertha's spectacles came down to Lynnette's face, her false teeth clicking, the odor of coffee and age on her breath. "Because I'm not going to let it. I'll lock you in before I let it happen again, Missy."

Harold's dark-rimmed glasses peered over Bertha's

shoulder. "Lynn, you really should be more considerate of our mother."

She cut him off by opening the stairway door and slamming it behind her.

"She always was wild. Hasn't changed a bit."

"Now, Mother . . ."

"Don't you 'now Mother' me, Harold Olson!"

The voices followed her up the stairs and she put her hands over her ears.

Just before falling asleep, Lynnette wondered whose mother was the most menacing—her own or Jay's. Nella might do murder, Bertha incited it. *Ridiculous. I'm acting as if Nella's ghost really exists. There's another explanation for what happened. I'm just too tired to think it out.*

But the memory of choking cold and screaming air and fierce pressure in her ears haunted her during the night. Lynnette finally rose to find an extra quilt in the cedar chest at the foot of the bed. As she pulled it up to her chin the subdued whooing of a turtledove sounded outside her window and she buried her head in the pillow. Even the mellow call of that gentle bird sounded eerie and threatening to her now.

Bertha did not speak to her the next day and in the evening, when Roger's car drove into the farmyard to pick her up, the doors were locked. Her mother stood by the sink with folded arms and a determined smile. Lynnette shrugged and walked back upstairs. She opened the window in the hall and crawled out onto the roof of the back porch.

Roger was just walking through the gate and he stopped short as he caught sight of her. "Don't you think you're getting a little old for that?"

"Roger, don't hassle. Just come help." She took off her shoes and handed them down to him with her purse. Just as she let go of them the roof tilted under her. So did Roger. She lay back on the slanting shingles and closed her eyes to keep the branches of the trees from tilting too. Her stomach pushed up at her throat and for an agonizing second, Lynnette thought she might vomit.

"What's the matter?"

"I feel dizzy."

"Well, if you'd use doors like the grown ups do . . ."

"I couldn't. Bertha locked me in."

"The hell she did."

She sat up when the world finally adjusted itself and half jumped and half fell into Roger's arms.

"It's a good thing you're little." The familiar lopsided smile, on the familiar lips . . .

Lynnette drew back but held on to his arm to put on her shoes. She ignored the grim face at the back-porch window as they walked to the car.

"Why'd Bertha lock you in?"

"I was out too late last night."

"Who with?"

"Jay Van Fleet, not that it's any of your business."

"Looking for another Prince Charming to take you out of Iowa? You'll never learn, will you?"

They drove around to the highway and then up the hedged lane that led to the front of the Van Fleet house. The corn of the surrounding fields peeked over the tall bushes of the hedge. Roger parked by the gatehouse and honked for Hymie. While they waited, Jay drove the Bentley around the circle of dead elms. He looked very much recovered from the night before, very combed and groomed, handsome and relaxed in a white turtleneck.

"Looks like Prince Charming is going after another Cinderella tonight."

"Why shouldn't he, it's Saturday night and he's no monk."

"So I've heard."

The house sat contained and brooding in a fading rose twilight, with one garage door left open like a yawning mouth. Lynnette shivered in spite of herself.

She sat between Roger and Hymie on the way to Minturn as she had often in the past. They'd known one another so long that words were unnecessary. It was almost as though she'd never lived with Joey and then on her own for those four years in Colorado. Her Aunt Vera had once dubbed them the Unholy Trio.

She sat between them again after the movie in a semicircular booth at Hud's a dive outside town where they'd often gone when they wanted to feel wicked.

"If I ever go to a flick with you two again, we'll take a vote on which theater first." She moved her beer aside as the aging waitress flopped the pizza in front of them.

"Name of it sounded good, you'll have to admit." Roger wiped hot stringy cheese from his chin. "*Meadow of Sex*," he said, gesturing with a pie-shaped slice of pizza.

Hymie snorted. "Wasn't even a meadow. Some old rocky pasture."

"You missed the deeper meanings."

Roger and Hymie snickered over the deeper meanings of *Meadow of Sex* while Lynnette looked down the narrow crowded interior of Hud's.

The door, padded in black leather, meant to give a certain impression, but that was dispelled by the store-front window next to it. The light from Hud's outside neon sign blinked on the night in flashing pink, blinked off, blinked on . . .

The bartender plugged in the jukebox that sat against the window and it lit up like a roller coaster with lights zipping in fluid pastels across its top, down its sides and back up again. Dim lights in the ceiling dimmed further and a lavender spotlight shone on the floor in front of the jukebox.

A dark shadow jumped out of the restroom area into the spotlight, becoming a gyrating fluff of silver feathers that parted to reveal a woman with hair bleached to albino white. The music came suddenly but late and never quite caught up with the dancer.

"My God, what—"

"Hud's a Go-Go. Didn't you see the sign?" Roger turned away from the scenery at the other end of the room long enough to answer her.

"I thought go-go was long gone."

"In Iowa we hang on to the good stuff."

"Well, Hud seems to have trouble hanging onto the *young* stuff."

The face under the white hair was past its time for spotlights. As more agitated feathers parted and some even parted company with the dancer, it became apparent that the body was also. Costume and movements were more suited to striptease than go-go.

Roger watched intently, barely nibbling the pizza he held to his lips. Hymie ate and drank steadily, occasionally glancing at the performance.

Lynnette giggled then leaned against the booth and gave up on the pizza. This unbelievable dancer had at least broken the depressing spell that had refused to leave her since the night before.

Because of the narrowness of Hud's, the jukebox and dancer were very close to the door and several times it opened to let in new customers and a wind that stirred the feathers about on the floor.

Then it opened again and the attention, riveted on the swirling feathers, was diverted to a sleek brunette who made a startled movement to back out again but was ushered around the door by the protective arm of Jay Van Fleet.

"Prince Charming and Cinderella out slumming after the ball." Roger's chuckle held no mirth.

Jay slid his arm from the brunette's waist to her shoulders, then waited for a break in the dance to guide her through the feathers to the bar.

She wore tailored slacks and a fitted white jacket with a scarf at the neck. Whoever she was, she didn't buy her clothes in Minturn. The dark hair fell straight and glowing down her jacket. Jay leaned against the bar beside her stool and spoke to the bartender.

The white turtleneck sweater set off the tan he'd acquired, and the dusty-blond hair was swept across his forehead in a neater fashion than she'd ever seen it.

Jay might not look like a rich playboy in the dining room of the Van Fleet house, but he certainly stood out from the crowd at Hud's.

So did his date.

Lynnette looked away to find Roger and Hymie watching her. She reached for her beer and hoped the slight but surprising surge of jealousy hadn't shown on her face.

Roger rasped his hand across the dark stubble on his chin. "Where does he find chicks like that?"

"Just hope he doesn't take her out to the house. Lynn

tell you what happened last night?" Hymie told of having to rescue her from the Van Fleet library.

Roger's disbelief wrinkled his forehead, turned down the corners of his mouth. "A ghost tried to kill you?" Just as he spoke, the music stopped and it sounded like a shout.

Jay Van Fleet stiffened and turned. His high spirits seemed to drain away as he met Lynnette's eyes. He carried his glass to the booth. His expression was shuttered as he looked down at Lynnette. "Are you okay . . . after last night?"

"Yes . . ."

"They've been telling me some crap about a ghost." Roger cut her off. "Tell me it's a big joke."

"Whatever it was, Jenson, it was no joke." Jay turned back to Lynnette. "You're sure?"

She nodded, feeling uncomfortable with the girl at the bar peering at her.

Jay drained his glass and, walking back to his date, motioned that it was time to go. He stooped to pick up a silver feather and stuck it behind his ear. As he opened the door for her, the brunette turned to look up at him. Jay smiled and slapped her on the rear. They were gone without a backward glance at the trio in the booth.

"Now, if you told me *he* attacked you, I'd believe it. But Nella Van Fleet? If you couldn't see anything, how'd you know it was her? What'd she do, introduce herself?"

"Roger, I don't know what it was. Hymie and Jay assumed it was Nella because it was so . . . unexplainable. But I don't believe it either."

"Tell that to Chris Gunderson. Lynn would've been dead too if I hadn't got her out of there."

"What was Van Fleet doing all this time?"

"Couldn't get to her. Nella got between them." Pizza sauce smeared the end of Hymie's blunt nose.

Roger blew smoke rings into the clouded air of Hud's. "Why?"

"He was kissing Lynn."

"That must have been a shock to find old Hymie was watching. Next time you take guard duty, Hym, invite me up. Might see more than kissing."

They teased her all the way to the car and then to the gatehouse, but Roger was quiet and thoughtful for the rest of the drive home.

As she stepped out of the car in the farmyard, the ground swayed and she had to cling to him for balance.

"Dizzy again? How long have you been getting these spells?"

"Since last night."

"When Nella was supposed to have attacked you?"

She nodded into his chest as he drew her against him, felt the heat of his body through his thin shirt.

"I've been in that house a few times with Hymie since the old man died. And I could swear there's something wrong with it." He stroked her hair, held her tighter to offer the strength of his hard body. Trust Roger to protect her from anyone or anything but himself. "The thing is, Lynn, Hymie's filled us with stories about that ghost ever since he could talk and we could listen. Maybe you got a health problem and that was a fainting fit you took up there. In that house, with all those stories, you could have been scared into thinking it was Nella."

"I've thought of that, too." The earth leveled, her stomach settled back into place. She was ready for his steel grip when she tried to pull away. "If this doesn't stop in a few days, I'll go see a doctor."

"Could be just low blood pressure. I've heard of that." The steel around her back tightened.

"Roger, Bertha's probably waiting up." But she held herself very still.

"Van Fleet got a kiss last night." He grasped her hair and pulled her head back. "Of course, he's not a farm boy." His tone was silky with warning and she stared back, trying not to show her fear and excitement.

He had grown leaner, harder, stronger, hotter. She enjoyed his lips as she knew she would. Roger's reputation with women was not built on fantasy. But she knew him too well to be comfortable there. Roger Jenson didn't play games.

He released her when Bertha turned on the yard light, shattering the night clear to the barn. Roger slid into his car and drove off without another word.

Lynnette wondered if Jay Van Fleet knew how lucky he was to lead a roaming unattached life. He'd never stick in one place long enough for people like Roger to use him.

She closed the gate behind her and sighed. Of course, with a man things would be different. If Joey had lived and she were not alone, no one would dare suggest that she come back to Roggins. In town there were so many spinsters who had dropped out of life to care for aging parents and were too old and dispirited to drop in again when the parents died.

Bertha met her at the door. Her wrinkles sagged, but her eyes were afire. "Hardly get the smoke wiped off your face from one night and you're at it again. Lettin' men put their dirty hands all over you . . ."

"Bertha, I'm very tired and so are you. So I'll say this quickly and we can both get to sleep. It's no use. You're making no attempt to adjust and you're not about to give me any freedom as an adult." Helpless tears gathered in her voice if not in her eyes. "It's . . . Bertha, our lives don't seem to have anything to do with each other's."

"Freedom, you want. You call that freedom? Some would call it sin."

"I'm leaving." The salty-pepper taste of pepperoni came bitter to her tongue.

"You're doing no such thing. I won't hear of it."

"I'm going back to Denver and I'm leaving Monday morning."

16

*L*ynnette, dreaming of Chris Gunderson, jerked awake as rough fingers closed over her shoulders and shook her. "Whaa . . ."

"Get up, girl, or you'll never be ready for church. I milked the cow for you, but I can't eat and get dressed for you. Been calling up the stairs over an hour."

"I'm not going to church this morning. You go ahead. And it's your cow anyway." She rolled over and rubbed her face in the pillow.

"Of course you're going to church. What would people think?"

"It won't matter because I'm leaving tomorrow. Remember?"

"What's the world coming to? Young girl galavanting around so late at night she can't get up for church." Bertha yanked off the covers and let in the chill. "No more talk of leaving. You just get some clothes on. Elaine'll be here any minute." The clicking of her teeth accentuated every other word.

"Bertha"—Lynnette pulled the covers back up to her chin—"I am *not* going to church. I *am* going back to Denver tomorow. Now, *get out!*"

Her own shock at the sincere venom in her voice was mirrored in her mother's eyes. Bertha walked to the door, and when she turned, her mouth was so puckered it drew her nose down and the spectacles slipped further. "We'll see. We'll just see about that." She stomped into the hall, jarring the old bare boards of the floor.

I know we'd get along better by mail. I know it! Lynnette listened to the stairs squeak under Bertha's determined feet.

And then a soft moan and the unmistakable thump and bump of a body falling against the wall, onto the stairs, the gasps of pain as Bertha thudded from stair to stair and crashed to the kitchen below. . . . Silence.

Lynnette was across the bed, onto the floor, into the hall. "Bertha!" Looking over the wooden railing, Lynnette could see only a shoulder of the Sunday print dress against the door to the stairwell, one relaxed hand palm upward, propped on the bottom step. "Bertha?"

She'd leaped to the rubber treads of the third step down when the hand with the slightly curled fingers moved. Bracing herself between the two walls, she took a step down but the stair tipped and Lynnette grabbed the handrail and sat down, lowering herself from one teetering step to the next.

"Bertha?" It was only a whisper and there was no answer.

She sat on the bottom step. Gradually the kitchen righted and Bertha's body felt warm against her bare foot, but her mother lay horribly still, her head resting on the threshold of the bathroom.

Lynnette touched the bodice of the motionless blue and white print. *Is she breathing? I don't know. Do something!*

The spectacles dangled unbroken from one ear.

Lynnette stepped over the mound of print and, shivering, looked around the kitchen. Every other breath came as a little grunt. *What's the first thing you're supposed to do? Blanket or telephone?*

She started for the telephone but changed her mind in midstride and dashed through the living room to her mother's bedroom and grabbed a wool blanket out of the cedar chest. She tucked it around the still form. Bertha moaned faintly.

Lynnette had just picked up the telephone, wondering whom to call, when Elaine's car came down the lane. She ran out to the gate and waited for the car to pull up.

"Lynn, you're not dressed."

"Hurry. Bertha just fell down the stairs!"

Her sister rushed past and Lynnette was aware of her niece, Alice, gaping at her transparent baby-doll pajamas.

Elaine was on the phone when she arrived in the kitchen. "Just cover her up and don't move her. Get dressed, Lynn. There's an ambulance on the way."

Dr. Lindstrom arrived in the waiting room of Minturn General Hospital just after Harold and Margaret. He announced that Bertha had a slight concussion, a broken leg and a broken hip.

"Broken hip!" Harold flushed and paled alternately. "That . . . that's pretty serious, isn't it, Doctor?"

"I won't mince words. With someone her age it's critical. She's being prepared for surgery right now." He softened as he looked from one stricken face to another. "If it had been anyone but Bertha Olson . . . I don't know why . . . with her weight and blood pressure . . . but that woman enjoys the most outrageous good health of any seventy-year-old I've come across. I can't imagine someone as cantankerous as Bertha Olson succumbing to such a mundane thing as a broken hip, can you?" When he noticed all the sober faces lighting up, he sobered himself. "Of course, it will all depend on whether or not she survives the surgery and anesthetic. . . ."

Lynnette sat eating ice cream with her brother and her sister-in-law in the breakfast nook of Margaret's kitchen. Elaine had gone home and sent Dennis back with a few essentials and the message that they would take care of Lynn's chores while she was away.

My chores! Lynnette chewed on the ice cream as if it were a tough steak. "What'll we do with Bertha when she gets out of the hospital?"

"For now, Lynn, let's just pray that she does get out." Harold piously rolled his eyes.

"Oh, she will."

"I should hope so," Margaret said. "Mom has used those stairs most of her life. Why should she tumble down them now? They're steep, but she knew that. And Harold had rubber treads put on when Dad was . . . wandering around so much."

"She and I had an argument. She was furious and didn't watch where she was . . ." *Why do you insist on being so damned honest?*

Four eyes widened across the table.

"Well. That answers my question, doesn't it?"

"Argument about what?" Harold forgot to take the spoon from his mouth.

"Because . . . I wouldn't go to church." *And I told her I was leaving and I ordered her out of the room and I yelled at her.*

"Whyever not? Lynn, what got into you?"

"What I asked was, What are we going to do with Bertha after the hospital? She'll be in a cast next to forever and I'm no nurse and she's too big for me to move. Can she stay with Elaine, do you think?"

"No. Leroy starts working at the cement plant next week and Elaine has lined up a clerking job at Stewart's General Store. They have to, to make ends meet, Lynn. Farming on a small scale won't support a family anymore. Leroy has been working out in the winter these last few years, and this year they feel Elaine must, too."

"How about here then? She'd be closer to her doctor and—"

"She couldn't possibly stay here! Why, I'm never home." Margaret looked as if she'd been insulted.

"You've got a job, too?" Lynnette's eyes roamed the shiny automatic kitchen. "To support your family?"

"No, of course not. Harold manages very well. But I do have a position to maintain in this community, and I'm deeply involved in more charitable committees than you can imagine." She'd gone pale behind her pink powder mask.

"Well, it's either here or a nursing home. I don't see any other choice."

"A nursing home would eat up every cent of the estate." It was Harold's turn to look insulted.

"Well, that's what the estate is for, isn't it? To take care of Bertha in her old age? Or were you planning on inheriting . . ."

"Mom would never consent to a nursing home."

"Then you'll have to take her, because I'm going back to Denver."

"You wouldn't . . . not now. Not after causing her to break a hip by arguing with her."

"Margaret!"

"Harold, don't you see? She might as well . . . as well

110

have pushed your mother down the stairs."

Lynnette didn't wait to carry her dish and spoon to the sink and rinse them, as was the rule in Margaret's kitchen. She didn't follow the newly directed traffic pattern across Margaret's dining-room carpet, so that it might not have a path worn in the plush shag. Instead she trod as heavily as her light body could across a pile so high it had to be raked back to attention with a garden rake after vacuuming.

Threatening Margaret's cozy life-style was like doing a Mexican hat dance around a coiled rattlesnake. *But no one thinks twice about ruining my life.*

She stomped up stairs so cushioned by carpeting that falling down them would be similar to floating over a corrugated foam scrubboard. *But Bertha gets rubber treads.*

Once in the guest room, she closed the door and leaned against it, as if holding it shut against her brother and sister-in-law.

The next day she again stood pressed against a door, the inside of the lobby door of the Good American Nursing Home, her face against the cool glass, her sweating hands clutching the metal bar to keep her upright. The mealy smell of bland foods kept too long on a steam table had just about overpowered her when Harold came up behind her.

"Seen enough, I take it?"

"Get me out of here."

"I'll find someone to unlock the door."

Outside she sucked in carbon monoxide gratefully.

"Can you see Mother in a place like that?" Harold checked his watch and led her to the car. "Come on, I'll take you to lunch, and then I have to get back to the office."

"What about Margaret?"

"She has a bridge luncheon on Mondays. She's never home at noon. I eat out," he said pointedly.

Lynnette made an appointment with Dr. Lindstrom for herself and kept it several days later. He listened

111

patiently to her complaints of dizziness, examined her everywhere he could reach and then sent her to the laboratory where she was x-rayed and pricked and her blood smeared on myriad glass slides. She was told to come back in three days.

When she did, Lynnette was conducted to Dr. Lindstrom's office instead of an examining room.

"Well, you are not pregnant," he said as she sat down across from him.

"I knew that."

"You seem to be a healthy young lady."

"Then why do I get dizzy?"

Dr. Lindstrom leaned back in his swivel chair and adjusted the venetian blinds at the window behind him. "Have you fallen recently? Say, just prior to these dizzy spells? Or hit your head?"

"No."

"Have you been doing any swimming, say, diving off a diving board?"

"I was swimming in a pool the night this all started, but it didn't have a diving board."

"Um hmmm. What I'm getting at, Mrs. Stewart, is that the only thing we've been able to come up with is some possible irregularity of the inner ear, which often causes imbalance. It can be caused by a sharp blow to the head or some sort of extreme pressure on the ears. I feel that if this is the case, the problem will be temporary and will adjust . . ."

"It couldn't have been caused by choking on something? Or a seizure of some kind?"

"I certainly don't see how. Are you subject to—you're looking suddenly pale—do you think one of these spells is coming on? Mrs. Stewart? Is something wrong?"

How about screaming cold air forced into the ears and down the throat? How about a ghost crawling into the body, Doctor? But, of course, she couldn't tell him about that.

"No, there's nothing wrong, Dr. Lindstrom." Lynnette did not believe in ghosts.

112

17

*J*ay Van Fleet studied his face in the mirror and sloshed the brush about in his shaving mug.

He whistled one of the robust little tunes that he and Harry used to sing on their treks. But the whistle sounded thin and reedy in the stillness and he stopped.

Setting the mug on the sink's generous edge, he heated a washcloth until his hands stung and washed his face. The warmth felt welcome against the chill of his skin.

Jay turned slowly to look at the knob of the bathroom door. It didn't move. He crossed to touch it. The knob wasn't any colder than anything else.

Back at the sink, he lathered his face and wiped a space in the steam on the mirror so that he could see the self-contempt written on his face.

It was just that in this house it took a superhuman effort for him to turn his back on a door, open or closed. He wondered how much more he could take.

Jay made the shaving process last as long as he could and then stepped out of the bathroom. A white dove stood in the center of the floor of the master bedroom.

"How the hell do you birds get in anyway?" He crossed the room and pulled the French doors open. "Out. Scat!"

It turned to follow him with a red-eyed stare.

Jay circled back around it to drive it out the door. "Stinking birds. Crapping on everything."

It pivoted again to watch him and he found himself returning stare for stare.

It was a striking bird, with the snowy purity of the albino, a lustrous sheen to its feathers, a regal manner of holding its head and neck. When you got close, the eyes were really more a dark pinkish than red, the black pupils compressed to such tiny dots they were almost nonexistent. Was albinism rare in doves?

"You may be a special-type bird, I don't know. But you

don't belong in here. Now out!" Together they listened to the echo of his voice in the cavernous room. The dove spread a graceful wing to preen one long feather with its beak, moving the wing to pull the feather through.

Jay took a step forward. The dove puffed its neck feathers until its beak was hidden in them; its beady red eyes peered over the snowy necklace.

"Now look, lady . . ." Somehow it did seem feminine, soft. Perhaps they all did. He'd never taken much notice of doves. The rug seemed colder under his bare feet as he approached her. She stood her ground.

He removed his pajama top and swung out with it. "God damn you, get out of here!" He flailed the pajamas in her face and heard a click as a button struck her bill.

She grunted and strutted toward the balcony, head and neck pumping as she moved.

Must be somebody's pet. They aren't that tame, are they? He slammed the doors behind her and looked through a square pane to find her staring back. Jay drew the drapes against her and dressed.

On his way down the curving stairs he checked his watch. Only 8:30. And he thought he'd wasted so much time. How long ago had it seemed that there was not enough time?

Coffee growled comfortably in an electric percolator in the breakfast room. His complaints about cold coffee must have penetrated. He tinkled the silly bell and stared at the lonely place setting. He was beginning to understand why men tied themselves to a mate.

Mrs. Benninghoff appeared with half a grapefruit and a motherly smile. "Good morning, Mr. Van Fleet. Did you sleep well?"

"Like a baby. But there was a dove in my room this morning. I thought Hymie fixed the roof."

"He did. Yesterday. There was a hole next to one of the chimneys." As she poured his coffee, the sleeve of her coat-sweater brushed the butter. It was so old the sweater came away clean. "The dove could have been in the house when he covered the hole."

"How did it get down from the attic?"

But she had returned to the kitchen. When she came

back with a plate of fried eggs, sausage and potatoes, he'd tired of the dove and didn't renew the subject.

"I hope you don't mind, but Hymie's helping Roger Jenson again today."

"I know. Soybeans."

"Oh my, no. The soybeans were in long ago. They've been combining corn for a week."

"Do they need any help? I haven't got anything to do."

"No. You just eat your breakfast and have a restful day." She quickly disappeared through the swinging door.

What she meant was they didn't want a greenhorn anywhere near Jenson's fantastic machinery. He turned to watch the combine cutting tan-dry cornstalks on the other side of the lawn. It picked the corn, stripped the kernels off the cob and showered chewed-up husks, stalks and cobs into the rows of mutilated half-stalks still standing in its wake.

Hymie drove up beside the combine on a tractor pulling a wagon, and the beast spewed clean kernels from a narrow head on a long neck. It resembled a green sea serpent vomiting gold.

Jay turned back to find his breakfast congealing on his plate. No, they didn't need him. Did anybody?

He pushed the plate away. He could remember wistfully describing just such a breakfast to Harry as they chewed llama charqui and drank water. That seemed a long time ago.

Lighting a cigarette, he took his coffee and passed through the dining room, the narrow hallway with the putrid wallpaper, across the black marble and out the front door where the ivy had turned the darkness of old blood.

The trees on either side of the house wore glaring splashes of yellow, orange, red and brown. It made the elms in front look even more hideous, black . . . dead.

Jay turned toward the tennis courts.

There was a startled movement in the shrubbery at the corner of the house, and he spilled half the coffee down the front of his sweater. If it was that damn dove sneaking around, trying to get back in the house, he'd . . .

But the widow Stewart rose from behind a shrub, wearing a sheepish grin and blue jeans.

"You're supposed to be in Colorado."

"There have been complications." She stepped out of the shrubbery to walk beside him. "My mother's in the hospital."

"Sounds like a good time for a getaway."

"Somebody has to look after her when she gets home— she broke a hip and a leg—and, of course, I'm elected."

They came to the path through the trees that led to the tennis courts. Weeds, still summer green, fought with the scarlet of poison ivy for possession of the path. They stepped carefully.

"So you decided to have a chat with a fellow prisoner." He set the cup on the fissured surface of the court and stripped off the sweater that had felt so good in the house.

"No. I was trying to avoid you."

"Come to think of it, I noticed that." He lay flat in the sun with the sweater rolled under his head. "So you came to see Hymie."

She stood above him and her coloring blended with the autumn of the trees overhead. She should have been a wood sprite.

"No, I spent a great deal of time hiding in the ditch and among cornstalks so that Hymie and Roger wouldn't see me."

Part of the roof line showed through a break in the trees, doves perched along it, bunched in groups. Jay wondered idly if there was a shotgun in the house. "I'm out of guesses."

"I came to . . . to sneak into your house."

"Why would you want to get near it after last time?"

"To prove to myself there's nothing there." She sat beside him, her back to the house and poked her finger into a hole that had once held a pole to support the net.

"You're just bored, alone on the farm. Let's get the Bentley and take a ride to Minturn."

"Jay, I have to get into that house." It was just a whisper, but the force of it, the bravery and defiance in the small face made him want to laugh. It also made him want to slap her. Why? "To prove to yourself that there's nothing there!"

"Yes."

Anger burned somewhere deep and it was directed at the girl beside him. Merely because she had not gone to Denver? "What if there is something there? There is, you know."

"There can't be. Don't you see? Why could your mother return from the dead and not your uncle? Why not my father or Roger's or Hymie's? Why not a whole world of them?"

"Maybe she wanted to and they didn't. Maybe she was too young to die."

"Joey was twenty-four. If anyone could have come back, he would have. He'd have come back to me."

You've got a point there. "All right, so you don't believe in ghosts. So there can't be one in that house. Let's go into Minturn." He stood, picking up his sweater with one hand and yanking her up roughly with the other, then letting go quickly. Touching her could make him burn in ways other than anger.

"Listen. This is very important to me." She reached down to retrieve his coffee cup. "I have been hauled off to church from my cradle days. And I'm not sure I've ever even said this out loud before but . . . I don't believe there's anything after death. I don't think I ever did."

Jay turned and started down the path but she kept on close behind him.

"So?"

"So I have to know."

"You already know. You don't believe in . . ."

"I've been disoriented ever since that . . . that night here." She put a hand on the sweater held in the crook of his arm and looked into his face. "Don't you see? If Nella Van Fleet exists after thirty years . . . it blows all the beliefs of a lifetime or at least the basis . . ."

"You're not that old."

"Jay, you might as well cut off my feet and leave me nothing to stand on." The defiance was there again, in her stance, as she turned and eyed the door. "There can't

117

be something that I haven't known all this time. I refuse to believe it."

She turned back to him, her eyes searching his as if she could look through them to his mind. "You really don't have the least idea of what I'm trying to say, of how I feel, do you? Here I've been yakking my heart out and you stand there without a live emotion in your body." Her hand balled into a fist.

Wrong on both counts, little widow. I know exactly how you feel. And he did, because he felt the same. But Jay could not understand why, given the same fear of being forced to give up a basic belief, they should have opposite reactions. His reaction was to run. Hers was to face it. Why? He admired her for it, but at the same time it fed his anger. She was wrong about his emotions, too.

"Do you know what you are? You are a cowardly . . . bastard. You . . ." Tears welled in her eyes. "You . . ."

"All right, go. Go on in." She was wrong about his lack of emotion. He was furious. "And if anything happens to you, don't expect any help from me."

When she hesitated, he gave her a shove toward the door. "Go on, damn it!" But he was surprised when she walked up to the house without a backward glance, just a squaring of her shoulders.

Ivy whispered as the door closed behind her.

"Lynnette?" The sweater fell to the drive at his feet. He left it there. "Come back out here!"

Clever little bitch had made him mad on purpose, just to get into the house. "Lynnette!" He'd brought other women in. Nothing had happened to them. Barbara what's-her-name and two others he could think of. But the widow Stewart was different. And Hymie was a long way off this time.

Jay found the doorknob cold as if the warmth of her hand had not touched it just a moment before.

The front hall was empty, silent. His cup sat on the black marble just inside the door.

Her arguments had sounded so logical, unarguable out in the sun. But in the house they sounded foolish.

The library was empty. And the sunroom. "Lynnette!"

Why don't you advertise her presence, Van Fleet? Keep yelling out her name. Better yet, you could hand her to Nella on a platter. Here, Mother dear, have her for dinner.

He moved quietly, listening now, through the dining room, the breakfast room. He peered into the kitchen . . . not even the housekeeper. Back through the shrouded, dusty living room . . .

Jay broke into a run. Sweat beaded cold on his skin as he reached the stairs, took them three at a time.

Hymie's words haunted him all the way up the circular staircase. *You making time with Lynn is a threat to Nella's getting her baby back.*

He stopped at the top of the stairs, not daring to call out, trying to still his breathing so that he could hear. *A pretty young woman is liable to take you away from your mother.*

The door at the end of the hall was open. He could see a corner of the gray blanket on the bed. The spread had so deteriorated that Mrs. Benninghoff had discarded it. *Be careful, Van Fleet. Nella's waited thirty long years.*

Lynnette wouldn't go into that room. Would she?

Jay started down the hall toward his mother's bedroom. Yes, Lynnette would do just that. She was brave—and stupid. And if Nella didn't get to her first, he was very tempted to throttle the widow Stewart himself.

Perhaps Nella had already . . .

Except for the sound of his own breathing and the bare swish of his shoes on the carpet, there wasn't the hint of a sound anywhere.

A picture of himself crossed his mind. Jay Van Fleet, thirty years old, creeping down a hallway in his own house, clammy sweat standing out on his face. The picture and the thought brought him to a stop halfway to Nella's room.

This whole thing was stupid. Lynnette was right.

But then again, around this place, logic stopped where the bugs did. Hymie had been right about the bugs, too. Jay covered the last half of the corridor on the run, illogically afraid of what he might find at its end.

He half expected to see another body stretched out like Gunderson's, with staring eyeballs . . .

119

The floor, its carpet cleaned now but faded to an unhealthy gray, was bare, even of bird crap. Lynnette was not there. Of course, Gunderson's body had been hidden by the bed. Jay could swear he still smelled him as he moved into the room, trying to sense any change in the atmosphere. But things seemed as normal as they ever did in the Van Fleet house.

Lynnette Stewart did not lie staring up at the ceiling on the other side of the bed.

The housekeeper and Mary Jane Gunderson had kept the room clean. Where the wallpaper had peeled, they'd sliced it off, leaving patches of plaster showing. The queer old radio, with vertical arches of faded gold fabric under the dials, and the ugly black credenza glared with polish.

Jay gave in and peered under the bed. Nothing.

When he honestly thought about it, the whole situation looked like a con game. Nothing really fit. Why get so worried about one woman and not the others? If your mother was a ghost and jealous, why not jealous of any woman?

Had he touched or kissed the others in the house? No, he hadn't even fed them. He'd shown them around just long enough to impress them with his "mansion" and then whisked them off to more comfortable surroundings. They had not fallen to the floor, writhing . . .

Jay opened the double doors of the wardrobe and pushed aside aging dresses. All he saw were aging shoes, neatly arranged in pairs. He felt the softness of one of the dresses in his hand, a lavender dress, and a long buried memory surfaced. He'd had a mother once . . . and long ago he'd imagined a woman much like the older Nella in the photograph album.

The dress tore at the waistline. It came away in his hand.

Jay dropped it and closed the doors. He'd outgrown the need for a mother long ago. If he could just outgrow the need for women altogether. . . .

He crossed to the French doors and found himself staring into the red eyes of the fat white dove on the balcony. But no Lynnette Stewart.

Could the "thing" that inhabited this house with him sense his interest in Lynnette? The interest that made her different from the other women who came here? The interest was only physical, he told himself, and easily replaced. He'd known it before, often.

He looked beyond the dove to the balustrade. He couldn't see his uncle taking a dive off that balcony in the dead of winter. But his death, however managed, would bring a penniless nephew home if the will . . .

He turned from the French doors, started across the room and stopped. That was Hymie's thinking, not his own. Hymie was behind all this, a clever man in his simple way. He stood to gain much if Jay became too frightened to stay.

Take away Hymie and what did you have? A cold house, full of doves. Jay resumed his progress across his dead mother's bedroom feeling a good deal better . . .

The cold impenetrable air met him face on at the doorway.

No warning change in the atmosphere. It was just there. And he could not pass through it. It wasn't exactly solid. It was thick, squishy, like fighting an invisible piece of foam. He could see the hall clearly . . . but the air would not let him pass. Just as it had not let him reach Lynnette when she fell to the floor in the library. . . .

He buried his face in it and couldn't breathe. It seemed to pulsate.

His fists sank into it, but not through it.

"Let me out!"

The door to the attic stairs opened slowly and Lynnette Stewart stood on the hall carpet brushing dust off her hands.

"Get away. Get out of the house." He flailed harder at the air in front of him. "Lynnette, run!"

Lynnette bent to brush dust from the knees of her jeans.

"For God's sake, she's here. Run!" His scream ended in choking as his face came in contact with the barrier.

Lynnette closed the attic door and looked down the hall to the master bedroom as if she hadn't heard him.

She turned toward the door of Nella's room, her lips pursed, her expression thoughtful.

"Go back!"

She wasn't looking at him. She was looking through him.

As she walked toward him, Jay held his breath and backed away. The thickness in the air came with him. He backed carefully, testing it, till the edge of the bed hit the back of his knee.

When Lynnette stood in the doorway, she seemed unaware of his presence . . . or the other presence. She glanced about the room and shrugged.

Jay moved his hand and felt the cold still in front of him. His heart kicked at his chest as if trying to break out. He swallowed the dryness in his mouth and inched sideways along the bed. If he could draw Nella away . . .

Lynnette turned and walked down the hall.

He moved back to the foot of the bed and watched until she reached the stairs. Then he backed slowly to the French doors, feeling behind him for the bolt that unlocked them, the handle that opened them.

Jay let himself out of Nella's room and slammed the doors. He turned and stepped across the balcony so quickly that he almost tripped on the dove lying on its side.

His breath made a noise in his throat as he crawled onto the balustrade and straddling it, he glanced again at the white form. What was the matter with that bird? She'd been alive and well only minutes before.

He put his other leg over and lowered himself until he was hanging above the shrubs, clinging to the balustrade.

Jay's eyes were even with the floor of the balcony and he was looking through the space between two of the posts that supported the railing, looking directly into the eyes of the dove. The pupils that had been tiny dots in the master bedroom were now so dilated that only a bare rim of the red-pink iris showed.

Jay dangled a moment and let go. He fell into the shrub that had caught his uncle one snowy night three years ago. He could hear branches snapping under him, feel the pain in one heel shoot up to the ankle and then to his knee. Piny bristles scraped his skin as he fell out of the bush onto the lawn, the protest of old wounds in his chest making him grunt.

He stood and backed away till he could see the French doors of Nella's room. They were still closed. A smear of white dove showed between the balustrade's posts. Jay limped around the house.

Lynnette stood on the drive. "I was looking for you. Nothing happ—"

"Get away from the house."

"What?"

"Get your ass over here. Here, where the bugs stop. Now!"

"Well, you don't have to get mad." She started toward him. "What happened to you? There's blood on your face. Jay?"

He grabbed her and jerked her in the direction of the gatehouse. "If you ever go into that house again, I'll—"

"Jay, nothing happened. I felt weird, I admit." A hint of doubt crossed her face and she glanced back at the house. "But nothing happened." They stopped in the shade of the gatehouse. "You have scratches all over and your shirt is soaked. . . ." She put a finger to his chin. It came away with the stain of his blood.

"You're wrong. Something did happen. Something you wouldn't believe, but . . ." A thwap of wings against air and a streak of snowy white flew over the roof of the Van Fleet house.

She leaned toward him, flecks of gold glinting in amber eyes. "Jay, you weren't there. I was. Not a thing happened."

This time it was Jay Van Fleet who backed away.

18

*B*ertha sat propped against three goose-feather pillows, munching green seedless grapes. The pillows were so much more comfortable than those hard foam things in the hospital.

She adjusted her bifocals and turned her attention to the television set. The lawyer was explaining that the raped daughter would have to appear in court, and Bertha began to forget the itch under her cast, when the local Minturn station broke in for a special weather bulletin.

Tornado watch.

Oh well, they were always having watches. Hardly ever had tornadoes, but lots of watches. In seventy years she'd seen only two near Roggins. But she couldn't ignore the icy doubt playing along her spine, the hardness in her swallow.

By the time the game show came on, the sky had darkened. By news time it looked black as night, and spittles of rain tapped at her window. Awful being so old and helpless . . . and trapped.

Lynn finally came in carrying the supper tray and placed it on the dresser to close the windows against the rain, her movements slow and graceful.

How could two raw-boned people like herself and Olaf have produced this fairy creature? Now that the unbecoming tan had faded, her skin was milky white, so thin that veins showed faintly blue at her temples. If only she had roses in her cheeks instead of the shadowy darkness under her eyes that made them look so large and lonely.

A gust of wind hit the house and old wood creaked. Lynn pulled the window shades. Did she look worried?

As her daughter placed the old kitchen tray across her lap, Bertha reached out to touch her soft cheek. *I'll never understand her, but I love this strange child to my very bones.*

Lynn looked up startled, but didn't pull away.

Then Bertha saw Rachael Stewart's brat put his hands on her child, and that bright-eyed Roger Jenson, and Nella's boy—so many. She pulled her hand away and looked at the tray. "What in the Sam Hill is that supposed to be?"

"It's an omelet."

Bertha took a bite and mulled it on her tongue. "Humph! Tastes like scrambled eggs with air in 'em."

"That's about it."

"What's the matter with meat and potatoes?"

"The doctor wants you to eat light because you're bedridden and overweight."

"Who wants to be scrawny like he is anyway? Like to see him get out of a warm bed in the middle of February to help a sow litter. He'd freeze solid halfway across the bedroom floor."

"You don't have sows anymore. But you do have high blood pressure. Watch the salt . . ."

"Fancy falutin' thing don't have no taste to it. 'Course, what cooking you can expect from a person with the appetite of a sick mouse, I don't know. What's for dessert?"

"There is no dessert. I'll get the coffee."

It certainly sounded quiet outside, the rain must have stopped. As if in answer to the thought, the windbreak of pines groaned and wind thudded against the house. It moved on, leaving broken leaves to whisper across the shingles. Bertha's eyes searched the wallpaper and came to rest on the wheelchair by the door. It wouldn't go down the steps to the fruit cellar . . . not with her in it . . . not upright.

Lynn carried the coffeepot and two cups. That meant she'd stay awhile. The froth of her hair feathering around her face, matching eyes flecked with gold . . . What was it Grandma Maud used to call her? October child. October? "Lynn, I just remembered we forgot your birthday. What with everything happening."

"Don't worry about it." Lynn handed her a steaming cup. "I'd forgotten, too."

"Bless me, you're twenty-five now. Don't seem possible."

"And what have I got to show for it?" It came as a soft sad whisper.

"Got your health and a roof over your head. And family. There's plenty in this world would love to be in your shoes, Missy."

Another rolling gust that made the bed shiver and then the funny dead silence. "Lynn, turn down that TV for a minute. I want to tell you something. Remember when you were little we had that bad storm that took the old machine shed and we were all in the fruit cellar when the storm went over? I want you to try to think about that rumbly sound and then the high keening sound . . ."

Lynn's face went even whiter making the dark patches under her eyes stand out as if they were painted on. "That's what it sounded like . . . I couldn't remember what—"

"What are you talking about, child?"

"The screaming air in the Van Fleet house—Hymie thought it was Nella."

"Nella! Nella Van Fleet? She's dead and buried long ago. What I'm talking about is now and I want you to listen close. If you hear that sound in the night, head for the fruit cellar and don't worry about me. There's a storm watch out . . ."

"Bertha, I couldn't just leave you here."

"You have to. And I don't want back talk. If the watch isn't called off before bedtime, maybe you should take a blanket and just go down there."

"Couldn't we get under the bed in here?"

"*I* couldn't. Now you do as I say. Probably won't come to anything—never does."

They both sat listening to the quiet outside while the TV flashed pictures without sound. Lynn's cup trembled when she picked it up.

Nella Van Fleet. How could Lynn give a thought to her at a time like this? Why wouldn't that woman stay buried? Spoiled rotten, she was, and turned out wild, too. And now her son was hanging around Lynn. He was probably as wild as his mother. Bad blood's all that ever ran in Van Fleet veins.

At least he didn't look like Nella. But he did remind her of someone. Who? Wasn't Clayborne.

"Bertha? Did Nella really try to run you over in the Bentley?"

"Might as well have. . . . Listen to that wind, will you? She drove a car as crazy as she did everything else. I was at the box getting the mail and she came down the road like a horse out of a burning barn. Had to jump for the ditch she was swerving so. What keeps putting Nella into your head?"

"I don't know. Why is it you never talk about her?"

"Now, why should I bring her up to you? She was dead before you were even born."

"But she was your childhood friend. I'd think . . ."

"Friend! Nella Van Fleet? Who told you a thing like that?"

"The night I went swimming with Jay, he showed me a picture of you and Dad and Aunt Vera at Nella's birthday party. You must have been friends to be invited to her party."

"Oh, her mother was always trying to get us neighbor kids up there to play with Nella. Didn't happen often, I can tell you. Fancy Nella had everything done for her and had nothing to do but play. The rest of us had to work." The quiet outside . . . so very quiet. "Lynn, raise up that shade and see what color the sky is." No branches scratching at the roof.

"But it's night."

"Do as I say now." No rain on the window. No sound. The silent TV made glowing flashes on the wallpaper.

"It's just black . . . like night, no stars. I really can't see anything." Lynn turned with a smile. "Let's have some more coffee and talk." She was trying to make light of everything but she didn't fool Bertha. There were little drops glistening on the pale skin above that smile.

The telephone rang in the kitchen and Lynn poured coffee all over the nightstand instead of into Bertha's cup. She left to answer it while Bertha used the tea towel that had covered her dinner to wipe it up.

Lynn came back to the door of the bedroom. "It's

Elaine. She wants to know if they should come over."

"No."

"But they could help get you up if . . ."

"And they could get blown across the county on the way. You tell her to keep her family near her cellar. We'll manage."

"But . . ."

"No buts!"

Lynn shrugged and left the doorway. Bertha could hear the soft voice talking in the kitchen.

"I don't like the quiet," Lynn said as she came back in the room. "It's like this all the time up at the Van Fleet house."

"Oh, pshaw. That house—There's a weather bulletin. Turn up the sound."

Just as Lynn turned the volume dial and brought sound to the inside of the house, the wind slammed into the outside as if it were trying to drown out the man's voice. "Change in status from tornado watch to tornado warning." Bertha could feel the cold dampness on her body even under the hot cast. "All residents in a fifty-mile radius of Minturn, Iowa, are advised to seek shelter. I repeat there is a tornado warning . . ."

"You head for the fruit cellar, Missy."

". . . basement . . . southwest corner . . . cyclone cellars . . . sight a funnel cloud approaching, leave your car . . . nearest depression or ditch . . . move at right angles to the path of the funnel . . ." Thunder drew suddenly close. Interference kept interrupting the man's voice. The picture slipped into horizontal lines. ". . . away from windows . . ."

Lynn sat staring at the horizontal lines, her cup suspended in front of her mouth.

". . . doors and windows to north and east to equalize pressure . . . no basement, crouch under strong table or desk . . . transistor radio near . . . further information . . . two funnel clouds have been sighted in the area, one at . . ."

The crack outside shook the floor and the bed. It lit the drawn window shades. It turned off the man's voice and

128

the lights and the horizontal lines. Thunder slammed close behind.

"You get to that fruit cellar or—"

Wind-driven rain hammered at the house so hard that shades rustled at closed windows.

She could hear Lynn moving about the room. "What are you doing?"

"Looking for the matches." Her voice came strangely calm out of the darkness.

"I told you—"

"Bertha, I am not going to the fruit cellar and leave you alone and helpless. Where are the matches?"

"In the top drawer, in the old cigar box to the left. But you'd go off to Denver—"

"If I weren't here, I couldn't do anything."

"You can't do anything now either." Bertha covered the panicked catch in her voice by clearing her throat. She had to sound calm to get her child to safety, to convince her. "What was that?"

"I think a tree limb broke and fell against the house." Lynn's shadow leapt up the wallpaper as she struck a match and lit the oil lamp that Grandma Maud had given Bertha for a wedding present.

Lynn brought the wheelchair to the side of the bed, her movements slow and deliberate, only the tightened lips showing that she might feel fear.

"You can't get that contraption down the cellar steps with—"

"I know. I'm taking you to the kitchen."

"The kitchen. What for?" But she raised herself up with both arms, biting off the pain.

"We're going to get under the kitchen table." Lynn slipped cold hands under Bertha's armpits to help lift "Rest a minute now, I'll move the cast around."

"What good's the kitchen table if the house comes down?"

It was a slow process, but they were both afraid enough to get the job done. In the kitchen Lynn pushed the table against the wall beside the refrigerator.

"Now how do you expect me to get out of this chair onto the floor?"

"Let's see if we can get you onto a kitchen chair, it's lower, and then onto the kitchen stool and then the floor."

Bertha's nightgown was sticky by the time she sat on the kitchen chair, her leg resting on another one. "Wait, I have to catch my breath. Lynn, if I get under the table, will you go to the fruit cellar?"

"No. Where is the transistor radio Dad always carried around?"

"He broke it when he fell on it . . . in the machine shed."

"Let's get you onto the stool."

Each successive move became harder to bear. Something hurt deep inside the cast, like the grinding pain of a bad tooth. Somehow pain didn't get any easier with age. Bertha rested on the stool, the end of her cast on the floor.

Lynn pulled on the blanket and pushed on her until Bertha was under the table, her head propped on pillows against the wall, her ear touching the cool but silent refrigerator. "Better blow out that lamp. If something should happen that could catch on fire." The light hadn't been much but the dark was sudden and uncomfortable.

Lynn crawled in beside her and covered them both with blankets. Bertha put an arm under her daughter's shoulders and drew her close as lightning lit up cracked linoleum.

"I thought tornadoes only happened when it was hot and muggy."

"Hot weather's the season for them, but they can happen anytime. They have to warn a big area because they don't know where they'll hit. Chances are it won't be right here. Only seen two in seventy years." But she'd spent countless hours in the fruit cellar just in case.

Lynn stiffened against her and she realized the trees had stopped scratching at the house, the wind no longer slapped rain against the windows. It was so quiet she could hear the alarm clock ticking clear from the bedroom and she imagined she could hear a restless mooing from the barn. Cows and horses always knew for sure. . . .

"Why did Nella stop traveling and come back to live

130

with her brother?" Lynn startled her by whispering close to her ear.

"Clayborne cut off the money. She had to come back. She bought that car and it was the last straw. Spent all the money her mother left her." *And she had to come swishing her fancy skirts around my Olaf.*

"Bertha, you're squeezing me." Lynn pulled away. She was always pulling away just when you thought you were getting close to her. "But didn't she inherit half the Van Fleet estate?"

"No, just her mother's money and the right to live in the house for life. Clay had her on an allowance for a while after her own money was gone. And that's all I'm going to say. Wish you'd get that whole family out of your head for good."

The floor creaked beneath them for no reason and they both made little startled sounds. Bertha *could* hear the cow in the barn. She kept thinking about Nella Van Fleet because she didn't want to. Drat the child for digging her up.

Vera had sat in this very kitchen, drinking coffee at the same table that Bertha was lying under now. "I think you should know . . ." Vera had said. "Have you heard the rumors?" Vera had said. Had there ever been a rumor that Bertha hadn't heard?

Well, she hadn't heard this one and she was astonished that Olaf's own sister could sit in his kitchen and tell his wife such things. And that Vera could believe her own brother capable of foolishness with a known chippy like Nella Van Fleet.

Then one afternoon she'd left Harold cleaning out the hen house and little Elaine scrubbing the kitchen linoleum and had taken a fresh pie across the road to the Jensons. On her way she saw the silver glint of Nella's car in the sun. It sat in the field that surrounded the one-room schoolhouse. It sat next to the half-filled hay wagon that Olaf had driven out of the farmyard after lunch.

She'd hidden in the Jenson windbreak, as if Olaf and Nella and Vera and the whole world were watching and laughing at her confusion.

Here it was some thirty years later and she could still remember that awful day.

Lynn's head rolled onto her shoulder and she breathed soft regular sleep. A barn cat mewed from the crawl space under the house.

How long had she stayed in the protection of the trees, hurting? She could feel that hurt even now. No, pain didn't get any easier with age. . . .

Finally she'd walked across the road and stopped automatically at the mail box, and Nella's car had careened down the road toward her. Nella hadn't even seen her . . . she'd looked crazy, angry . . . still wore her hair down like a little girl . . . and she was forty by then, same as Bertha . . . hair blew around her face . . . looked like a rat's nest . . . putting on weight, she was . . .

Bertha awoke to the vibration of the refrigerator tickling in her ear, sun on the linoleum. Lynn no longer lay beside her.

Elaine peered under the table, her stout legs looking like barn supports. "She's awake now. Mom, we're going to move the table and help you up. Leroy's here."

"Storm warning over?"

"It's been over since midnight."

19

L ynnette squinted against the raw wind and shifted the empty pack on her back.

She took long strides, bringing the heavy hiking boots down hard as if to punish the gravel road for being there. Her hands were stuffed into the pockets of her windbreaker, which didn't break the wind, even with the thick ski sweater under it.

Stopping at the driveway with the historical marker beside it, Lynnette looked across the empty field to the one-room school. Her parents and Nella Van Fleet had gone to school here and even her grandparents. But it hadn't been used since the 1920's.

She turned into the narow drive that ran through the plowed, harrowed, disked and barren dirt. When the corn was high, you could hardly see the little building, but now it looked ridiculous sitting in the middle of a field. Roger had plowed right up to the front door.

Engraved on the block above that door was 1873, the year Grandma Maud was born. The trim needed painting. Someone had been shooting at the bell, but only one small windowpane was broken. She could remember trees, a well, a playground and outhouses. Now all was leveled but the school itself. The precious black soil could not be spared for nostalgia when it was worth so much money in cash crops.

She peeked in a window at the side of the building and shivered as she met the glassy stare of the teacher behind the desk. A dirty cobweb hung from the dummy's wig to the puffed shoulder of the faded dress. Evidently Rachael Stewart's Historical Society had not held a meeting here for some time.

Olaf had kept this building in a state of semi-repair for years, either out of sentiment or because it was on Olson land. When the roof started to cave in, her father gave up on it and Joey's mother put on a new roof and donated it to the State Historical Society. The stiff cobwebby teacher must have been her idea, too. Somehow the dummy reminded Lynnette of her mother-in-law.

Wind whistled with her around to the back of the building where her father had once stood and pointed out to her the track that Olson children had beaten down for years across the fields to the school. It hadn't been there then, but the way he'd described it, she had seen it. She still could.

At one time a cold upstairs bedroom in the Olson farmhouse had been reserved for the schoolteacher. Poor things could not have had much of a life of their own. . . .

A ghostly echo came to her on the hollow whistle of wind. An echo of squealing children at play, the squeak of a swing, the faraway ringing of a school bell. She had heard it before . . . and denied it.

But she moved quickly around the school to the drive and along it to the road. The sounds came once again on the wind, whispered past her and were gone.

Lynnette walked down the road toward Roggins, looking over her shoulder often. *If I can still do that to the old schoolhouse, remind me not to visit a cemetery for a while . . . or the Van Fleet house.*

Leafless trees around clustered farm buildings dotted a desolate landscape waiting for snow. In the distance the grain elevator rose gray in a dirty sky, a sky the color of cold dishwater. She tried to concentrate on enjoying the crisp air and a few hours of freedom.

Harold and Margaret had come for lunch that day and after Lynnette finished washing their dishes, she'd startled them by coming downstairs in her hiking boots and carrying her backpack.

Bertha sat by the oil burner in her wheelchair. "Where do you think you're going?"

"I thought I'd walk into Roggins."

"What for? Elaine just brought out groceries yesterday."

"I'm going to the library, poke around a bit."

"Into Roggins? That'll take too long." Harold fished the car keys out of his pocket. "I'll drive you in and back."

"No thank you. The walk'll do me good. See you later."

Harold followed her out the back door. "Lynn, you don't understand. Margaret and I are due at a bridge-buffet gathering at three thirty and we have to change and . . ."

"Oh, I understand perfectly."

"But if you walk, you won't get back in time. What are we supposed to do, leave Mother alone?"

"That's up to you."

He stopped her by grabbing her arm. "Lynn, we can't break this engagement. It's—"

"Then you'll have to leave her alone, won't you?" She had pulled away and walked off down the lane.

Lynnette grinned at the memory and then closed her lips tight because cold wind bit her teeth.

Well, she *did* deserve a little time off. Myrtle Jenson had come to sit one night so that Lynnette could go out with Hymie and Roger. Other than that she hadn't been off the place since Bertha had come home from the hospital.

She hadn't seen Jay Van Fleet since the day she'd explored his house. He was probably still angry with her, and if he could come up with girls like the sleek brunette she'd seen at Hud's, he would forget about Lynnette soon enough. Still, she'd found herself looking up the hill to the Van Fleet house wistfully and often during the long boring days. How had he come through the tornado watch?

Lynnette reached Roggins all too soon. She slowed her pace as she came to the picket fence, the large white house at the end of Main Street. The windows of Joey's home reflected the gray of the day and the jagged barrenness of the trees. She touched the points on the picket fence, standing long minutes while her eyes searched empty windows for nothing. Finally she turned away to Main Street.

It was busy. Three cars were parked in front of the pool hall, one of them was the Bentley.

She stopped before the wooden war memorial, one side of which creaked against loosened, rusty bolts. A brown weed hung around the neck of the weathered eagle perched atop the fading names. There was no handle on

135

the drinking fountain next to the empty flagpole, and reddish-brown stained the bowl where water had once dripped from the spigot.

A flag whipped above the door of the post office, its chain ringing crisply against the horizontal pole.

Joey's father, Joseph Stewart, stood at the window of the newspaper office watching her through painted gold lettering outlined in black, ROGGINS SENTINEL. He moved to the door and opened it before she could disappear.

"Lynnette. I was wondering when you were going to take the time to visit your old father-in-law." Joey's voice gone mellow and uncertain.

"I wasn't . . ."

"Come in, come in. You look pinched with cold."

The office was dark but warm; it smelled of printer's ink and pipe.

"I was sorry to hear of your mother's accident. It must be hard for her to be inactive." He relit his pipe and puffed sweet smoke around them.

"Yes." They were alone. The *Sentinel* was a weekly, supported by the Stewart-owned hardware store, grocery, lumber yard, feed store and several lucrative farms outside town—all managed by others while Joseph Stewart concentrated on his desire to be a newspaperman.

"Sit down, won't you?"

"I can't stay . . ." She turned her face to the slated wood of the wall.

"Can't even stand the sight of me?" he asked gently and drew her to a chair beside the desk.

"It's just that you remind me so of Joey."

He handed her a Kleenex from a box on the desk. "You make me think of him too, Lynnette. Something ended forever for Rachael and me when he died. But not for you, my dear."

"That's what you think."

"No. You can begin again and we can't."

"In Roggins? I seem to have trouble getting away from here."

"Anywhere." He lit the pipe again. The ashtray on the desk was full of burned matches but held little ash. "I'm sorry about Rachael. Believe me, if she'd felt different,

I'd have had you over to the house. I feel that a little of you belongs to us through Joey, but Rachael . . ."

"I know . . . I understand." She managed a smile for him. He returned it and began to talk of other things —local news of Roggins, questions about Colorado, her schooling after Joey's death.

As she left, he bent to kiss her forehead. "Keep only the good memories, Lynnette. Build from them. Don't let them be a barrier. Joey wouldn't have wanted that. And come back and see me sometime."

When she stepped out onto the sidewalk, Roger Jenson and Jay Van Fleet stood by the Bentley. Jay hunched his shoulders and rolled the sheepskin collar of his jacket up to warm his ears.

Roger wore a black cowboy hat, looking comfortable in nothing more than a plaid long-sleeved shirt. They were discussing "cylinders" and "cams."

The earthy grin and the phony smile greeted her simultaneously.

"Have an audience with the king, Cinderella?" Roger looked past her to the windows of the *Sentinel*. "Not even a king can help you now. God, that was beautiful. Did you hear what happened? Lynn wanted to leave town so her mother fell down the stairs and broke her hip. Now she can't even leave the house. Who's staying with the invalid?"

"Harold."

"Hear you haven't been feeling too well yourself." Jay's glance was cool. "Hymie says you've had dizzy spells."

"Not lately. They stopped several weeks ago."

"Good." He hunched his jacket again and blew on his hands. "See you around." He crawled behind the wheel of the Bentley.

"Hey, Van Fleet. Will you let me drive that thing sometime?" Roger put a possessive arm around Lynnette's shoulders and pushed the pack askew.

Jay looked from one to the other, something questioning in his expression. "Sure."

"No, he'll never make another Prince Charming, Cinderella," Roger said as they watched the silver antique pass the pier without stopping. "Maybe he doesn't like farm girls." He crossed the street with her. "Need a ride? My car's getting a new battery at Torgeson's."

"No thanks, I'm going to the library." They parted company without good-byes. She walked past the empty bank building, its chipping columns jutting onto the sidewalk and turned the corner at the hardware store. Behind it shiny farm implements sat in the weather awaiting sale.

Lynnette crossed to the vacant lot next to the building housing the library and the general store. Wooden stairs ran up the side of it to her Aunt Vera's apartment and intersected a large rectangular sign painted on the bricks. Lettered in blue across fading yellow was STEWART'S GENERAL STORE and beneath that, UNION-MADE GUARANTEED LEE OVERALLS AND WORK CLOTHING.

A marquee spread over the building announcing ROGGINS THEATER. It had been a library for only ten years. Change came slowly to Roggins.

Vera Olson had given up teaching in a little town in Southern Iowa at fifty-five and let Rachael Stewart talk her into becoming a librarian. Aunt Vera, who had hated teaching, seemed to enjoy the library, maybe because it was never very busy.

Today was no exception.

Roddy Gunderson, the late Chris Gunderson's youngest, sat on one of the old theater seats that lined the walls. He gave her a dark look and went back to his comic book. Other than Aunt Vera he was the sole occupant of Roggins library.

"Hi, Lynn. Who's with your mother?" Vera dropped her glasses from her nose and they dangled on the chain that hung from her neck.

"Harold and Margaret." She whispered it more out of habit than necessity. "Comic books?"

"We aim to please all comers."

"Do you run to porno?"

Aunt Vera replaced the glasses and looked her over carefully, then grinned.

"Actually, we take all donations. Half the fiction would probably be frowned upon by an investigating committee —if Roggins read enough to need one. What are you looking for? Or have you just dropped by to talk to an old lady?"

"Think I'll browse. I'm going out of my gourd out there."

"I'll bet you are. Take a bunch home. Nobody will miss them."

Because this had been a theater, there was a slope in the floor and the last two-thirds of the stacks slanted so that any books in shelves not filled tended to lie flat. At the end of the stacks the stage remained, the screen covered by a dusty maroon curtain.

"Good heavens, can you possibly get all these in your pack?" Aunt Vera asked when she brought her selections to the desk. "Lynn, you didn't walk?"

"Afraid so. It's going to be a hard trudge home."

"Let me drive you. My one other customer has left."

"No thanks, I'm trying to kill time." She grinned sheepishly. "Harold and Margaret hadn't planned to stay."

Aunt Vera surprised her by leaning back in her chair and laughing. "Bless me, you're the only child Olaf had who turned out to be an Olson. Give me five minutes here to close up and come up to the apartment."

"Isn't it a little early?"

"On Saturday afternoon? Since the advent of television, my dear, the old-folks home of Roggins has taken to closing up early. Especially on Saturday night."

She managed to get the books in her pack and the pack on her back. The problem was walking under the load.

Lynnette left Aunt Vera to tidy up and stepped into Stewart's General Store.

Her sister, Elaine, stood behind the counter looking very important in a sea of overalls and canned goods. "Who's with Mom?"

"Harold and Margaret."

"Oh." Elaine relaxed with a smile and poked her glasses back up on her nose. "I thought they had that bridge marathon thing on Saturdays."

"So did they." Lynnette reached behind her sister for a pack of cigarettes and hunted in her purse for change.

She counted what was left. Two dollars and forty-seven cents.

"Lynn, you're not going to smoke these!"

"It's called pathetic rebellion. Bye, Elaine."

In the apartment, Lynnette dropped her pack on the overstuffed black couch and settled beside it while Aunt Vera fussed about, making tea, finding cookies, chattering from the kitchenette.

"I take it you came through the tornado watch all right. Those are frightening things." Vera Olson had to turn sideways to get the tray and herself through the accumulation of several lifetimes. She'd managed to stuff most of Grandma Maud's house into two rooms. "Other than that how are things on the farm? I expect your mother feels trapped in that awful cast."

"So does her daughter on that awful farm."

"And where would you rather be? Hum?" Crinkles around her eyes scrunched together as she laughed. "Lynn, Lynn, you remind me so much of me when I was young—and your father, too." She nudged a stack of books aside to set down her cup and saucer. The stack next to them fell to the floor. "I couldn't wait to get out of Roggins myself. I can remember taking the teaching job in Atlantic because it was the offer that came the farthest from Roggins."

"You could have married or something."

"As it happens, I wasn't asked, but then I'd have just been in another trap—diapers, cub scouts, and the privilege of cleaning up after others. Have you seen Elaine since she started working in the store? She acts like she's just been let out of a cage."

"I'm sorry, but as soon as Bertha's up and on her own, I'm heading for another and distant trap."

"That's too bad. You're about the only answer to your family's problem. Bertha has had a hard life. She quit school when her mother died to keep house for her father. Then she married young and had to run a farm. Your father was no manager. She had one miscarriage after another before Harold. Then her aging father to nurse and my mother for years. Just as life was settling down a bit you came along at a late date and, more recently, Olaf's mind going. The woman has had nothing but burdens."

"At least Bertha had a life of her own, a happy marriage, her own children, a farm she loved . . ."

"Happy marriage? Well, hardly."

"What do you mean? She was happy with Dad."

"Lynn, what you don't know about life wouldn't fit in my library if it was on microfilm. Have some more tea and don't glare at me." Vera poured her another cup. "I would not call my brother a philanderer. But he had a crush on the glamorous Van Fleet girl."

"Nella?"

"Yes, Nella. She was unattainable, could never have been the farm wife to him he needed. So he married Bertha. Your mother let herself go to fat with the first ill-fated pregnancy. Everytime Nella returned from college or her later travels, Bertha presented a greater and greater contrast—grooming and dieting were not Bertha's specialties."

"I don't believe all this."

"Lynn, I'm not saying that Olaf had an affair with Nella. All I am saying is that whenever Nella visited Roggins, your father lost no time in seeing her and without the company of your mother. Rumors raged in a small place like this and of course Bertha was the last to know. But what I wanted to tell you was that no matter the job —teacher, housewife, store clerk—you'll soon be in a rut little different than the one you feel you're in now."

"Some people find work they like doing in places they like living. Everyone should have the chance to try." Lynnette lit a cigarette and watched for her aunt's reaction.

Vera passed her a decorative dish for an ashtray without blinking. "I suppose at your age it looks that way. But Nella Van Fleet traveled all over the world and was never happy or satisfied. She certainly didn't escape her trap. Oh well, I wouldn't have listened to this at your age either. Just remember that when you leave, you won't enjoy it because Bertha—and your leaving her when she needed you—will haunt your dreams. I should know. You'll be just as haunted as Jay Van Fleet and for better reasons. By the way, I hear you had a date with him."

"That was months ago. Are there no secrets in Roggins?"

"You know there aren't. You'd do well to remember that. The ghost of his mother is supposed to be hooting in the night or something?"

Lynnette told her of the attack in the library, the coldness of the house, Hymie's theories on both. "I can't explain some of it . . . but I've been up there since and didn't really find anything wrong. I'm not convinced that there's anything more than Hymie's stories."

Aunt Vera didn't laugh but stirred an empty teacup thoughtfully. "You know . . . if anyone could do it, Nella could. That woman was unbelievable. And the stories about the house have been around for years."

"There are always stories in Roggins. About everything."

"True, but most have some basis in fact, no matter how tenuous. Tell me, do you know if Jay has ever tried to make contact with her?"

"Are you kidding? Aunt Vera . . . are you a medium of something?"

"No. But I know one. Lynn, I can't see any harm in looking into it, at least. There have been two deaths up there in the last few years that could be questioned if anyone bothered to. And if she's going to attack people, well . . . it couldn't hurt to try to find out what she wants anyway. Of course, as I remember Nella, she never knew what she wanted."

20

*N*ella paused in the sunroom before the wall of glass panes.

How long since she had flown with the dove to the little schoolhouse sitting gray now, on black earth? Or to the farmhouse at the bottom of the hill? What had drawn her there once? She could no longer remember. Time meant only to confuse her.

The housekeeper, strands of hair flying about her face, polished the table in the dining room with swift, sweeping strokes. There was strength there. Strength for the taking.

Nella considered the housekeeper.

But no. She needed a more lasting source that would bring color and fun to her drab world, perhaps even freedom from the dove. And she needed it soon.

Nella left the sunroom to prowl through familiar rooms, slightly out of focus. Upstairs and down, everything was shades of gray and the shadows were black and were flat. The house was empty of light and color and warmth.

Her son was not home.

She wandered restlessly about the master bedroom, into the bathroom where his toothbrush lay beside his shaving mug.

When Clay had lived, the strength of her hatred had brought color and form, revenge and the planning of mischief had brought fun. Now all was boredom, boredom and agony.

Where was Jay?

Nella whirled into the hall, hovered above the staircase. She'd had to fight boredom all her life. It was not fair that she should have to fight it in death. Her anger formed a hiss on the air that only she could hear.

The housekeeper was dusting in the entry hall now. Nella moved back to the sunroom, to stare again at the schoolhouse far away. Why did it have meaning for her?

She had vague memories of attending it as a child. But there was more. She must go there again soon, to discover what it was.

Something moved on the road by the school, moved toward her.

It focused into the Bentley.

The Bentley . . . she'd had it made especially and then had it and herself shipped home to Clay—C.O.D. clear from England. He'd been gloriously horrified.

A bright blue chair emerged from a flat shadow.

He was coming home!

The figured wallpaper in the hallway had once again become the yellow of memory as she moved toward the front door to wait for Jay.

The housekeeper was still in the entry hall, but Nella barely noticed her as she passed to the front step so quickly that remnants of dead ivy rustled.

Jay. She would have named him Joy, so delighted an unwed mother was she. But she had named him Jay because it was the closest to Joy she dared name a boy. At least Clay had not changed the name.

How she had laughed at Clay when she announced that he was to become an uncle. Why could she remember some things so vividly while others were only hazy hints of things forgotten?

The Bentley was turning off the highway into the lane.

She must give Jay time, must not be impatient. But whenever she tried to reach him, he would pull away.

The Bentley passed the gatehouse.

At least his belief in her was firm. She knew because without it she would not exist.

The Bentley didn't stop at the garage but pulled up in front of the house. It sat there long minutes with its engine running while Nella waited for her child.

And then it started forward, gaining momentum after it turned the circle around the elms, to pass the gatehouse and roar back down the lane.

Mrs. Benninghoff dusted the delicate figurine and set it carefully on the corner table in the entry hall. Just as she straightened she heard what sounded like a sigh and, from the corner of her eye, saw someone walking slowly up the staircase.

But when she turned to look directly, there was no one there.

21

L ynnette reached the end of Main Street and had turned onto the road home before she realized that the load on her back was too much for her. She'd been so intent on mulling over the astounding conversation with her aunt in that overstuffed apartment that she didn't feel the straps on her shoulders biting in until the strain began to pull at her neck muscles.

She stood across the road from Joey's house and took off the pack. Perhaps if she adjusted the strap again . . .

The Bentley flew by and left her in a dust cloud with pieces of shattered golden leaves scurrying down the road. It came to a noisy halt and made a U-turn.

As it came back, Lynnette grinned and stuck out her thumb.

The Bentley stopped and Jay reached across to open the door for her. She juggled the pack into the backseat and crawled in beside him. They started moving before she could close the door.

Jay's face looked as bleak as the sky. "Is it always this cold in November?" There was a restless edge to his voice.

"It isn't cold yet. The cold starts in December."

"I wonder what that house'll be like in the dead of winter." He nodded toward the hill at the end of the road. Except for giant firs, the back of the Van Fleet house had taken on the barren appearance of the front.

"The only difference is you'll have dead winter outside as well as in." Her pack fell onto the floor as he braked and turned into the driveway of the one-room school.

"What the hell is that? I didn't even know it was here until the corn came down. . . . What's so funny?"

"I've never heard the expression, 'the corn came down,' before. It's a historical shrine to the old one-room school. One teacher, eight grades, eighteen or twenty pupils. Didn't you read the sign?"

"I don't read signs." His hand moved from nowhere to the nape of her neck, turning her head so that he could study her face. "Unless they're written in people's eyes."

"What sign do you read here?"

"I read 'Desperate Boredom.' What do you read?"

"I read 'The Cat in The Creamery.'" Lynnette drew the forbidden pack of cigarettes from the pocket of her windbreaker and offered him one.

As she expected, the motion of lighting two cigarettes took his hand from her neck. They smoked, sitting apart. The cigarette tasted to Lynnette like hot gasoline filtered through an old bedroom slipper.

"My Aunt Vera wants to know if you'd like to communicate with your mother."

His eyes went empty. "Just how would I do that?"

"Are you ready for this? She knows a medium."

She waited for a laugh or at least a grin, but Jay Van Fleet stared grimly at the schoolhouse, blunt fingernails tapping the steering wheel.

"Why? To make her go away?"

"At least to find out what she wants—although Aunt Vera doubts that Nella the ghost knows what she wants, since Nella the living never did." The Bentley smelled of ancient dust. Combined with cigarette smoke, the effect was smothering. She opened the door for air but the cold had dampened, deepened; it reached into the car for them.

Jay put out his cigarette, impatiently. "Let's go take a look at the school."

"Just promise me one thing," she said as they walked down the drive. "That if you get Aunt Vera's medium up there, you'll let me watch. We desperately bored creatures are curious."

"I don't want you in that house again."

"I was safe the last time. You can find Aunt Vera at the Roggins Library. You'll find the library under the theater marquee."

"Where's the theater? In a gas station?"

"No, it's long gone. Jay, I've never seen a medium at work. I've never seen a medium at all."

147

In a lightning change of mood he took her cold hand in his and smiled down at her.

"Don't get your teeth chilled when you do that?"

"Most women are pleased when a guy smiles at them. From you I get insults." He touched the weathered brick of the building, his eyes telling her he could care less what she thought of his smile. "Did you go to school here?"

"No. Farm children are shipped into the school in Roggins now. It used to be the high school when this was in use. High school kids are bused into Minturn." She shivered and folded her arms across her chest. "That hurt Roggins. What community spirit existed was centered in its high school."

He tried the door, but the lock held. "Who's the Grand High Keeper of the Key?"

"My mother-in-law has one. She's the president of the Roggins Historical Society." She laughed at his expression. "Rachael Stewart's maiden name was Roggins. The town is named after her great grandfather and Stewart's General Store was once Roggins' General Store. The Stewart money came from Rachael's side of the marriage. She's what driving force there is behind Roggins."

"I'll probably see you at the Stewart's Thanksgiving Day then. Some broad called me yesterday and invited me to dinner. You'll be there, won't you?"

"You were invited because you are all that's left of the local aristocrary. The Van Fleets are the only romance Roggins has known." She looked away. The sky had darkened. "After Joey's funeral I was asked never to grace the door of the Stewart house again."

"Why?"

"I took Joey away from his momma so that he could be murdered in a car crash in Denver. And I wasn't even in the car."

Wind blew Jay's hair across his forehead as he moved around the corner of the building. He reached up to push it into place, then stood back to look up at the school bell in its squat little tower on the roof. "What was that?"

"The wind."

"I thought I heard it ringing." He gazed across empty fields. "And kids laughing . . . far away."

"And swings squeaking?"

"Yeah, what was it?"

"The wind. Let's go." But as she turned away, his hand on her arm turned her back.

"But if you heard it and I heard—Christ, is it the whole countryside? I thought it was just the house." His grip on her arm tightened. "Tell me."

"I don't know. I honestly don't . . ."

"Then why did you say it was the wind?"

"It was the only explanation I could think of that I could accept. Okay? I'm cold, let's go."

"No."

She sighed and followed him to the rear of the school. He paced the crumbly dirt, looked across the level field and turned to scan the building. His expression suggested that he suspected her of playing a joke on him. She waited, shivering, as he walked around to the other side of the school and back. Their eyes met as the wind echoed the sounds again.

The sky had darkened even more, hiding the grain elevator and Roggins. A gray-white mist tumbled in slow motion over the fields toward them.

"Think it'll snow?" he asked behind her.

"I doubt it. It'll fool around like this for a month and then all hell'll break loose."

"What's this?" Jay tried to pull up on a flat panel set in wooden runners against the brick. It didn't budge.

"A hole."

"For what?" The fact that it wouldn't open seemed to spur him on. He strained against it until his face reddened.

"Could have been a primitive fire escape or a ventilation hole. There's no window on this side. It opens at floor level. Everything below it is foundation."

Jay straightened, squinting at her. "You've been in this way?"

"Roger, Hymie and I got into a little trouble here when we were kids. Hymie got stuck halfway through."

"Does it still open?"

"It probably just hasn't been moved for a long time."

Lynnette took hold and helped pull upward. It slid an inch and jammed but the inch gave them a better hold. "Do you think you want to go in? It's kind of a spooky place. You seem spooked enough already."

"You calling me a coward?"

They jammed again at two inches and her knuckles scraped on brick. It was impossible not to brush against Jay somewhere.

"This is getting to be a challenge I can't resist. Thought you farm girls grew lots of muscles milking cows and slopping hogs. Pull!"

Another inch and then the panel moved unexpectedly, sliding out of its runners. He leaned it against the building and bent to peer inside. "What's that rustling noise in there? The wind again?"

"Rats." *We shouldn't go in there, you and I.*

By turning his shoulders at an angle, Jay was just able to squeeze through. As his feet disappeared, Lynnette poked her head inside and found herself looking at the interior through his spread legs. The dust smelled like the dust in the Bentley, but mustier. From her vantage point the most obvious obstacles were the legs of double desks and the legs of their benches, nailed to the floor and fuzzy with dust.

She could see down one aisle to the teacher's desk, hollow in the middle for its occupant's legs. The black hem of the teacher's dress jerked up as two shining eyes stared straight at her down the aisle. It fell back to the floor as the rat disappeared.

She had to crawl between his legs and ended up flat on her stomach in the dust. The legs on either side of her didn't seem to notice her arrival.

Lynnette stood and brushed herself off. Turning, she found Jay staring straight ahead, his eyes wide. "Oh-oh, I should have warned you. It's just a dummy."

A shutterlike blink and then he shook his head and focused on her face. "Christ," was all he said in that whispery voice.

Wind no longer rustled around the building, and the squeak of a floorboard under his foot as he moved to the windows sounded startling in the sudden hush. Light grew

150

dimmer as the fog approached, dulling dust-covered colors, making the buff of his jacket and blond of his hair the brightest colors in the room.

Lynnette stood where he'd left her, watching his back as he faced the windows and the movement behind the teacher's desk caught only the corner of her attention but it was enough to make her breath come sharply, noisily.

She felt his fear across the room, felt it rush toward her to meet her own. "She won't fall."

The teacher had tilted in her chair and the rat stood with its back feet on one of her shoulders, its head poking out from under the wig. "She's wired to the chair."

But Lynnette felt crawling skin on her own neck as she came up behind Jay Van Fleet.

The rat tittered high and sharp and leaped to the floor to disappear in shadow. The teacher tipped even more; her wig came askew. Lynnette's hand reached for the buff of Jay's jacket.

"Whose creepy idea was that, Mrs. Stewart? Your mother-in-law's?"

Lynnette felt the softness of suede brush against her hand as he turned suddenly. "I expect so." She held tight to his jacket, her other hand brushing the soft suede.

She listened for the rat but was aware only of his warmer fingers moving under her hair, spreading thumb and little finger, placing slight pressure on the skin behind each ear, a hand so large it warmed her neck, her face against the cold zipper of his jacket, his breath moving the hair on top of her head.

She imagined she could hear the fog wisping over the roof, moving toward the Van Fleet house. She dreaded the thought that Jay might say something brittle.

"So lonely," he whispered above her. Did he mean himself of did he mean her?

She slid her hands up under the suede jacket and then her arms. She needed warmth, needed to feel him, needed to feel.

Dry coarse lips scraped a tear from her cheek. Did the fog cover up the Bentley?

"Jay?"

"Don't talk." He drew her down with him to the floor.

Winter's coming. And I can't get away. I need to get warm before winter. How would the Roggins Historical Society interpret the misplaced dust on the floor of the one-room schoolhouse?

Jay was heavier than Joey; the heaviness felt good the entire length of her, the floor uncompromisingly hard beneath her. Did Harold and Margaret stay with Bertha?

Lynnette had to force her ribs up to give her lungs room to breathe under him, had to concentrate. . . . She needed . . . What shame was there in needing?

She opened her eyes to fog-darkened twilight, to the colorless intentness of the eyes above her.

Her windbreaker unzipped. She felt the pull of her slacks over the crest of her hipbones, the surge of herself inside them, the prickle of skin exposed suddenly to cold damp air.

The clumsy groping, of two people who hadn't known each other, eased as she sensed his assurance that she wouldn't reject him. She didn't intend to.

But as the massaging of his lips and fingers became less gentle and her own need threatened to engulf the fine balance between them, a vision sharp and unbidden, flew across the fog twilight in front of him. . . .

The pallor of the dead seeping through the mortuary makeup . . . Joey.

A tiny cry from her throat. Her spine scraped the dust of the floor. The rat, the staring dummy, the crippled form of her mother invaded her.

Jay Van Fleet's voice sounded remote. "You don't want to quit now."

"No."

His hands burned her skin as they opened her. *Think of now, Lynnette, now.*

"You need me."

The cramping at the hard pressure inside her spread through her. "Yes."

Still, unbidden thoughts fought her struggle to reach that commitment she knew she was to make . . . and he was not.

Light from the fog glanced off the plane of Jay's

cheekbone. Uniform upper teeth showed through a grimace of effort as he fought his own battle to stay with her.

But then he forgot himself in himself. He groaned and lunged. Sweat dripped past her and she was lost in his chest. The final lunge brought her own commitment, soundless, tortured. . . .

Then she lay luxurious and quiet, treasuring the weight that wanted to bow her rib cage even though she needed to breathe fully the dusty air of release.

Even in the gloom Lynnette could see that Jay's expressionless mask was down. His vulnerability lay naked in fog-gray eyes.

It confused her. She was ready for her own vulnerability. But not for his.

He kissed the end of her nose and drew away. And the drawing away hurt more than the entering.

She clung to him as they huddled together in the jacket with the sheepskin collar, sitting with their backs against the shelves that lined the wall under the mist-drenched windows.

Jay began to tell her in a husky voice about his partner in South America, a man called Harry.

22

*J*ay was late arriving at the Stewarts' on Thanksgiving Day. He stood on the welcome mat and pushed the doorbell. Chimes trying to sound like Big Ben could be heard on the porch.

The door opened just as the chiming finished and a slender man with graying hair greeted him. "Mr. Van Fleet, we were afraid you weren't coming. I'm Joseph Stewart. Won't you come in?"

"Sorry. I lost track of the time." He almost hadn't come, but stepping into the warmth filled with spicy cooking odors, he was glad he had.

"Here, let me take your coat. Everyone is settled in the living room and dinner's soon ready."

He motioned Jay into a room where a fire crackled and a woman with great somber eyes rose from a chair next to it. "Well, here you are after all. I'm so glad you could come. I'm Rachael Stewart. This is Evelyn Birmingham. You've met her husband, our minister . . ."

Jay nodded at the Birminghams, as he stole glances at Lynnette's mother-in-law, her hair swept away from a face so carefully made up it defied classification as to age.

". . . and John Henson is your lawyer, too, I believe."

Old Henson sat on the couch with a Siamese cat on his lap. As he extended a limp hand to Jay, the cat arched and jumped to the floor. "Good to see you again, Jay. How are things up at the house?"

"Chilly."

The Siamese gave him a cold cross-eyed stare, then sniffed his shoe and pant leg. Hissing, it backed away as if it had been kicked and tore from the room.

Rachael linked her arm in his and led him to a chair across the room. "That was Petula. Her exits are usually more dignified. And here is someone I particularly wanted you to meet. Lue Ann, this is Jay Van Fleet, our prize man about town. Jay, this is Lue Ann Schroeder, my niece."

He'd wondered why he'd been invited.

Lue Ann rose with a practiced smile and a hint of that unsure expression worn by the uninitiated. "Hi."

Pushing eighteen, pretty, not quite ripe, was his quick appraisal of Lue Ann Schroeder, but his hostess watched him expectantly and so he said, "Nice."

"I thought you'd think so. Lue Ann is a beauty queen. We're very proud of her." Rachael's eyebrows were permanently arched high above her eyes, her look one of constant irritated surprise. "I'll help Mary Jane dish up the food. Dinner has been ready and waiting for an hour. Lue Ann, entertain our guest, will you?"

As her mistress left, Petula slid around the door into the room. Her ears back, her tail jerking, she settled under an ancient treadle sewing machine and eyed Jay as if he were a crippled mouse.

"Sorry I held up your dinner."

Lue Ann cleared her throat and brushed an invisible speck from her dress. "Aunt Rachael was afraid you wouldn't come at all. You're a kind of a celebrity around here."

"So are you. What are you, Miss Iowa or something?"

"Oh no, I'm this year's National Pork Queen." She tossed a pale strand of hair over her shoulder.

"Really? Do you live around here?"

"I'm from Ricketts. It's a town way south of here."

"I thought it was bad bones or something." He smiled down at her to soften the sarcasm, wishing he hadn't come after all.

"You have the nicest smile. Have you ever thought of acting?"

"No . . . no, I haven't."

"I have. I . . ." She went on to a lengthy discussion of the contacts she'd made in her travels as National Pork Queen.

Jay cocked an attentive ear in her direction and tuned her out. A cow bell hung from the mantel, and an old-fashioned coffee grinder, like those he'd seen used in South America, had been converted into a table lamp.

155

". . . the offer is good enough, I'll take it."

"Dinner's ready." Rachael stood in the doorway.

In the dining room Reverend Birmingham intoned grace and as Joseph began carving the turkey, Petula scuttled over the threshold and hid under the buffet. Every time Jay looked up from his plate he found himself staring into the widened and crossed eyes just to the left of the minister's elbow. The cat was either crazy or constipated, Jay decided, and kept his eyes averted.

He was, of course, seated next to Lue Ann. Mary Jane Gunderson smiled at him as she poured his wine.

"I thought that the only way to get Mary Jane to help out today was to invite all her other employers to dinner." Rachael passed him the mashed sweet potatoes. Or was it squash?

"Haven't seen you in church, Jay." Birmingham's laugh wrinkled his forehead. "I hope you aren't afraid it will crash down on you. No, really. I hope it's . . . not because of our mutually unpleasant experience . . . finding Gunderson that way."

"I'm jealous of the Reverend." Rachael rested both elbows on the table and rubbed one hand over the back of the other in a curious and apparently unconscious gesture. "I haven't been in that beautiful house since I was eighteen. Your uncle didn't pass out invitations. The Christmas holidays are coming up. You should have a party. That house is so unique."

What would Nella do with a house full of guests? Would guests warm up Christmas? Jay had never liked Christmas. "Maybe I will. Might be fun."

Rachael raised her glass, her orange-red lipstick standing away from the shadows of her face. "Well then, here's to the holidays, in hopes that you will."

"I understand your house is a real mansion with acres of lawn and a swimming pool," Lue Ann said.

"Yeah. You'll have to come up and see it . . . and meet my mother . . ."

"Oh, I'd love to," Lue Ann gushed into the sudden quiet. "I'd just love to."

Joseph Stewart cleared his throat. "Mr. Van Fleet is

156

teasing you, Lue Ann. His mother is . . . no longer living."

"You remember my telling you that his house was supposed to be haunted, dear." Rachael's eyebrows rebuked him. "Well, his mother . . . the stories are . . ."

"My mother's a ghost. Should have had a Halloween party."

Lue Ann Schroeder was startled into silence, but she tried again over the pumpkin pie. "Aunt Rachael said you'd lived in Peru. What do they eat there on Thanksgiving?"

"Guinea pigs."

"Thanksgiving is a national holiday, dear. Coffee, Jay?"

"Please. Guinea pig tastes a little like turkey. The food on this table would feed a small village there. Petula would feed a family."

"They don't eat cats and guinea pigs?" Evelyn Birmingham peered around the dried-weed centerpiece.

"You would too if you were hungry enough." Jay had eaten too much because food tasted so good hot. Even the coffee felt good burning his tongue. But the pleasant warmth was growing stuffy.

Petula ventured out from under the buffet, crept along the floor and disappeared under the table. Jay moved his foot slightly and she spat, careening into Mary Jane on a mad flight for the kitchen.

"She's certainly taken a dislike to you. I've never seen her act this way," Rachael said.

"Maybe I picked up some ghost dust on my shoes."

That evening as he was getting into his coat in the hall, he found himself standing next to a china cabinet that held no china. It was filled instead with trophies, framed scholastic certificates of honor and a picture of a young man with Rachael's eyes in Joseph's face.

"My beautiful son," Rachael said beside him. "He's dead." Her dark eyes misted.

"I know. I'm sorry." He looked again at Lynnette's husband. "I've met his wife."

"He made an unfortunate marriage. He showed great promise before that, a gifted boy . . . could have married

157

well . . ." She drew in her breath in an attempt to regain her composure.

Jay changed the subject quickly. "Did you know my mother?"

Rachael stared at him blankly, then blinked as if mentally changing gears. "Nella? I had met her. She was older and traveled a great deal. Why?"

"Just curious. It's natural isn't it? I don't know anything about her."

Her eyes searched his face. "Jay, is there really something strange going on up at that house?"

"Yes, there is."

"It could be . . . just leftover unhappiness. I do know she was unhappy when her brother made her come back here. And I'm sure, speaking as a mother who has lost her only child, that losing you couldn't have been easy. If she hadn't gotten herself mixed up with an Olson . . ." She ran a finger down the corner surface of the china cabinet. "Romantic relationships with that family lead to disaster, believe me."

The heavy dinner was forming into a bowling ball in his middle. "Olson? You mean my mother and . . ."

"The farmer across the road. There was some kind of involvement there. I'm not saying you are the result of that involvement, Jay. But Olaf Olson was one of the names linked to your mother before her death."

The homey warmth of the house had turned stuffy again. Jay started to move around her to take his leave.

"Wait. There's something else I can tell you . . . a closely guarded secret that can't really matter now that everyone but you is dead." She looked over her shoulder where her husband was helping the old lawyer into his coat. "Which of the stories have you been told about your birth?"

"I was born in a New York hospital. My mother died giving birth . . ."

"No." She lowered her voice. "You were born in the Van Fleet house."

"How do you know?"

"I drove the midwife to the house. My grandmother delivered you in Nella's room. She had been a midwife

158

years before. Clayborne didn't want a doctor." An earring reflected light flashes on the glass of the china cabinet. "He'd told everyone that Nella went East when she began to show. She stayed in the house. All the servants except the housekeeper were let go."

"Mrs. Benninghoff?"

"The Benninghoffs didn't move to Roggins until after Nella died. And Nella didn't die right away. When you were two weks old, the housekeeper took you away . . . to New York, I suppose. Your mother died the next day. I don't know how he arranged the death certificate and birth certificate, the mortuary business and all. But the body was supposedly flown back and the funeral was held a few days after the notice of death made the papers. I'll never forget the night your uncle called my grandmother, and she asked me to drive her out. There was a blizzard . . ." Her eyes fixed on his but focused inward.

He wanted to leave before this story finished but found himself riveted to the movements of the fiery-colored lips.

"There was so much snow I had to spend the night there. My grandmother told me about what was going on and swore me to secrecy. She . . . used your mother as an example of what happened to women who . . . well, you know. It's probably one of the few secrets that's been kept from Roggins since it was founded. I've never told . . ."

Joseph Stewart walked toward them. He'd been holding a similarly hushed conversation with the lawyer. "Rachael, you are not bending this young man's ear with the fantastic exploits of our late son, are you?" He nodded toward the china cabinet.

Jay used the interruption as an excuse to leave, thanked the Stewarts, nodded to the pork queen from Bad Bones, Iowa, who stood uncertainly in the doorway to the living room, and escaped.

On the porch Henson was putting on thick gloves, breathing frost onto his coat collar.

"How long before I can get out of here?"

"Takes time, Jay. It's difficult to push the tax people. I've told you . . ."

159

"Just try to hurry it up, will you? Do anything you can. Anything!"

He was off the porch, down the walk and through the gate in the picket fence before the old lawyer could go into his patient explanations of the complexities of the law.

But once in the Bentley, he drove slowly. As he approached the one-room schoolhouse, he was barely moving at all. He turned the Bentley into the drive and switched off the ignition.

The roof of the old school was outlined in frost, the rest sunk in night shadows. A thin icing of frost looked like mold on the crinkled surface of surrounding field, broken only by the dull glow of ice on an occasional shallow puddle.

Jay sat for a long time, staring at the darkened building in front of him, chewing on the knuckle of his glove, hunched into the collar of his jacket while the hot meal and the warmth of the wine cooled inside him.

She certainly picked her own time and the damndest places. He'd chalked Lynnette Stewart off as interesting but unattainable. Why had she turned to him suddenly and with no softening up? And she hadn't needed to say a word, make a movement except to reach out for him. His glance strayed to the lighted farmhouse across the field. Car lights moved away from the Olson house, turning in the other direction as they reached the road.

The little widow had lost her tan. The soft shadows under her eyes made her look older and should have ruined her looks. But they didn't.

Jay lit a cigarette. The trouble with being alone was that there was too much time for postmortems.

Frost on the Bentley's windows slowly clouded him in with his thoughts.

Is that why he could talk to her so easily? Is that why he thought of her when loneliness swamped him? Had he laid his own . . . Was the little widow his sister? He stubbed out the cigarette so hard he broke it.

She'd lived here most of her life. Surely Lynnette Stewart would have heard the rumor he'd heard tonight. Or wouldn't it matter to her? He'd been out of the country so long, he didn't know what mattered to people here anymore. Everything had changed so quickly he felt like a stranger in his own country. But how fast could things change in Roggins?

The cold merciless attack on Lynnette in the library . . . a warning? Was Nella warning him away from his own sister? Had the thick air at the door to Nella's room sought to keep them apart?

Jay slowed the Bentley again as he passed the lane to the Olson farm.

"Romantic relationships with that family lead to disaster. . . ."

He stepped on the tiny oblong gas pedal, as he rearranged his favorite four-letter words into new and wonderful phrases.

Jay turned the Bentley toward Minturn. Maybe Barbara what's-her-name would have a drink waiting for him. Another little party he'd been invited to and he would be late for and he'd almost forgotten about.

The house on the hill was peacefully dark as he made the turn. There was only a dull glow from the direction of the toolshed.

23

*H*oarfrost laced fence wires and telephone lines, weed stalks and grass blades, with a white shimmer. It crunched under Lynnette's boots as she crossed the farmyard. Frost and sun transformed the shoddy farm into splendid brilliance.

She squinted in the glare and listened to the brittle snapping and cracking sounds, watched the red flash of a cardinal, heard its delirious song and smiled to herself. Crisp air dried the lining of her nose and made her eyes water. The handle of the milk pail cut into cramped fingers through her gloves.

Almost two weeks now since she'd crawled into the old schoolhouse with Jay Van Fleet. She had neither seen him nor heard from him since, but the last two weeks had been easier to live because of him. She had even spoken kindly to the cow this morning. *He'll call. I know he will.*

By afternoon the sky had clouded over, but Lynnette still had a snug feeling of well-being and inner warmth as she settled on sofa cushions next to the kitchen oil burner. She lay on her stomach with a novel from Aunt Vera's library, a steaming mug of fresh coffee at her elbow. The world was blue-cold outside, the windows frosty. But in the kitchen the roasty smell of coffee and the richness of herbs and turkey carcass simmering together in the soup kettle heightened her feeling of coziness.

Having settled Bertha in her wheelchair in front of the television with some mending garnered from Elaine's workbasket, and the morning chores and household duties completed, Lynnette planned a long undisturbed afternoon with a book.

"Lynn, what're you doing?" The standard question when the sounds of work ceased in the house.

"Reading."

"Can't you read in here with me?"

"I can't concentrate with the TV on."

Quiet from the living room except for the weepy music on the television. Lynnette snuggled deeper and read the first page. This was going to be a ghost story, she could tell by the . . .

"Why do you want to read when there's television to watch?" The plaintive call of the lonely bird.

Oh, dear God. "I'll come at news time. Let me read awhile, will you?" Her toasty feeling was ebbing before the nudge of irritation.

By the second page she knew it was going to be a murder mystery as well and had just begun to visualize the main character and the house through which he crept when the phone rang.

She looked up at the squat telephone on the counter and received a mental image of tangled, streaky ash-blond hair and colorless eyes over a sheepskin collar. She pushed herself up, feeling silly about the smile she couldn't smother.

"Lynn, the phone's ringing."

"I know." *Cripes, I'm in the same room with it.*

"Well, answer it."

"I am. Hello?"

"Lynn? That you?"

"Yes, Aunt Vera." *Damn it.* "It's me."

"Lynn, I've just got to tell you what's happened."

"The hog market took a sharp rise and . . ."

"Hush, smarty pants, and let your old aunt talk, will you? Jay Van Fleet just now walked out of the library . . ."

"Lynn, who is it?" Bertha wheeled to the door of the kitchen.

" . . . so surprised, I . . ."

"Just a minute. It's Aunt Vera."

"Does she want to talk to me?"

"No. I'm sorry, Aunt Vera, Bertha's talking in my other ear. You lost me at Jay Van Fleet just walked . . ."

"Well, what does she want?"

"Bertha, the world will never know if you don't let me listen!"

"Lynn, he came to ask me to bring my medium friend and come to the party. I'm so excited. It'll be the social

163

event of the century for Roggins. Why didn't you tell me he was throwing a party?"

"What party?"

"The Christmas party. I expected you'd know all about it. Can't wait to see what'll happen when Dorothy walks in—she's my medium friend from Minturn."

"I . . . hadn't heard."

"I'd better ring off. He's probably trying to call you right now. Evelyn Birmingham came in earlier and said she'd been invited, so I knew about it but didn't dream I'd get to go. . . . Well, better get off the line, if he's trying to get a-hold of you."

"Bye, Aunt Vera."

"What did she say?" Bertha had jimmied the wheelchair into the kitchen.

"Jay Van Fleet is throwing a Christmas party up at the house and she's been invited." Lynnette went back to her sofa cushions by the oil burner.

"Have you?"

"No." She took a sip of cooled coffee and turned a page. As the quiet lengthened, she looked up to find Bertha staring at the telephone.

"If he asks you, will you go?"

"I don't know." *The hell I don't.*

"Those cushions are going to get all dirty there on the floor." The wheelchair thumped over the wooden threshold into the living room.

Lynnette stared at the black words on the white page and wondered what she would wear if Jay Van Fleet asked her to the party. Finally she poured herself some hot coffee and carried the percolator into the living room to refill Bertha's cup.

Her mother sat facing the window while the TV blahed at the side of her head. Still hands held the mending on her lap.

Why doesn't she want me to see him? The thought chased her back into the kitchen. Bertha didn't approve of her seeing anyone. It needn't necessarily mean that her mother suspected her father and Nella of . . . Roggins was full of rumors, always. Olaf had lived across the road, had known Nella all his life. It was only natural he'd see her sometimes in a place as small as Roggins.

The phone rang again and this time only once.

"Hello?"

"Lynn, that you? This is Myrtle. Say, I've just baked a batch of yeast bread. Why don't you run over and get a couple of loaves for your supper? Your mom'll be all right there for a few minutes."

". . . Uh, yes. Thank you. I'll be right over." She turned to find Bertha in the doorway. "Relax. Just Myrtle. She has fresh bread for our dinner." Lynnette reached for her hiking boots. "I'm going to run over and get it."

Outside the cold had changed from brisk to numbing. Feathers of snow on the wind floated wet against her face.

She paused at the end of the lane to look up at the Van Fleet house. It sat grim on brown lawns, dirty smoke coiling out of the chimneys into a dull sky. In the other direction . . . the schoolhouse looked cold and lifeless as if it had not known the heat of life two weeks before.

At the back door of the Jenson farmhouse she was met by Myrtle and the incomparable smell of homemade bread. "Wipe your boots real good, will you? Then come see what Roger's done now."

Royal blue carpeting covered every inch of the floor in a kitchen larger than most living rooms.

Royal blue? "Myrtle, it's beautiful. Isn't this a new dinette set?"

"Came this morning. Roger laid the carpet himself. You know, Lynn, when his father was alive, all the money seemed to go for seed corn and stock. I never dreamed I'd get kitchen carpeting."

"How does Roger do it?"

"He raises porkers only when the market's good, and otherwise it's all in corn and soybeans. Here let me take your coat."

"I can't stay, Myrtle, Bertha will . . ."

"Oh, let her fuss awhile. Do her good." She unzipped Lynnette's windbreaker and led her firmly to the new dinette set. "Baked doughnuts, too, and the coffee's fresh. Your mother is going to have to learn she can't shut a young woman up in an old farmhouse after she's been out in the world."

Lynnette could see that assembling Myrtle's conversation wasn't going to be any easier than it ever was.

"What are you going to wear?"

"Where?"

"To the party, of course. I just can't think what I'll wear. Probably have to sew up something. But I've never been to a house that fancy before, and if I make a dress that fancy, I'll never have any place to wear it again. Do you think if I made something nice enough for church it would be good enough to wear to the Van Fleet house?"

"I'm sure it would." *You too, huh?*

"I felt so guilty when he called yesterday. Do you know why?"

"No. Why?"

"I'd wanted to ask him over to dinner, but I thought maybe he'd think we weren't good enough for him. And —do you think we'll see the ghost?—and then he asks us to his party. Didn't I feel about an inch high?"

"I don't think you can see her."

"I've never been in that house. I'm really curious to see it. I asked him if I could bring anything, but he said no. Here's Roger, I knew he'd smell the doughnuts. Take your boots off."

"How come she doesn't have to?" Roger grinned at her from the doorway where the cold came in around him.

"She didn't come from the farrowing house, that's why."

"I didn't either." But he unlaced his boots. "Was down to the road talking to Hymie. He's got a mad on about the party. Figures his ghost'll act up and wipe out everybody or something." He came to the table where his mother poured him some coffee. "Suppose you're going, Cinderella?"

When she didn't answer, he exchanged looks with Myrtle. "No? Hum, maybe that dark-haired chick he had in Hud's that night. Remember her? Like to meet that one." He took half a doughnut in one bite.

Flat, silent snowflakes fell as Lynnette walked out of

the Jenson lane carrying two loaves of crusty bread in a paper sack.

She stopped at the road and looked again up the hill to the house. Jay had called the Jensons yesterday. She'd been home all day. Maybe he really meant it when he said she couldn't go into the house again. Maybe he just didn't want to see her anymore.

But Lynnette stayed close to the phone all week.

By the weekend she gave up and walked into Roggins with Aunt Vera's books. She was too tired to carry the new ones home, so she waited in Stewart's General Store for Elaine to get off work and drive her back.

"Did you leave Mom all alone?"

"Oh, Elaine, she's all right for a few hours, and she can get to the telephone." She helped Elaine turn off the lights and lock up. "Of course, you could chain me to the table leg or something."

"I'm sorry, Lynn. I just worry about her being alone. I don't know what we'd do without you."

Come the day, dear sister . . .

"Has Jay Van Fleet asked you to his party yet?" Elaine wanted to know as she started the car.

"No, why should he?" *If one more person asks me that, I'll . . .*

"Well, you went out with him and everything. I thought sure you'd be invited. I mean, if Aunt Vera's going." A thin layer of snow crunched under the tires.

Okay, you were horny, right? And you felt better afterward, right? Makes no difference that the whole world is going to his party but you, you still feel better. It was only his body you lusted after, you evil girl, not him—right?

But she didn't feel better.

Three days before Christmas she was looking upstairs for Christmas decorations and came across a wicker basket shaped like a treasure chest and full of old family photographs. Forgetting about Christmas and the deep chill of the room, she rummaged through the pictures looking for likenesses of her father in his youth. There were many. And in none of them could she see any resemblance to Jay Van Fleet.

167

24

Roger Jenson stood behind the plastic fern and watched the brunette at the bar shiver. Nella's bastard shook up ice and booze in a fancy shaker. He wore a blazer over a heavy white turtleneck and still looked cold.

Roger had not been in the basement of the Van Fleet house before. This room was all red and black. The entire wall behind the bar was mirror, with glass shelves across it for bottles. It reflected the back of the bastard and Rachael Stewart, who came to fawn over Barbara, the brunette. Barbara must be somebody.

Hymie edged through the doorway with a tray and carefully skirted the pool table. He wore his dumb-scowl look tonight.

"Hey, servant. Come here."

"What you hiding behind the fern for, clod?"

"Watching old Myrt get snockered." He nodded toward the black couch, where his mother sat with Lynn's Aunt Vera and another old biddy. All three looked distinctly happy.

Hymie grinned. "Didn't know she ever touched the stuff."

"Far as I know this is the first time she's even tasted it. She's on her second. Christ, I don't know what he's mixing, but this ain't no highball." He raised his own glass.

"It's a whiskey sour—not a whiskey and sour. Better take it easy, there's wine for dinner."

"What's this?" Roger picked one of the sticks off the miniature charcoal cooker on the tray. Pieces of meat and whole mushrooms were impaled on the sticks.

"Horse's duvers, dumbhead. You're supposed to wait till I take them off the skewer."

"Oh." Roger replaced the stick quickly. "Hey, Hym, who's the brunette that old lady Stewart's making such a fuss over? We saw her in Hud's."

"Barbara Shapperd. As in Shapperd Cement Company."

"Uh huh, that explains it." Shapperd Cement Company teamed up with the meat-packing plant to keep Minturn dirty, stinking and employed.

"Don't flick the ashes in the spittoons," Hymie said as Roger lit a cigarette. "There's ashtrays on the bar. Spittoons don't have any sand in 'em."

"Can I spit in them, servant boy?"

"You can pee in 'em if you want to. Just don't flick your ashes."

"You are gross, Benninghoff. Surprised you didn't wear your overalls tonight."

Hymie put his scowl back on and took the tray to the bar. He slid the meat and mushrooms off the sticks onto a plate. As he was carrying the tray out of the room, he stopped at the fern again. "Keep your pants up tonight, Jenson. Might need your help."

"What, washing dishes?"

"No. You see anybody looks like they're getting clobbered by heavy air, grab 'em and get 'em out of the house. A good ten feet out."

"Any particular direction, Inspector Ghost-Catcher?"

Hymie held the tray in one hand, rubbed his nose significantly for Roger's benefit with the other and left.

"Need a refill, Jenson?" the bastard called from behind the bar.

"Yo." He drained the foam from his glass and moved to join the company. On his way he stopped off at the black couch. "Need another boost, Myrt?" But his mother didn't hear him because she was so absorbed in the conversation next to her. He slipped the empty glass from her hand.

"Something, definitely something," said the old lady who had come to the party with Vera Olson.

"Evil do you think, Dorothy?" Vera asked. She wore her coat over her shoulders. It was maroon and clashed with her orange hair.

"I don't know." Dorothy looked around with eyes that weren't looking. She had a shape like a small pregnant pear. "But definitely strong. So strong, Vera, I'll be

169

honest. I think I'm frightened." She might be frightened, but she still looked happy to Roger.

He gave up trying to entice his mother's attention and carried her glass to the bar with his own. "Another for the mother, too."

Jay peered around him to the couch. "She really puts it away."

"Yeah. Tomorrow I'm going to introduce her to the world of tomato juice with Tabasco and ice packs."

"Might slip a raw egg in the tomato juice when she isn't looking," Jay suggested as he poured.

Roger slid his mother's drink into the hand that was still in the same position as when he'd taken the glass from it.

"Why, thank you, dear." Myrtle glanced at him briefly and then leaned back into the conversation.

When he went back to the bar, Rachael Stewart acknowledged his presence with a lift of her eyebrows. ". . . coat. Would you like yours, Barbara?"

"Yes. Thank you."

Rachael rubbed bare shoulders. "You really should have that furnace checked, Jay."

Roger took her place next to Barbara and reached for his drink. "Hi, I'm Roger."

"I'm Barbara. We met at the door."

"That was a long time ago."

"Why were you hiding behind the fern?" Barbara was one of those lean, leggy types with smooth skin.

"I was planning on hiding in it if the ghost came along."

Barbara laughed as smoothly as she did everything else. "You don't think she'd take on a whole crowd, do you?"

"If he keeps mixing these things, Old Nella won't have much trouble. She's crafty, you know. You'd have to be to figure out how to come back from the dead."

"You mean there are no dumb ghosts?" Her eyes were laughing into the bastard's.

"No such thing." What did Jay Van Fleet have that attracted a luscious dish like this? Money?

"Roger, why do you keep licking your lips?"

"Nervous, real nervous." Someday he'd have money, too, and acres of land to spend it on.

Old Henson, the lawyer, left Reverend Birmingham and wife at the meat-and-mushroom plate and walked over to get acquainted with Barbara. Apparently the Van Fleets owned a piece of Shapperd Cement and Henson had done the dealing. Roger moved away to talk to Jay. "Van Fleet, when do I get those acres for my very own?"

"Soon as the estate's cleared, you can have the whole business. How about pulling down the house and covering it over? Plant corn on it?"

Hymie appeared at the door wearing a white jacket like those the busboys wore at the hotel restaurant in Minturn. Clunking a wooden spoon against a tray, he snarled, "Dinner is served!"

Roger choked on his whiskey sour and the bastard doubled over behind the bar. Roger didn't really like Jay Van Fleet, but he could appreciate his sense of humor.

"Drink up, everybody. Might as well eat while the food's still cool." Jay, the laughter still in his eyes, moved around the end of the bar to take Barbara's arm.

In the dining room the table stretched forever. There were candles burning and too many spoons and forks.

Roger felt good. No, Roger felt wonderful. He realized he was high and looked at his mother. He gave her a half hour of consciousness.

Jay began to place them all at the table and came up one guest short.

"Where's Rachael?" Mr. Stewart asked. "I thought she was up here."

"She went to get coats . . ." Barbara started.

Van Fleet tore off some beautiful profanity and ran out of the room.

Hymie set down a dish. "Come on, Rog!" And he followed Jay.

"Want to meet a smart ghost?" Roger whispered to Barbara.

"Wouldn't miss it."

They raced for the door to the hall and followed Hymie up the curving stairs and into the largest bedroom Roger had ever seen.

Jay stood in front of the open doors to the balcony staring back at a dove with red eyes. Snow floated down around the dove and onto the carpet.

"Was it just me or did I hear our host talking to that dove?" Barbara whispered.

"Cussing it out I think. Anybody who can string them together like that can't be all bad. Hey, has anybody thought of calling for her?" He squeezed Barbara's hand. "Mrs. Stewart? Mrs. Stewart?"

"Who is it?" A muffled voice from somewhere.

Hymie upended to look under the bed.

"Half the party's up here looking for you, Mrs. Stewart. You can come out now."

The door on the other side of the bed opened slowly and Rachael Stewart stood there blinking, hugging her fur coat around her. "Oh, thank heavens!"

Jay turned to stare at Rachael as if she were the ghost then flopped into the nearest chair. The color had left his face and eyes.

The doors to the balcony closed, slowly. The drapes fell back into place with a sinister whish. Van Fleet was on his feet again.

"Who closed the doors?" Barbara snuggled close to Roger and he put his arm around her, hugging her and laughing.

"The curtains. Relax, everybody. The curtains are heavy and forced the doors closed," Roger explained.

"I'm sorry to cause so much trouble." Rachael stood uncertainly in the doorway, staring at the drapes, rubbing one hand on the back of the other as if she had an itch. "But I came up to get my coat and Barbara's and when I got to the head of the stairs I was suddenly afraid and . . ."

"Why?" Jay sprawled in the chair for the second time.

"I don't know. I didn't see or hear anything really. I just felt frightened. I found my coat and then hunted under the others for Barbara's, trying to remember which was hers, telling myself I was being silly and desperately wanting to get back downstairs with the rest of you . . . and then those doors and draperies flew out and I . . . I ran into the bathroom." She'd eaten away most of her

172

gaudy lipstick. "I've been huddling on the floor in there trying to work up the courage to come out." Her pale lips tried a wobbly smile.

Barbara began pawing through the coats on the bed. It *was* cold. When Roger helped her slide into her coat, she didn't seem to notice the extra rub his fingers gave her neck as he pulled the glossy hair from beneath it. "What say we join the party, troops?"

Hymie looked around. "Think we better."

There was a rush for the door. Roger found himself beside Hymie as Jay went ahead with the women.

Joseph Stewart met them at the bottom of the stairs. "There you are, Rachael. I was about to come up for you, too. That Tripp woman who came with Vera Olson suddenly announced you were in great peril. A strange creature." He waved his unlit pipe at them. "How could she tell from down here?"

"She's a little late," Jay told him as he led Barbara into the dining room.

"I know of her. Dorothy Tripp." Rachael put an arm through her husband's and leaned against him. "She's a medium, Joe."

"Good God, don't tell Birmingham. He'll have a scizure."

Hymie stopped Roger outside the dining room door. "Well?"

"Chicken shit, Hym. Old Rachael's been hearing stories for thirty years. Finds herself all alone and the wind blows the door in and she thinks Nella Van Fleet's after her." He followed the others, wondering when Hymie stopped making up his stories and started believing them.

Mrs. Benninghoff was rewarming the food, so they started on the wine. By the time the dinner arrived again, no one seemed to mind the way it cooled on the plates before it could be finished.

Jay cleared his throat often, but said little. Rachael Stewart was silent, evidently having forgotten about impressing Barbara. Dorothy Tripp huddled in her chair across from him, her happy look dried out. But the booze had done its job on the others and the conversation roared.

Reverend Birmingham sang Christmas carols in the library after dinner, finally persuading most of the party to join in.

Roger pretended to examine the droopy Christmas tree so that he could get away from the singers. The one thing he hated more than hearing other untrained voices singing, was to have to sing himself. They'd pulled chairs up to the fireplace and lighted a fire that threatened to burst the screen.

They'd turned off all of the lights except those on the tree. Suggestions of wild shadow dancers leapt across the floor and the furniture. Roger grinned as the shadows made the carolers look like dancing natives around a cooking missionary in an old Tarzan movie.

The cold crept through Roger's shoes and socks to his feet, the last warm place on his body. It irritated him to have the temperature of this house get to him.

But this . . . this was a different kind of cold. Not the kind that hit him in the face when he walked out of a warm house into a frosty morning. This was a seeping cold that moved through him as if the air were solid and he wasn't.

"Oh, come all ye faithful . . ."

"Son-of-a-bitchin' chair!" Jay appeared suddenly at his elbow, almost knocking him over. "Sorry, I tripped over that cha—who's that?"

They peered through the dark into the chair between the Christmas tree and the party. "It's Myrt . . . she passed out." His mother sat with her hands neatly folded on her lap, her chin on her chest and her knees as far apart as her dress would allow. "Lasted longer than I thought she would."

"You're still on your feet. Want some brandy?"

"Never tried it." Roger was embarrassed at the shiver that reached his voice. "Is it warm?"

"Lot warmer than the coffee you just drank. Gulp it." Jay splashed good-smelling hooch straight into a glass, handed it to him and headed for Barbara.

"Oh little town of Bethlehem . . ."

They ran twice through everything everybody knew, and some that only the Birminghams could sing to the end. Then the quiet took over again and they shuffled around, keeping close to the fire and to each other.

Finally Rachael spoke up. "Perhaps we should play party games. Charades, for instance. What do you think, Jay?"

"How about the séance game?" Jay moved from glass to glass with the brandy bottle.

"Séance?" Birmingham laughed. "You're not serious."

"Why not? It's a great party game. Miss Tripp here knows all about it. She's a medium. Explain the rules so we all can play, Dorothy."

"I really do not think it wise, Mr. Van Fleet. We're all weakened by alcohol, and your spirit is very strong. I've never felt a stronger one."

"You said . . ."

"I said I'd look over the situation and I have. I definitely feel it would be unwise . . ."

"Claptrap! What's all this about anyway? Medium what?" Reverend Birmingham's boom was not happy.

"I am not a recognized medium, nor have I ever claimed to be. I do not hold seances, play with Ouija boards or anything like that." Dorothy Tripp pulled her funny little shape straighter in an attempt to appear insulted. But to Roger she sounded phony.

"What do you do then?"

"I am more what you would call a sensitive. Through no effort on my part I seem to be able to sense the presence of spirits. Occasionally one of them will use me to communicate with the living."

"How?"

"I don't know. They use me . . . use my voice. This is a gift I did not ask the Lord for and would gladly give away if I could."

"The word 'Lord' hardly seems appropriate."

"The point is, Mr. Van Fleet," Dorothy said, ignoring the Reverend, "you definitely do not need a sensitive to sense the presence of a spirit in this house. I doubt there's a person in this room who has not felt something this evening. The spirit could have spoken through me at any time since my arrival and has not chosen to do so. Apparently he does not wish . . ."

"She. It's my mother." Jay hurled another log on the fire.

Myrtle snored softly in her chair. People began to shuffle again. Roger was thinking of moving to the fire when Lynn's Aunt Vera spoke up.

"Dorothy, Mr. Van Fleet does need your help. This . . . spirit is making life very unpleasant for him. At least try."

"Well . . . I guess I can try." Miss Tripp gave in a little too easily for Roger's taste. "But I doubt it will do any good. I can't force the spirit. And I'm worried about all the alcohol consumed tonight. If this is an evil or violent spirit, we might have trouble."

"Just try . . . please." Jay sounded like a drowning man. "Might be strength in numbers, you know, even tippling numbers. Tell us what to do."

"First, is everyone here agreeable?" Dorothy asked.

No one answered. Roger could see heads turn toward each other and then away, shoulders shrug. Expressions were hard to gauge from where he stood, but he was sure that the Stewarts and Lawyer Henson were awaiting word from Reverend Birmingham.

"Are you sure you can pull it off with several nonbelievers in the group?" The minister's tone suggested that he took the whole thing as a bad joke, but it held a touch of curiosity as well.

"The beliefs of anyone here will have little to do with it. The spirit must be willing." Her voice reminded Roger of a wounded bird caught in a roll of fence wire. "I'm sure you have faced similar lack of belief in your own work—with varied results."

"Ah . . . but the Holy Spirit is always willing . . . I will consider it merely as a parlor game," Birmingham said primly.

"Tell us what to do, Dorothy."

"Everyone sit down and be still. Do nothing distracting." Chairs scraped as they were pulled closer to the fire in a semicircle. Dorothy Tripp sat in the center, facing the group with her back to the fire. "Now, if I seem to fall asleep, Mr. Van Fleet, you may ask the questions that trouble you. The spirit, if it chooses, will answer through me."

No one seemed to notice that Roger and his mother hadn't joined the crowd. Roger moved closer to the chair where Myrtle slept to get a better look at the show.

Dorothy took several deep breaths. Her face stood out against the shadowy dark blue of the chair and her black dress. Her head, the V of her throat and her hands and wrists seemed to stand alone in the air. Roger could just make out the outline of her clothes against the chair.

"Please be very quiet." She sounded sleepy. "I must concentrate."

The cold seemed to deepen. Jay and Barbara, side by side, leaned toward the old lady. Reverend Birmingham yawned aloud. Roger couldn't see the others clearly.

He looked longingly at the fire but didn't move. He didn't want to stop the show. Not yet anyway. She was good, this Dorothy Tripp. By making everyone sit still and be quiet, the heavy silence of the house itself was impressive enough even if nothing else happened. He could see nervous heads turn slowly and had the desire to look over his own shoulder.

When something brushed his arm, Roger dropped his empty glass and it fell with a thunk to the rug. It was only Hymie.

The small woman's head dropped suddenly so that Roger could see the thin place in the curly gray fuzz on top of her head.

The quiet continued until Jay Van Fleet cleared his throat. "What do you want, Nella?" he asked weakly.

The gray head with the thin patch on top didn't move.

Roger felt his mother's leg brush against his own and looked down to see her straighten from her drunken sleep.

Jay's voice sharpened. "What do you want, Nella?"

But Roger was watching the dark shape in the chair beside him as it arched then fell back. Myrtle was mumbling and Roger didn't want her ruining the performance so he bent over her and put his hand on her shoulder.

177

"Hey, quiet, it's all right," he whispered close to her ear.

"My son . . . my son . . . my son." His mother's eyes were open.

"I'm right here. Now be quiet, will ya?"

"My son, my baby."

"Myrt, that's enough. You want to make a fool of yourself?"

Hymie knelt beside her. Myrtle's lips moved but she made no sounds.

"Ask her another question." At Barbara's voice Roger straightened, still holding his mother's hand.

Jay stood and walked up to Dorothy Tripp. "Who was my father? Who?"

Myrtle's hand tightened in Roger's; he put his other hand over her mouth, keeping his eyes on Dorothy. Not answering the questions, Roger decided, made her somehow more convincing.

"Who was my father?" Jay repeated.

Roger shook uncontrollably and so did Myrtle. It seemed as if the chair and the floor did too. He nudged Hymie.

Hymie wasn't watching the group by the fire. He pushed Roger's hand away from Myrtle's mouth as he bent over her. Myrtle was acting strangely, her head rolling back and forth against the chair, her eyes still open.

"Hey, stop it. You all right?" He was worried about her but couldn't take his eyes from the scene at the fireplace.

Jay Van Fleet had grasped Dorothy's shoulders and was shaking her. She didn't seem to notice, her head lolled back and forth.

"Why did you kill Gunderson, damn it?" Jay shouted.

Barbara tried to pull him away. Everyone else sat still as if they were tied up.

"Why Gunderson? Why?"

Myrtle was moaning, "Left me . . . left me . . . left me . . ."

Jay released Dorothy Tripp and stood back. She started to breathe heavily, her small frame heaving, and then

178

opened her eyes, letting them roll around. "Well?" she asked breathlessly.

"Well, nothing!" Van Fleet threw himself into a chair rubbing the back of his neck and swearing softly in Spanish.

"What do you mean?"

"He means, my dear lady, that nothing happened." Reverend Birmingham laid a hand on Jay's shoulder. "There now, my boy, you didn't really expect anything to happen did you?"

Jay shook his head. "I don't know." He put his face in his hands, and Roger could feel every women in the room lean toward him in motherly sympathy. Every woman except Myrtle. She'd gone back to sleep.

"I don't understand. I never know till afterward, but I could swear I'd just had an . . . experience. Are you quite sure? The spirit is just filling this room. Are you sure something didn't happen?"

"Nothing, I'm afraid, Dorothy." Vera Olson let her glasses fall to the end of their chain. "Is there anything else you can do?"

"Perhaps this spirit doesn't talk." Lawyer Henson reached for the brandy on the mantel. "We might ask her to knock on a table or something."

"Or rattle and clank." Luscious Barbara stretched and shook her hair.

"How about materializing as a wavering light on the ceiling?" Rachael took the brandy from Henson, and Evelyn Birmingham held out a trembling glass.

They all moved with a studied ease, a bravado that told Roger they were relieved nothing had happened, that they only pretended disappointment.

Retrieving his glass from the floor, Roger whispered, "Lights," to Hymie and headed for the roaring warmth of the fire and the brandy. Pitching his voice low in an imitation of Birmingham, Roger intoned, "Nella Van Fleeeeet, show thyself, shooooow thyself." The lights came on. He reached for the brandy. "Give us a siiignnnn, Nella Van Fleeeet, a signnnn . . ."

It was just as Roger began to pour the brandy into his glass that it happened . . .

179

The brandy didn't pour, at least he couldn't hear it pouring or filling the glass.

Normally he would know because he could see it. But he saw nothing. Nothing.

The upended bottle in one hand did not seem lighter nor the glass in the other heavier, because he could feel neither. He couldn't feel his clothes against his skin or his weight on his feet and legs. An absence of feeling, except for the unbearable cold.

It was as if a giant cloud of black ice had suddenly lowered on him, sucked away sensation of any kind, absorbed the fire, the lights, everything. He was not aware of breathing, blinking. But he must not be dead because he was still thinking.

The last time he had been aware of such a complete vacuum of sensation, such total isolation, was during a white-out in a blizzard. Wind-driven snow had so isolated him that he hadn't realized he'd continued to walk until he'd brained himself against his own silo.

Was this what it would be like in a closed coffin if you could still think?

The blackness of void continued, but the lack of feeling was relieved by a sensation—uncontrollable—inside him. A feeling in his guts that seemed to rise when he was really falling—the upward lurch of his stomach, the tingling in his genitals—like the first drop on a roller coaster or coming over the crest of a hill in a speeding car. He'd expected to fall but felt that he was rising . . . or that everything else was falling out from under him . . . a strange weightlessness . . . an ecstasy filled with panic.

And it did not end. Roger was alone, terribly alone with his thoughts. He tried to speak, but couldn't feel his mouth to move it, couldn't vibrate his vocal cords. Totally alone with thoughts that would not stop. It was worse than smothering, worse than anything.

Lynnette Olson married Joey Stewart again and again. The letter from his mother that he read under mortar fire, telling him of Joey's death. His return home to find that Lynn had not waited again, had returned to Denver, a widow. She hadn't waited and he'd hurt. Lynn jumping off her porch roof into his arms. Lynn's giggle that tinkled like the wind chimes Myrtle had hung by the kitchen window.

Mortars exploding fire at night . . . the surprising slipperiness of fresh blood under his combat boots . . . the way his mother had moaned when they lowered his father's casket into the ground. . . .

All sights and sounds and sensations from within. Nothing from without. . . .

Roger finally found his voice but the sounds he made were hollow, far away, swallowed up in the black vacuum. No feedback or echoes or vibrations bounced off walls or furniture or the world outside the black cloud.

Once he'd started the sounds, Roger found he could not stop them. And the black hell and the black thoughts went on and on . . . to scenes he had permanently shut away from him . . . horrors and agonies too horrible and agonizing to remember. Vietnam mixed with long-forgotten childhood fears and dreams whirled around the black cloud inside his head until the sounds he made were screams sucked away from him into the void.

The pain of sudden light, the jolt of his weight upon his feet were his first indications of the abandonment of the cloud . . . and the dampness of brandy on a hand that shook so that the glass overflowed. He dropped the empty bottle and heard its thud on the rug with relief . . . heard the groans of his own breathing, and realized he was hyperventilating.

Roger sat on the floor before he looked around at the others. He expected them to rush to him, hover over him, ask him what was wrong, at the same time that he mentally thanked Whoever was listening that he was still alive, that he had come through whatever had happened.

It was not until he looked into the wildness of the eyes around him—saw Rachael collapse into the arms of her husband as both fell to the couch, saw the beaded sweat that looked frozen on Birmingham's face, saw the old lawyer sprawled on the floor next to him—hugging himself with tears on wrinkled cheeks, saw Evelyn Birmingham sobbing into her hands, Vera Olson and Dorothy Tripp reaching for each other—that Roger realized he had not gone on the wild and intensely personal trip alone.

Jay was shaking Barbara Shapperd as he had Dorothy earlier. "Barbara, what is it? What is it? What's the matter with everyone?" But Barbara was stiff, her hand over her mouth, her eyes staring.

"Rog?" Hymie knelt beside him. "Can you talk? Are you okay?"

Roger drank deep of the brandy and glanced quickly at Hymie and then at Van Fleet. They alone of those in the room looked concerned, worried for the others.

Everyone else looked inward, terrified.

"How's Myrt?"

"Still asleep like you left her. What happened?"

"It didn't happen to you?"

"What? Seemed like everyone froze for a minute and the fire went out . . ."

"A minute!"

"Not even that long."

Reverend Birmingham held onto his head with both hands. "My God, my Lord, God . . . no." His wife put her hand on his arm, but he turned away.

"Oh, Joe." Rachael twisted in Joseph Stewart's arms. "I saw him, Joey. He kept reaching out to me . . . over and over . . . I couldn't help . . ."

"Dorothy," Vera Olson asked, "can a ghost do that?"

"I . . . don't . . . I've never known anything that could do that . . ."

"Do what?" Jay sat Barbara in a chair. "What happened to everybody?"

Roger took another swig of brandy and savored the burning. The others stared at Van Fleet, their mouths hanging open.

"I want to go home. Joe, take me home." Rachael voiced everyone's wish. She started toward the door and the rest of them followed in a rush.

Hymie brought the coats from upstairs. With brief mumbles of apology and no "thank yous" for a "lovely" party, the company cleared the house.

Myrtle seemed undisturbed in her chair, but Roger couldn't get her fully awake. Hymie helped him half walk and half drag her to the car. Roger wondered if he'd be able to make the short drive home. He'd never felt so drained, so exhausted in his life.

"What *did* happen in there, Rog?" Hymie asked over Myrtle's lolling head.

Roger didn't know how to answer that question, so he didn't try.

He just couldn't get the vision of the charred logs in the fireplace out of his mind. Not an ember left glowing, not a wisp of smoke. Just dead cold ash . . . How in the hell. . . ?

25

The day after the Christmas party, Christmas Eve day, Myrtle Jenson suffered a heart attack.

Roger called Lynnette from the hospital in Minturn. His mother hadn't awakened in the morning, her breathing was funny. He'd bundled her up and rushed her to the emergency room.

Myrtle was in intensive care, her condition critical. Roger would stay in Minturn.

After throwing some food at Roger's boar from the safety of the manger, Lynnette crossed the road and made the beds at the Jenson house, switched off a light in the bathroom, turned back the thermostat and cleaned spilled tomato juice off the kitchen counter. Myrtle's new kitchen looked dark and forlorn without Myrtle.

She joined Hymie in the farrowing house, where they dished out pig starter to the young pigs and fed the sows. The day was frigid and the blower roared at one end of the aisle, sending warmed air through the pens. The din of squealing piglets was deafening after the empty farmhouse.

Finally she and Hymie sat close together on straw bales so they could hear each other.

"How was his lordship's party last night?" She couldn't keep the bitter note out of her voice.

"Lynn, if he'd asked you to that party, I'd've killed him." Hymie didn't smile.

"Hymie . . ."

"Listen to me for once, will ya? He could lay you on the front steps of the gatehouse if you was willing." The big face reddened anyway. "But if he gets you where Nella can get at you again"—his high voice dropped a good two octaves—"he's just another dead Van Fleet."

"Hymie, I don't need another big brother." *I may have two already.* She glanced at the bulging shoulders and upper arms, the short thick neck where the heavy muscles never seemed to relax. He twisted to spit over the side of his bale and she looked at the panel his mother had sewn up the back of his jacket to give his bulky shoulders room to move.

"I just want to hear about the party. Who was there?"

"Lawyer Henson, Mr. and Mrs. Stewart, Roger and his mom, the Birminghams . . . uhh . . . your Aunt Vera and her friend, Dorothy Tripp. . . . Let's see . . . oh yeah, Barbara Shapperd."

"Who's she?"

"Remember in Hud's—when Van Fleet came in with a date?"

"The gorgeous brunette."

"Right. Roger worked up a sweat trying to get her to notice him. But she could only see Van Fleet . . . stopped breathing every time he looked at her."

"And Dorothy Tripp is the medium?" Jay had promised she could watch the medium at work . . . well no, he hadn't promised . . . but . . .

"She says she's a sensitive. Old Nella scared her half to death. Probably the first time she's come across the real thing. Scared your mother-in-law, too . . . locked herself in the bathroom." Hymie found a toothpick in one of the deep pockets in the bib of his striped overalls and described the events of the night before. ". . . and then Jay started asking questions like 'Who was my father?' and 'What do you want?' But Dorothy Tripp just stayed asleep."

"So he didn't get any answers?" Had Jay heard about Olaf and Nella?

"Every time he asked Dorothy a question, Roger's mom would answer it. I was the only one paying any attention to Myrtle Jenson. Roger was standing right next to her but he didn't listen."

"I thought you said Myrtle passed out in a chair."

"She did. Answered anyway."

"What did Myrtle answer when he asked who his father was?" She had to remind herself that she was getting Hymie's version of this, as usual. But Lynnette clenched her hands in her pockets.

"What difference does it make?"

"Was it my father?" She drew in a breath filled with the peculiar sweet-sour pungency of pig manure. "Was it?"

The toothpick rolled to the other side of his mouth. "Olaf?"

"Aunt Vera hinted that . . . my father and Nella had been very close."

"And you got the hots for Van Fleet and think he might be your half brother?" Hymie scratched at tight fuzzy hair. "Lynn, why do women get themselves—"

"Hymie, what did she say?" Myrtle was probably just playing along, getting into the party spirit.

"Thought she said Gunderson. Never thought of Olaf."

"Chris?" Her hands unclenched slowly.

"Yeah. She could've been talking in her sleep."

Lynnette shook her head to clear it. Hymie made the preposterous sound so real. "Chris Gunderson wasn't even around Roggins thirty years ago. . . . Was he?"

"Don't know. He'd've been younger than Nella but plenty old enough. Went over to the house this morning. Van Fleet took Barbara Shapperd home last night and didn't come back. Nella got all stirred up in the night. Doors off the balcony were standing open. Had to shovel snow off the carpets. Same thing in the sunroom."

Here we go again. "Couldn't the wind—"

"Now you sound like Jenson. Never knew the wind to do that. I tell you Nella didn't like her son staying away all night. She pulled some books off the shelves, tipped over furniture. Broke a bunch of mirrors."

"Now Nella's a poltergeist."

"Lynn, you still don't believe there's a ghost in that house?"

Lynnette shrugged and stood up.

"She's getting stronger. She's dangerous. I don't think she wants people hanging around her boy. You in particular. If he don't get home pretty soon, she's liable to tear that house apart." He stood and held her by the shoulders. She felt like a kitten in the embrace of a grizzly bear. "If you do see him again, don't make it at the house."

"I have to get back to my albatross. It's time for her

186

lunch." She tried to pull away. "If I see Jay Van Fleet again, I'll try to make it somewhere else. Okay?" That wasn't a promise, was it? She wiggled free and moved toward the door.

"Hey, Lynn? I want to hear about Colorado some more. Take you in to the cafe for dinner tonight?"

"You've got a date."

"Pick you up at six," he said just before she stepped outside.

Lynnette broke the ice on a puddle in the Jenson farmyard with the heel of her boot and looked toward the window of Myrtle's kitchen. *Don't worry, Myrtle, it's probably just your gallbladder.*

The sky sat gray on top of the pine windbreak. More snow soon. About three inches covered the lane and she walked in the car tracks. Wind had piled most of it in rolling shadow drifts under the pines.

Where was Jay Van Fleet? With Barbara the brunette? *Why the hell should I care anyway?* But Lynnette reached into the mailbox so hard her gloved hand slammed against the back of it, and then she remembered the mail wasn't due for two hours. She started running down the Olson lane.

Lynnette rounded the turn of the fenced house yard out of breath. She didn't notice the car in the farmyard until it was too late and she'd collided with the startled man about to open the gate.

"Good heavens, child! What's wrong?" Reverend Charles Birmingham looked past her as if to see who was chasing her.

"Uhhh . . . just . . . running." She tried to smile but grunted instead.

"Is something after you?" He looked almost frightened.

"No. Just . . . running." She fought to get the cold air into her lungs.

"Oh." His shoulders sagged as if in relief. "It must be wonderful, youth." Reverend Birmingham appeared unlike himself . . . different. "Evelyn is ill today, some bug. She'd planned to visit your mother. So I decided to take her place." He opened the gate for her.

"Oh, the Christmas pledge." She was still confused

by the change in his appearance. His hand shook on the gate, his breath came foul even across the cold air. *That must have been quite a party last night.*

"Well, she did pledge a certain amount at Christmas, but as her minister I feel I want to visit her in her illness. What are ministers for?" His skin was the color of the sky, which had now dropped almost to the roof of the old farmhouse.

"You realize," she said as they followed the narrow sidewalk to the back porch, "that Bertha has no money. It's all tied up, and she has no income."

"It's difficult to serve a congregation when the people have no income. Social Security, I'm afraid, affords only enough to feed the stomach and not the soul. . . ."

"But the elderly need you. . . ."

"I know," he said. "They need me more than anyone. I do know that, Lynnette."

She turned on the back step to look up into his face and felt an unexpected relief. He meant it.

Lynnette prepared sandwiches for the three of them while he sat at the table talking quietly to Bertha. Talking quietly. The resonance was the same, the deep chesty quality. But the heartiness, the exaggerated enunciation, were gone.

He slumped with his elbows on the table, his hands supporting his chin. Reverend Birmingham looked ill, tired and—what? Humbled?

Bertha repeated her thoughts when he asked her how she felt. "A darn sight more chipper than *you* look, I can tell you that. You should be home in bed like Mrs. Birmingham. Looks to me like you're getting her flu."

"I'm just very tired. I have Christmas Eve services in Jewel tonight and Christmas services in Roggins tomorrow morning. Evelyn's too sick to help out tonight and I'm afraid Rachael Stewart has the same bug and won't be able to play the organ tomorrow. And at Christmas, too."

"Well, it's no use your expecting this year's pledge because I'm living on borrowed money now."

They went on to speak of Myrtle Jenson's sudden illness and the weather. Charles Birmingham ate little but stayed to talk with Bertha. Lynnette cleaned up the dishes and started meat stewing for dinner. When she asked him about the party at the Van Fleet house, he shrugged and changed the subject.

"Never known that man to make a sick call unless you was dying or in the hospital," Bertha said when he'd left.

"He does seem different today, doesn't he? Say, I'll fix dinner tonight, but Hymie's taking me to the café . . ."

"On Christmas Eve?"

"Well, Aunt Vera will be here for dinner. I won't be gone long."

Bertha spent the rest of the day complaining about being left on Christmas Eve, about the pain in her leg, about the pain in her hip.

Lynnette met Aunt Vera at the door with relief. Her aunt did not seem to share that relief. Bertha took one look at her sister-in-law and decided that Vera, too, was coming down with the "Christmas flu."

Vera's skin was the tone of Reverend Birmingham's with a touch of yellow added. The yellow tinge did not mix with the orange hair. "Lynn, I've brought my nighty. The way I feel I'll never make it back here for Christmas dinner tomorrow. Do you mind?"

Lynnette assured her she didn't and left her aunt staring at the stew and Bertha eating with a vigor, unseemly in an invalid, as Hymie's pickup sounded in the lane.

"Is Jay home yet?" she asked as she slid in beside Hymie.

"Nope. Haven't seen him or the Bentley all day."

He's staying with Barbara Shapperd.

By the time they parked in front of the Roggins Café, snow fell hushed and heavy as if intent on obliterating the Christmas lights bordering the café's square window.

The café was furnished with chrome kitchen dinette sets. The night's menu was written on a chalkboard hanging over the coffeepots. It was late for the Roggins dinner hour and they were alone. When Mrs. Borglund brought their water, she wore that familiar look Lynnette had encountered often when she went out with Hymie. *What's a nice girl like you doing with a creep like him?*

She felt hungry at just the thought of someone else's cooking and ordered turkey but was disappointed to

189

learn, when it came, that even this far from the world, potatoes had degenerated to instant and gravy to corn-starch.

Hymie listened closely to her promised descriptions of Colorado. But he soon returned to the subject that interested him most. "I'm wondering if Nella had anything to do with Roger's mom's heart attack."

"Hymie, people have heart attacks all the time."

He sat looking through her as if she hadn't spoken. "Last night, everybody started making dumb jokes about having Nella rattle chains and everything. Old Jenson asks Nella in a spooky voice to give them a sign. I was back at the light switch and everybody but Van Fleet and me stopped moving. Like in that game we used to play about statues. Roger poured booze all over the rug and the rest just froze. But, Lynn, the looks on their faces . . . their mouths were open like they was yelling . . . and the dots in their eyes got big while you watched."

Lynnette pushed her plate away. "Hymie, are you making up stories again?"

"I'm telling you this is real." He reached for her plate to finish up what she'd left. "They all seemed to come around at once and nobody'd say what happened except Mrs. Stewart said Joey had reached for her or something. Whatever it was, it sure stopped the jokes."

"Joey, but—I think we'd better go." There was nothing retarded about Hymie's imagination.

The sky had deposited about four inches of wet clingy snow while they'd eaten. The pickup had to plow itself a path out of town. They rode in silence to the farmhouse where Hymie pulled up behind a mound of snow that was probably a car. "Who's here?"

"Aunt Vera."

"I better stay and shovel her out."

"No, she's spending the night. She's got the flu. There seems to be a lot of it going around. Reverend Birmingham was out today and he looks awful. His wife has it and Rachael won't be able to play the organ because—"

"And Myrtle Jenson's in the hospital. Takes care of half the party."

"Bertha calls it the Christmas flu."

Hymie's high voice dropped to a lower pitch. "More like the Ghost of Christmas Nella."

26

*N*ella stood before an oval mirror in the narrow hallway. The figures in the yellow wallpaper behind her were all that was reflected in the mirror's surface.

She willed herself to appear, brought to bear all her newfound energy. What torture to pass countless mirrors for countless years and leave not even a fleeting image.

The mirror splintered. Shattered bits of glass fell from the ornate frame to become one with the carpet.

Nella turned in anger to pace the dining room, where shapes stood clear and colors swam vivid now. She knew that at this moment she had all the power she needed to reach him, perhaps even to appear to him if she could find the way.

But her son-was not there to reach!

The chandelier above the dining-room table swung out dangerously. Crystal facets lit hundreds of tiny fires that spun across the ceiling and swirled over the walls.

How long had he been gone? She could not tell. Time was her enemy. What was in their world a day, might be a week in hers. Or what seemed to her a minute could be hours to them. She could remember Clay aging in sudden bursts.

If Nella could make her child see her, then surely he could not deny her. Had she appeared to Clay that night on the balcony? Or the man with the veins in his nose? For an instant, at the moment of their deaths, she felt she might have.

But she could not appear to a son who was not home!

The captain's chair at the head of the table swayed and then crashed over backward.

Such a waste of power. She had never had so much before. It was heady.

But what marvelous fun that party had been. How long since she'd had fun? To enter that drunken old woman instead of the silly one by the fire. Brief but *glorious mischief. All that wonderful strength in one room. Nella had been desperate and now nothing tired her. How long could it last?*

What she needed was what any other mother needs, to feast on the lasting love of her child. But Nella needed it more . . .

A lamp toppled from its table in the sunroom.

She stood before the wall of glass panes and looked to the farm at the bottom of the hill and the little schoolhouse.

No Bentley sped down the road toward her. The road was empty.

Had her tiny bit of mischief frightened Jay away forever? How could he expect her to answer him in front of others? How dare he try to use his own mother as a party game? She who had died with her breasts still bulging with milk for him alone . . .

The French doors burst open.

Nella was outside before she realized it. Her strength flew off in all directions and she backed quickly into the house. Must not waste it.

But already colors were duller, shadows deeper. She must have a lasting source. . . .

Nella moved further into the house to seek the dove. Together they would fly to seek her son. . . .

Later, the dove looked down upon a dark form sprawled in a world that was drowning in white snow.

27

*I*t snowed all night Christmas Eve and all of Christmas Day, snowed hard and heavy from a darkened sky.

Lynnette could still feel the grease of Christmas goose on her tongue as she finished tidying up the kitchen and picked up stray ribbon from the packages.

Harold and Margaret had given her a power lawn mower, Elaine and family a Hoover vacuum cleaner, and Aunt Vera a cookbook. Everyone but her aunt had left right after dinner to get home, tire chains clinking against metal all the way down the lane.

Lynnette kicked the Hoover on her way by . . . something ominous in these gifts.

"Why did you kick the vacuum?" Aunt Vera asked sleepily from her makeshift bed on the couch.

Lynnette wondered how long she'd have two invalids to care for. As she prepared them both for bed that night, Hymie called. He didn't even wish her a Merry Christmas but asked abruptly, "How's your aunt?"

"Not good. She's about the color of a sick dandelion."

"Keep an eye on her, Lynn. Ma called the hospital to find out about Myrtle. Still unconscious."

"Is Jay home yet?"

"No."

"He's probably moved in with the brunette in Minturn."

"Nope. Ma called the Shapperds, too. They haven't seen him since he took Barbara home from the party. Barbara's sick. She was in the hospital overnight. She's improving. Called Dorothy Tripp, too. Talked to the lady who lives with her. Dorothy's sick."

"The Christmas flu?"

"She suffered a stroke. They put her in the hospital yesterday."

"Like Myrtle. And the Birminghams are sick." Lynnette shivered.

"Ma called them, too. Mrs. Birmingham is feeling

better, but he's down now. And the Stewarts have some kind of flu. And old Henson is sick and not having visitors." Detective Hymie had kept his mother busy. "Except for Van Fleet and me, that's the whole party, Lynn."

"And Roger . . ."

"Couldn't get a hold of him. But he wasn't at the hospital today. I've done his chores. You keep an eye on your aunt."

"Lynn," Bertha yelled from the bedroom when she'd hung up, "was that Roger?"

"No, Hymie. Poor Myrtle is still unconscious."

"Don't that beat all?" Bertha said as Lynnette crossed the living room to look down at her aunt. "Never known that woman to be sick a day in her life."

"Aunt Vera, what happened at that party?" Lynnette whispered.

Vera pressed her lips together and shook her head.

"Aunt Vera, your friend Dorothy had a stroke yesterday. She's in the hospital."

Vera moaned softly, turned even yellower and rolled over to hide her face in the back of the couch.

Cold woke Lynnette late Christmas night, and the shriek of wind blasting snow against the house. Her legs were stiff from curling herself into a ball to keep warm. She grabbed two blankets and her pillow then rolled up in the blankets in front of the oil burner in the living room and listened to Bertha and Aunt Vera snore while outside the wind arranged and rearranged the new-fallen snow.

Finally she slept again but only to dream of a scratching at the window glass and tiny eyes peering into the room from the night-white world outside.

"Is it still snowing?" Bertha asked as Lynnette helped her up the next morning.

"I don't know. The windows are drifted over. But I expect it's stopped. The weatherman said it was thirty-four below in Minturn."

At breakfast Aunt Vera played with a piece of toast

and drank some tea. Lynnette stuffed herself with hot oatmeal and coffee. She'd just carried her dish to the sink when the kitchen was sunk in an eerie twilight gloom.

No electricity meant no water. The oil burners would operate and the gas cooking stove, but not the pump. And the hand pump by the back door would be frozen up.

"Better call Leroy and see if he can shovel us out of the house," Bertha said dispassionately over her oatmeal.

"Bertha, he can't get himself out for hours and couldn't get here anyway unless he rode the snowplow. Besides the phone lines are down."

Bertha wheeled herself over to the phone, picked it up, listened for a moment and replaced the receiver. "Dead."

"The point is, Bertha, that we shouldn't even be here. You should have a house in town, with water and sewer and close neighbors," she said as she dashed up the stairs for her warmest ski wear.

Lynnette dressed in front of the oil burner, grabbed the snow shovel from the back porch and stomped back upstairs, closing the door to the stairwell behind her, almost losing her balance in the stiff ski boots.

Why didn't I sell my downhill skis instead of my cross-countries? At least she'd found some ski wax in a plastic bag when she'd unpacked. Funny . . . the things people hang onto when they lose everything else.

With hands already stiff from cold, she took a stick of green wax and applied it to the bottom of her skis.

Her teeth chattered convulsively as she slipped into a down parka, hood and ski gloves. Opening the air register, she yelled below, "Tell Aunt Vera to come up and close the window when I'm out!"

She wrapped a scarf around her nose and mouth and tightened the strap on Joey's goggles so they'd fit her.

Rapping the window frame hard with the end of the shovel, she managed to jar it from its bed of ice. She had to do the same with the storm window, which she hoped would push out far enough for her bulky figure to squeeze through.

Next her skis and poles. They slammed into the shovel and she groaned.

Sitting on the windowsill, she swung one monster boot out and then the other, turning so that her stomach lay across the sill, and lowered herself gingerly. Her puffy parka did not want to squeeze through the opening left by the storm window. Her feet met the drift while she struggled her shoulders through.

Just as Aunt Vera's face appeared at the window, Lynnette's gloves slipped their hold on the sill and she slid feet first to join the shovel and skis at the bottom of the drift.

"Lynn! Are you all right?" Her aunt looked even yellower from the white world outside.

"I'm terrific. Just terrific!" Her goggles had pushed up onto her hood and were full of snow. She tied the hood down to cover more of her face, cleaned off and replaced the goggles and rewrapped the scarf across her mouth and nose. She tried to stand but sank in above her knees.

The drift below her window dipped to where she'd fallen and then extended halfway to the barn where the tops of frozen ruts showed. The wind had taken most of the snow in the farmyard and slammed it against the house.

Her bindings, boots, poles and skis themselves were all wrong for cross-country skiing but perhaps she could use them as snowshoes.

With the two poles in one hand and the shovel in the other, she managed to get herself around the corner of the house to where the back door should have been.

The drift here came to the porch roof. The hand pump was buried.

The woolen scarf around her mouth felt wet and cold. She'd better get moving before she froze solid like Clayborne Van Fleet. *Don't think about him at a time like this. Dig yourself back into that house, girl.* She stuck her skis upright in the snow and began shoveling.

The racket of snowmobiles came over the suffocating drifts. The goggle rims grew icy against her face; her body became hot with exertion. But the cold crept through her gloves to her hands.

How had her grandparents managed winters like this without high-powered ski wear? *The minute my father was old enough to take over the farm they moved into town, that's how.*

When she'd shoveled a path to the door, she made her ungraceful way to the washhouse for pails, filled them with snow, and set them on the oil burner in the kitchen. She filled every container she could find and refilled them when the snow melted.

At last she had enough to haul a plastic water jug, strapped to a sled, across the mound that was Aunt Vera's car and out to the animals. She found only one chicken dead in the hen house, probably the lowest in the pecking order who had to sleep outside the group.

With the livestock watered and fed, she made lunch for the invalids and hustled them off to naps as soon as it was polite to do so.

Lynnette was buckling her boots when Aunt Vera peered around the doorway of the living room. "Where are you going now?"

"Over to check the Jensons'. Why?"

"I thought you might be going up to the Van Fleet house." Her aunt came around the oil burner to stand above her. "You won't, will you?"

"Why should I go up to the Van Fleet house? I'm going to have all I can do just to ski over to the Jenson farm before I freeze to—"

Vera's hand clamped down on Lynnette's shoulder. "Promise you'll never go near that house again."

"Aunt Vera—what did happen at that party?"

"I . . . I don't know. But I can tell you I'll never be the same again. It was horrible!" Her shudder reached along her arm to the fingers that gripped Lynnette. "There is something in that house, Lynn. Promise me."

"I promise that I won't go any farther than the Jensons' "—*this afternoon*—"now, get back to bed. When I get home, I'll fix some nice hot broth for you."

"Are you sure you should go at all? If you should fall and—"

"I'll be careful. I just can't stay shut up in this house."

"With two sick *old* women."

"It's not that, Aunt Vera. It's just . . . just that I have to get out, and I should check on things over there." But

Lynnette could not quite meet the accusation in her aunt's eyes.

Watery sun disappeared just as she stepped off the front porch and the gray gloom of winter settled in. It wouldn't dare snow again so soon. But the farther she skied from the house, the closer the sky sank toward the ground.

As she approached the nonexistent road across non-existent fields, her ski hit the tip of a buried metal fence post and she ended up on her back in a tangle of skis, poles and legs. She found herself staring back at the albino dove from the Van Fleet house. It sat on a black line of telephone wire that seemed so near the ground because Lynnette was so high above it on her bed of snow.

The dove left its wire and hovered above her a moment before it flew off to lose itself in the whiteness around it.

A hollow wind swept echoes across submerged farmland and swept the cold through her arctic clothing. She glanced up at the Van Fleet house.

It loomed blacker, larger than anything through her goggles. The air above its chimneys looked grayer than the sky. Smoke?

There was smoke from the Jenson farmhouse. When she reached the farrowing house, she was too numb to shiver, but a blast of warm air hit her the minute she opened the door.

Hymie knelt in the aisle, slitting a bag of feed. "How'd you get here? I was about to come over and see how you were getting along," he yelled above the din of squealing, snorting life.

"Not as well as everyone else, I see. We don't have any electricity. And I came on skis."

"I fired up Jenson's generator when the power went. We got one, too. When I'm done, I'll take you home in Rog's snowmobile."

"I feel outclassed." Lynnette shook the ice crystals off the scarf that had covered her mouth. "I wonder where Jay was when the sky fell."

"Holed up in a motel somewheres, I hope. Limeys don't build cars for this kind of weather. That Bentley'll have to be towed home."

They didn't try to talk over the snowmobile's racket.

She pushed her face against Hymie's back and used him for shelter, but without the exertion that had kept her at least half warm on the way over, the cold on the trip back was unreal.

"Come in and warm up before you go," she said the minute they reached the house. But she could get him no further than the porch, where they were out of the wind at least.

"Don't try to ski over tomorrow if it's this cold."

"I'll go crazy if I don't get out."

"I'll come get you on the snowmobile then." He turned to go.

"Hymie, wait. All those people sick after the party . . . their illnesses aren't even related . . . flu, heart attack, stroke . . ."

"Your dizzy spells, Gunderson's 'heart failure.' " Hymie shook his massive head. "Lynn, did you tell the doctor everything that happened to you that night up at the house?"

"No, but—"

"Well, you can bet nobody else did either. They've all had a bad shock and show it in different ways. All the doctors know is what they see and you better see that your aunt gets to a doctor when the roads are cleared." With that, Hymie left.

But he came back on the snowmobile the next morning as he'd promised and they did Roger's chores together.

The morning after, he did not come. Lynnette grew impatient. Finally she skied across the road under a misty sunlight. The temperature had risen to ten degrees below zero.

Roger's chores were done. Hymie had not come to pick her up first. The snowmobile was nowhere in sight. Lynnette skied back to the road.

Hymie did keep his promises if he could. She stopped to stare at the house on the hill. Something must be up.

There was the welcome sound of snowplows in the distance. The sun grew stronger above her and so did her courage. Was Jay home yet? Or was he frozen to death somewhere in a Bentley?

Lynnette turned her skis toward the Van Fleet house.

28

*L*ynnette stopped to rest on a massive drift that stretched across the lawn. It had a hole through it where the snow had caved into the empty swimming pool.

And every French door on the second floor, off the balcony, stood open. They opened inward, leaving sinister black holes all along the second floor.

The Van Fleet house looked a washed-out gray in the sun-snow glare that accentuated the blackness of the holes left by the open doors. It made them appear cavernous . . . deep . . . infinite.

Lynnette looked over her shoulder. Nothing but the two lonely tracks left by her skis, the pockmark of her poles on either side. The silence was intense even though there was a slight wind.

The last drift had piled itself against the house so steeply that it obliterated half the windowpanes of the sunroom. The contrast was a ghostly black and white. Painfully white snow, then the black doorways on the second floor, then the white of the snow-covered slant of roof, and finally the deadness of ancient elms on the other side of the house, their clawlike tips poised above the roof.

No smoke from the double chimneys. No sounds. Even under the clear sunlight it was horribly cold here.

Staring at the house in front of her, she sensed rather than saw the movement in the snow to her left.

Lynnette, forgetting her skis, tried to turn suddenly and fell hard on her arm, hurting her wrist, her pole jamming against her ribs as she landed on it. Snow worked its way into her glove, up the inside of her parka sleeve.

She lay between the two drifts, facing the corrugated toolshed. Something fluttered against the white of the snow.

Her legs felt feeble as she tried to stand on the skis. The trembling did not help her efforts to get to her feet. Her forehead and armpits felt chilly damp.

The white dove left the concealing color of snow and flew up across the balcony to disappear into one of the black holes.

Lynnette released her breath. Just a dove. She was so jumpy. Hymie was so damn convincing. . . .

But how else explain the night she'd had to be carried out of the house? All those people sick after a party? She pushed the goggles up onto her forehead and studied the house.

Why were all the doors left open? Were there really tables overturned and books pulled from their shelves in there? Mirrors broken?

But then . . . if a question seemed to have no answer, wouldn't it be easy to provide a supernatural one? Who could refute it? That was the way ignorance dealt with the unanswerable. And Hymie was not overly bright. She'd just peek into the windows of the sunroom before she went to find him.

Lynnette had stayed still too long. Her hands were numb and she could barely grip the poles.

Just as she decided she'd lost her nerve and would go find Hymie, the French doors to the sunroom opened with a strange cracking noise and her skies tipped forward.

Lynnette and part of the snowbank slid into the Van Fleet house.

The drift had become too heavy for the doors. It had pushed them open. It was just coincidence that the doors had opened while she stood outside. She pulled the scarf down off her nose and mouth and took a deep breath. The furniture was in place here.

Lynnette released her bindings casually.

I do not believe in ghosts. I do not believe in Nella Van Fleet. Her snow-dazzled eyes found it very dark inside the house.

More of the snow slid into the room and pushed her forward. She heard the sound of wood splintering behind her. *I do not believe.*

Her skis could have touched the door at the moment she'd decided to turn around. The latch may not have been tight. That was probably what had caused the doors to open at that particular moment.

She stood and slipped out of the skis.

The wood on the doors had splintered where hinges had torn away. Doors meant to open outward lay in pieces on the snow in the room. Cracked and broken panes had fallen out of their frames.

One could be afraid and not believe in ghosts. Scary movies were frightening, but that didn't mean one believed in them. The pressure of the snow could still have . . .

Unhurriedly she gathered her skis and poles together while her nerves fought with her common sense.

She would just crawl right back out the way she'd come in.

But when she tried it, Lynnette found herself on the floor again and she'd brought more of the drift with her.

Hymie opened all those doors upstairs himself. He's up to something.

Perhaps if she left the skis and poles she could get herself out without doing too much more damage to the room. She set them against the wall of snow.

She would crawl up more carefully, not try to scramble. There was nothing to fear, no need to hurry.

But the snow on the house side of the drift seemed more crumbly than that on the other side. No matter how she approached it she managed only to bring more of the drift into the house and it filled in sideways from the top, renewing itself.

She'd have to walk through to the front door. Lynnette retrieved her skis and poles and turned to face the sunroom.

She could see the inside of the front door from where she stood, through the corridor of grim wallpaper that formed the narrow hallway. The door was white, a swath of black marble beneath it.

Lynnette smiled. Anyone who grew up with Hymie would be afraid of this house. Childhood fears were never forgotten. They lived in the subconscious. She'd learned that in a psychology class in college.

She crossed the sunroom.

Now here was just the long narrow hallway and then

the entry hall. And then she'd be out and could find Hymie. No problem.

She stepped into the corridor. The library door stood open and as she came abreast of it, a thunder of crashing hit the hallway and her ears.

The sound of her poles and skis hitting the floor crashed in answer.

She stopped, unable to move.

Well . . . she *could* move. No one was ever really paralyzed with fear. One could think so, but that was just psychological . . .

Lynnette looked involuntarily from the skis on the floor of the hall into the doorway to her right.

The massive desk with the flags behind it was upended. It stood on its front, the desk lamp on the floor beside it, two of the flags lying against it at a funny angle.

Lynnette moved into the library. She raised her eyes to see a book fly across the room—an aqua-blue book—as if it had been thrown.

It flew through a window with a cacophony of shattering glass. Pieces of snow slithered to the floor from the broken window.

The floor was strewn with books. They lay littered among toppled couches, chairs, lamps, tables.

Two more books fell from nearly empty shelves. A third hurtled across the room, in a direct path to the doorway and Lynnette.

She felt the book strike her chest just as she felt the burn of urine flow down the inside of her thighs.

Lynnette fell back into the hall across her fallen skis, a sharp pain in her left breast where the book had struck her. Another crash where something fell—or was pushed over—in the library.

Hate. She sensed its approach without being able to see it. Hate was in the air. As clear as if she'd seen it in someone's eyes. And it was moving toward the doorway.

Nella Van Fleet exists.

She was on her feet and running as the air began to thicken around her, as the hate followed her.

The hate crawled up her back as she reached the front

door and pulled it open. She fell across the ice on the front step.

She drew in her breath and held it, clamped her mouth shut, put her hands up to hold her goggles and the scarf in place. She crawled forward on ice, slithered, using her elbows and knees, not daring to breathe.

The pressure was greatest on her back, her hood and face. It forced the goggles' rims hard into her flesh. She could feel it against her gloved hands holding the protection to her face. Her lungs ached as she refused to exhale. Exhaling would force her to inhale—inhale Nella.

She found herself head on with another snow bank just as breath pushed up her throat. She could never make it to where the bugs stopped. Never. The pressure around her became harder to bear.

Lynnette let go of her face to crawl on hands and knees across the snow and immediately felt the tug of goggles and hood. Nella was trying with such force to pull the tight hood back that the drawstrings were drawn choking against Lynnette's throat, her head was pulled back until she was staring up at the dark claws of dead elms.

The adrenalin had run its course, refusing to push her on any longer. She wondered languidly who would care for Bertha when she died.

The hood slipped back from her head, the goggles from her face. Her scarf felt as if it were tearing. The piercing, familiar scream penetrated her as something tugged at her wrists.

She closed her eyes as she was dragged, bouncing, across the snow.

The pressure pulling her wrists became painful even through the cuffs of her gloves. But the pressure on her face and back lessened and then lifted.

Lynnette was being carried. She opened her eyes to an unshaven chin. "Jay?" *I'm alive.*

"Shut up!"

"I'm so glad to see—"

"Shut up! Goddamned son-of-a-bitching, whoring—"

"What?" The gatehouse porch swung into view.

"Nobody deserves your luck twice. Nobody!"

Mrs. Benninghoff's face appeared above her as they

moved through the door. "Mr. Van Fleet, Lynnette. What happened? Where's Hymie?"

"He's down at the road with the Bentley. Is there a door around here that locks?"

"Well . . . the front door, the bathroom . . . What—"

Lynnette was set suddenly upon her feet, forced to walk. Scratchy wet-frozen ski pants chafed her soft inner thighs. Rock-stiff boots gripped her.

Jay held her up and pushed her into the tiny bathroom and seated her firmly on the lid of the stool.

She grabbed the nearby sink for support. *I'm alive.*

Nella's son locked the door and turned to face her.

This time Lynnette could see the hatred, as well as feel it. *Did he say whore?* "Jay?"

"You were in the house. You stupid—"

"Yes, but Jay she exists. She does . . . she . . . the library . . . Nella is really—"

"You think I don't know that?" He bore little resemblance to the lost lonely man on the floor of the one-room schoolhouse.

Would Nella's eyes have looked like that if she could have seen them? Her son's eyes had tiny red threads in the whites that lent power to their message, a puffiness beneath them. Jay looked as if he'd spent the last few days on the floor of a bar. He must not have shaved or changed his clothes since he had left the Van Fleet house.

Her body even after all that had happened to her, yearned to be held against him, comforted, soothed.

"She plays with others"—he unclenched his hands long enough to draw off his gloves and unzip his jacket—"but you, she means to kill outright."

"But don't you see what this means? There are ghosts, at least your mother. It's mind-boggling."

"I know that my mother hates you," he said through his perfect teeth. "I know you should be dead right now." He leaned over her, placing his hands on the wall behind her, forcing her to look up and stretch the sore muscles of her neck. "Who does that house belong to?"

"You." The hate in his eyes hurt more than her neck.

"Does that give me the right to keep you out of that house?"

"Yes."

"You may come to the gatehouse but never even near the main house. Do you understand me?" The gravelly voice filled the cramped room.

"Yes. I promise you I won't. But Jay—" She slid tired arms around his neck. "Please don't hate me. . . ."

Given his mood, Lynnette was prepared for anger but not for the revulsion that curled his lips. He straightened so quickly that he brought her to her feet. "Will you listen to me?" He tore her hands away from his neck, grabbed her by the arms and began to shake her. "You never listen, damn you!"

Something snapped at the base of her skull and her stomach answered with a twinge of nausea as the violent movement lifted her feet from the floor.

"Myrtle Jenson!" A strange wildness had replaced the revulsion and hate. He kept shaking her even as she fought him. "Myrtle Jenson!"

"I know, she's sick . . . in the hosp—"

He dropped her onto the stool lid and turned his face to the wall. "She's dead! She never regained consciousness."

29

Sun sparked tiny diamond fires on the snow, lighted the fringes of dark pines to chartreuse, and glared through Lynnette's eyelids when she closed them.

She could see just the corner of the roof of the Van Fleet vault behind the monstrous drift that had been scooped out to bury Myrtle Jenson and to provide standing room around the grave. Lynnette stood crunched between drifts to provide passage from the cars to the Lutheran pastor, whose prayer rose to heaven on a cloud of vapor.

Snow banks far higher than their heads walled them in on three sides. A narrow corridor had been shoveled between drifts to provide pasage from the cars to the gravesite.

A green rug, meant to resemble grass, lay across the hole under the raised coffin. *Don't they have a white one for winter?*

Roger was shivering. She could feel the vibration through his coat and hers. She put an arm around him and snuggled closer to offer what little warmth she could. He slid an arm around her shoulders.

Hymie flanked him on the other side. *The Unholy Trio rides again. Myrtle, I'm sorry. Truly sorry. It's just that I've stood in this cemetery so often, I'm numb to it. In fact, I think I'm standing on your husband right now.* Hymie's father had been her first funeral and then Grandma Maud . . . and Roger's father . . . Joey . . . her own father . . . who next?

Hymie squeezed the arm she had placed around Roger and motioned with his head for her to look in the other direction. Peering around the minister, she stared into the wide ice-colored eyes of Jay Van Fleet.

He wore the beige jacket with the sheepskin collar and leaned against one side of the snowdrift tunnel. The enormous sunglasses were propped up on his hair. The hate was gone from his eyes, replaced by the usual nothing that she found harder to bear.

Lynnette looked away and tightened her arms around Roger.

Reverend Stanglund must have finished. People were leaving, talking quietly.

"Lynn." Elaine motioned to her from across the frozen spray atop the coffin. "You stay with Roger now. We'll look after Mom. And Hymie, you stay with him, too." She looked up at Hymie uncertainly.

"You kids bring Roger up to the gatehouse tonight," Mrs. Benninghoff said as she turned to follow Elaine and Leroy. "When he's ready." Tears filled her eyes, "I'll keep a supper warm for all of you."

No one to prepare the repast for the mourners. Bertha probably would have been the one to do it if she'd been able.

Mrs. Benninghoff stopped to speak to Jay, patted his arm in a motherly gesture and entered the corridor.

Reverend Stanglund, his head bare, his gray crew cut looking frosty in the sun, moved away from Roger. "He doesn't seem to want me. You'll stay with him for a while?"

"Yes. Don't worry."

"Good. He needs friends now. Get him away from here as soon as you can," he whispered.

The sound of cars leaving and then only the wind in the pines. It fluttered the yellow ribbon on the funeral spray, picked up a yellow rose and set it down gently. The rose snapped from its stem and fell to the snow.

Lynnette winced. "Roger, let's go now."

Roger was staring at the rose in the snow.

"I'm sorry, Jenson." Jay rubbed his chin on the sheepskin collar and shrugged. "I shouldn't have asked her to the party."

Roger didn't look up. "Something's got to be done about your mother, Van Fleet," he whispered.

"I know."

"Roger, let's go," Lynnette said gently.

Roger looked up to stare at Jay. He turned finally to

209

gaze across the snow to Roggins. "Buy us a drink, Van Fleet?"

"Sure."

Lynnette and Hymie had accompanied Roger in the mortuary limousine because there was no one else. When they emerged from the snow tunnel, it sat waiting. A new dark blue car was parked behind it.

"That your Olds?" Roger asked.

"Yeah. I needed it for two reasons. One of them is that the Bentley tends to freeze up. And the other . . ." Jay glanced at Lynnette but didn't finish his sentence. Instead he waved the driver of the limousine on and ushered them into the Oldsmobile.

Lynnette felt strange walking into the Roggins pool hall. This was the first time she'd ever set foot in it. Roggins was that kind of town. "Bertha will kill me when she hears of this."

"Why?" Jay asked.

"No place for ladies." Hymie directed her around a pool table that filled the center of the room. "But today's kind of different."

Jay ordered beer and sandwiches for four and slid into the high-backed booth beside her. Roger sat across from her and she could feel his knees tremble where they met hers under the table.

"So you're not supposed to come in the pool hall where the nasty old men hang out, huh?" Jay turned to her, his arm brushing her shoulder, their thighs touching. Above the showy smile his eyes were cynical, reminding her that although she was afraid to be seen in the pool hall, it didn't bother her to get laid in the schoolhouse.

She moved as far away from him as she could against the polished wood at the end of the booth. Had he really called her a whore?

They munched cheese sandwiches, a subdued little group. Roger motioned to Woody, the bartender and owner, for a refill before the rest were halfway through their beer.

Besides Woody Hill, they were alone. The pool hall had no other name that she knew of. The only signs out front read, "Hamm's," "Budweiser" and "Schlitz."

When the sandwiches were gone, Jay ordered scotch.

Silent tears slid down Roger's cheeks and disappeared into the dark beard. He'd brought his mother breakfast in bed last Mother's Day . . . hard-bitten old Roger. It didn't seem possible. Neither did the wet beneath those silken lashes. There had been a strange but comfortable relationship between Roger and Myrtle Jenson.

She felt the sympathetic welling of tears in her own eyes. *How would I feel if it had been Bertha we buried today?* Was Myrtle a ghost now? Lynnette had had too much to think about the last few days. It was exhausting.

"Been in the house much since the party?" Roger asked Jay, finally breaking the silence.

"Just to scoop out the snow and chase birds. I moved into the gatehouse with Hymie and Mrs. Benninghoff. *She* has been throwing doors open and furniture around. Pipes are frozen. Everything's shut down. She's getting stronger." There was a tired defeat in Jay's voice. He lit a cigarette and leaned his head back against the high booth, one hand clicking the edge of the matchbook on the table top. "No more parties, that's for sure."

"Something's got to be done about her." Roger looked up from his drink, his dark eyes dry and leveled at Jay.

"Like what, Jenson? Go into the vault and run a stake through her heart? Burn down the house? She's good at putting out fires. Did you notice at the party?" He laughed bitterly and low. "I just hope for your sake, your mother stays dead."

"There's been enough murder up there," Hymie said.

The door opened to admit a swirl of cold in off Main Street and Joseph Stewart, too. He stopped at the sight of them, but it was too late to back out. He looked thinner, perhaps his hair was grayer. The darkness around his eyes made the aristocratic nose appear grotesque.

Joseph tried a smile that didn't fit. His hand went out to Roger. "Sorry about your mother. We weren't able to get to the funeral but . . ."

"That's all right. Don't like them myself." Roger and Lynnette's father-in-law shook hands across Hymie.

"I hear that you and Rachael have been ill," Lynnette said.

"Yes, but hopefully we're on the mend. It's a bad bug."

"My aunt is in the hospital, recovering from it."

"I'm sorry to hear that, but glad she's recovering." He wanted to get away from them. He kept glancing over his shoulder at the door. "The Birminghams have had it also."

"And Barbara Shapperd was in the hospital overnight." Hymie watched Joey's father closely.

"Oh? I hadn't heard."

"And Dorothy Tripp had a stroke the night of the party. Heard how Mr. Henson feels?"

"As a matter of fact he has the flu, too. He's at our house now. There's no one to care for him at home. He's—"

"And Myrtle Jenson's dead. Funny everybody at the party got sick—or worse," Hymie said into his glass.

"There are three of you here who were at that party, who aren't sick." Joseph's voice was stronger than before, but Lynnette noticed that he stuffed trembling hands into his coat pockets and backed away a step.

He's rejecting it because he can't understand it even though he knows. And I know just how he feels. . . .

Roger and Jay were staring at each other as if they'd just met and didn't want to.

Jay turned to Hymie, all color draining from his face. "Everybody?"

"I was sick too. One day I couldn't get out of bed to visit her in the hospital." The creamy whites of Roger's eyes seemed even yellower.

Joseph Stewart ordered a drink at the bar, took a sip and left.

"Your mother was in the house, Hymie," Roger said.

"Not at the séance."

"Why not you and Jay?" Lynnette asked.

"She wouldn't hurt him. I was back at the light switch. Maybe out of reach. Maybe she's just used to having me around."

After that the three man drank heavily and in silence. Lynnette's tailbone ached from sitting so long on the hard

212

seat. But the side of her that didn't quite touch Jay Van Fleet felt warmer than the other side. A thrill would run warm through her body at the sound of the low voice. He all but ignored her.

She took a token sip of lukewarm scotch and tried to clear her head. It was preposterous, but four people sitting in this pool hall knew for sure there was a ghost in that mansion on the hill. There were a number of other people about town who knew it also. But it was still preposterous.

"Anybody got a shotgun?" Jay asked suddenly.

"You can't shoot a ghost," Lynnette said.

"No, but"—he sat up and stretched in that deceptively nonchalant manner—"I know a few doves that aren't looking for this world."

"I got a four-ten and a twenty gauge," Hymie said, lowering his voice. "That's one apiece." He set his scotch down suddenly. "I get the one with the red eyes." Then he leaned forward and placed a hand on Jay's wrist, pinning it to the table. "And I think you've got yourself an idea."

"You've noticed it, too? How long has that white one been around?"

"As long as I can remember."

"White dove?" Roger asked. "You mean the pigeon on the balcony when we went hunting Rachael Stewart? I don't get it."

"I don't either. But there's a connection." Jay poured scotch in each glass, spilling some of it. "Shoot them all to be sure."

"Are you out of your minds?" Lynnette pushed her glass away. The table tilted and so did her stomach. "There's been enough death without killing innocent doves, surely."

"Might be a connection, Lynn," Hymie said. "It's worth a try."

"You think Nella's a bird? Doves can't open doors and throw books and push over furniture." *Or crawl into your ears and mouth or give you heart attacks or strokes or flu—but then, what can?*

"Might be a place to stay . . . maybe to rest." Hymie

213

drained his glass. "Or a way to move around or . . . get strength . . ."

"She took a lot of that from me at the party. And she took it all from Myrt."

"You don't have any proof. Kill those poor doves and in the shape you guys are in—" Lynnette screwed the top on the bottle and put it on the floor under the table. *I can't believe this is happening.*

"There's three graves in that cemetery that are proof enough—my uncle's, Gunderson's and Jenson's mother's." Jay's mouth tightened. "And but for your stupid luck, there'd have been a fourth. Let's go."

She was not surprised to see Jay and Roger weave, but Hymie showed his drink also. She'd never believed there was enough alcohol to get through all that body to Hymie's brain.

"Give Lynn your keys, Van Fleet," Hymie said.

"You want me to drive because you are all drunk but you'd handle shotguns? You'll end up killing each other instead of doves."

The sky was dark with early evening and falling snow. Jay stumbled against the Oldsmobile and fumbled in his pocket. "Now I know why people around here are always talking about the weather," he said acidly and handed her the keys. "There's so much of it."

He slid into the front seat beside her as she started the car. "Tornadoes, heat, tons of snow." He laid his head back against the headrest. "When do the heavens open up and rain fire?"

"If all this snow melts too fast in the spring it could flood," Hymie offered from the back seat.

"Great."

"I've never known it to flood in Roggins or fire either," she said. "At least we don't have earthquakes."

"That was before I came. Walking disaster area, remember?" Jay fell against her as she turned the corner in front of Joey's house. "Sorry." He pulled away but not before he'd added in a bitter whisper, "Sis."

The car swerved toward a towering mound of snow at the roadside.

"Watch out, Lynn!" Roger said. "I thought you were still sober."

She fought the car back into the plowed lane. "Jay, that's not true."

"What's not true?" Roger asked as they tunneled between the drifts that blocked from sight everything but their own headlights.

"Nothing." She stole a glance at the hardened profile beside her. *So that's it.*

When she stopped the car at the darkened farmhouse, Hymie left with Roger to find the shotgun. Jay and Lynnette sat alone in the chill.

"I am not your sister."

"Why didn't you tell me about your father and my mother? No wonder Nella wants to keep us apart."

"Murder is a little drastic. Don't try to vindicate your mother to me. She tried to kill me twice. And I'm not your sister. It's an old rumor. Who told you anyway?"

"Your mother-in-law."

"Good old Rachael." She turned in the seat to face him in the dark. "Is that why you called me a whore when you were carrying me to the gatehouse? Is it?"

"Forget it." He shifted uneasily. "I . . . I swear sometimes, that's all. It's just that women—oh, forget it." He turned away from her. "But I didn't hear anybody yelling rape in that old schoolhouse."

Lynnette took a deep breath and held it as she had when fighting off his mother.

"Forget it . . . I'm sorry. Just—"

"—forget it." The steering wheel felt icy through her gloves. Her head ached worse now than after Nella's second attack and Jay's subsequent shakedown. She leaned forward to start the car as the lights went out in the Jenson farmhouse. "Tell me, do you really believe in your double standards?"

"I don't know what you're talking about." His eyes seemed enormous in the glow of the dashboard.

Dead elms looked like upright shadows against the snow as they approached the gatehouse and parked beside the pickup.

215

"She won't hurt you, Van Fleet. You go in and scare 'em out."

The main house stood dark and remote amid piles of softly luminescent white left by Hymie's plowing.

Mrs. Benninghoff was silhouetted at the gatehouse window as she drew back a curtain to peer out.

"The garage door," Roger said suddenly as they got out of the car.

One of the four garage doors opened slowly, as they watched. It left a hole that was a deeper black than the rest of the house.

The light over the front door turned itself on, shone yellowish on the drifts to either side, made the black nude tendril stems of the ivy appear to be leggy spiders hanging onto the limestone blocks above the door.

"She's waiting for you, Van Fleet."

30

*T*he Van Fleet house was a blur of lights through great slushy snowflakes. Jay must have switched on every light in every room. The headlights of the Oldsmobile and pickup were trained on the house. There was more than enough light for her to see the sacrilege at her feet.

She had pleaded with three drunken men carrying shotguns. They hadn't listened.

Lynnette had *known* Nella Van Fleet, felt her power. And she knew that Nella was not a dove.

She shuddered as another volley of shots exploded the quiet of the Van Fleet Estate. *I'm not sure what I believe in anymore, but this is wrong.*

The gray and white dove at her feet lay on its side, its claws curled stiffly to its body. Its wing on the upward side lifted as a breeze caught dead feathers, its head a black stain on the snow, unrecognizable except for the open beak and sliver of tongue.

Her mind still saw it when she looked away. She held onto the fender of the teetering pickup.

"Lynnette, come in here with me." Mrs. Benninghoff opened the door just enough to talk through it and the steamy aroma of something meaty poured into the night. "I don't think you're safe out there."

She brushed a snowflake from her eyelashes and walked up the steps to the porch of the gatehouse.

The sound of heavy wings thrashing air stopped her just as she reached for the storm door. A dove landed on the porch railing so suddenly it almost overbalanced, fluttering its wings in panic to maintain a perch in the dislodged snow.

"Shoo! Don't stay here or they'll shoot you. Fly away . . . far away!" She moved toward it, waving her arms but was stopped by the snow-covered mound that was a metal porch swing under a winter tarpaulin.

It must have been too panicked to fly because it let

her approach without moving. Its white feathers blended with the white background. Both the dove and the snow behind it seemed to glow dully in the dark.

"If it weren't for your red eyes, you could just hide quietly in the snow. But they give you away. And you're the one they're really looking for. Please get out of here fast." She reached toward the dove. It made a sound, shuddered violently and fell forward into her arms.

Lynnette stared at the limp body she held, wanting to drop it but afraid she'd hurt it more.

There had been no shots for the last minute or two. What had happened to the dove? Had it been literally scared to death? But it still seemed to be breathing, slowly, shallowly.

The men's voices sounded very close and she looked up to see the three of them walking toward the gatehouse.

Lynnette ducked quickly and pushed aside some of the snow at the base of the tarpaulin and slid the white dove under it. Would it freeze to death in its present state? There was no time to do more.

She slipped through the storm door, afraid to look back at what she had done.

31

A week later, Lynnette propped her skis against the gatehouse porch and turned to sniff the air. A strange odor came strong on the wind. Roger Jenson's car was parked between the Oldsmobile and the pickup. She hadn't seen the three men since the night of the great dove hunt.

Curiosity and something else had brought her back.

She crossed the porch quickly and knelt to lift the tarpaulin that covered the porch swing, afraid she'd find a snowy, frozen carcass.

The dove was gone.

She stood up guiltily as Mrs. Benninghoff stepped out onto the porch, a woolen scarf tied babushka-style under her chin. "Oh, Lynnette, I'm glad you're here. Maybe you can talk some sense into them."

"What are they doing now?" She followed Hymie's mother to stand by Roger's car. The front door of the Van Fleet house stood open and so did many of the windows.

The housekeeper put an arm through hers and leaned on it. "They're trying to burn the house."

"Kerosene?" That was the funny smell.

"They're soaking down rugs and piles of paper." Her sigh came softly. "That beautiful house. I've cared for it so long it's become a part of me."

"Killing all the doves wasn't enough?"

"There's been more mischief done since then, and you can still hear doves in the attics." Mrs. Benninghoff took a damp Kleenex from her coat pocket and blew her nose. "I've lived with . . . her for thirty years now. We've gotten along in our way. But they say she's a killer and must be destroyed like some wild animal."

"What makes them think they can destroy her by burning the house?"

"Ahhh, they're beyond thinking, those three. They

read in some book of old Mr. Clayborne's that ghosts haunt places, that they're tied to a place. But only the Lord knows that for sure, and He hasn't thought to write a book on it."

"Look, there's fire." Lynnette pointed to a window in the living room where she'd seen a brief flash. "They've started it."

Sudden wild shouting and all three men rushed out the front door. Hymie held his arm stretched in front of him, and it looked as if Jay and Roger were leading him.

They crossed the drive, stopping under the elms to watch the house. Another flash accompanied by a muffled explosion and the library windows shattered. Mrs. Benninghoff drew in her breath and put her hand to her mouth.

Lynnette expected to see flame leap from the shattered window but the hole remained dark.

The three under the elms huddled together talking, then Jay left them and walked into the house.

Don't go in there. She might be angry with you now.

But in a few minutes he emerged safely, shaking his head and they walked toward the gatehouse.

"Told you she'd just put it out," Hymie said as they approached. He still held his arm in that awkward way.

"Hymie, you're hurt!" His mother rushed to him.

"A burn. Not too bad." But he let her and Roger lead him into the gatehouse.

"What are you doing here?" Jay asked coldly, brushing the ash-blond hair off his forehead. "I don't want you near that house."

"I came to talk to you, not the house." Lynnette tried to revive the courage that had brought her here.

He turned to look over his shoulder. The Van Fleet house was not burning. When he faced her, his lips were pressed in that stubborn line. "Talk about what, little sister."

"I am not your sister."

"Look, be reasonable. So we had a good time in an old schoolhouse. That doesn't give you the right to hound—"

"Jay, I'm not your sister!" She could hear Bertha in

her voice even when she tried to soften it. "I couldn't be
. . . not . . . not the way I feel about you."

He squinted at her and then at the sky, shifted his
weight, lit a cigarette and threw the match at the snow
as if he'd like to stick it down her throat. "Look, it's
no good . . . it's . . ."

"Hey, Mrs. Benninghoff says she's got hot soup for
everybody, homemade!" Roger yelled from the doorway.

"I don't want any soup," she managed to say before
she had to turn away.

"Yes, you do want some soup. Then I'll take you
home." He took a no-nonsense grip on her shoulders
and pushed her ahead of him. As they reached the porch
they heard a soft hollow *cooooo*. Jay swore under his
breath and stopped, his hands tightening on her shoulders.

She thought then of telling him about the dove she
had saved from slaughter. But his rejection of her and
the fact that she would merely be marking another bird
for death stopped her.

A quiet group gathered over soup in the gatehouse.
Hymie's hand and wrist were greasy where his mother
had spread ointment on the reddened skin. He and Roger
stole curious glances at Jay and Lynnette over the steam
of the soup.

A car sounded in the drive before they'd finished and
Hymie went to the window. "Mary Jane Gunderson."

"I thought I told you to tell her not to come back,"
Jay snapped at Mrs. Benninghoff.

"I did, Mr. Van Fleet." She replaced a stray pin in
the bun on the back of her head and opened the door.

Mary Jane was obviously embarrassed to see them all
there. The housekeeper took her coat and scarf and
insisted that she sit down for a bowl of soup. "I just came
to find out why I was let go." She looked from Jay to
Mrs. Benninghoff. "I mean . . . if it was that I didn't do
good work . . ."

"Oh no, you do a beautiful job. It's just that . . ."
Hymie's mother nodded helplessly in the direction of her
employer.

"It's just that it's no use to clean the place anymore
because my mother messes it right up again and I don't

want anyone in it. I don't even let Mrs. Benninghoff in anymore. Look, Mary Jane, you've got eight kids to raise. You don't need Nella Van Fleet."

"I'm not afraid of her." Mary Jane began to cry. "But I do need the money. And I'm not afraid, honest I'm not."

Roger and Hymie moved discreetly into the living room and turned on the television. Mrs. Benninghoff brought a box of Kleenex and joined them.

Lynnette stayed in her chair. "Mary Jane, you told me Chris never did much providing and you were getting along."

"I lied a little, Lynn. And everything costs so much now. We were all right until Mr. Van Fleet died . . . the old Mr. Van Fleet."

"What did he have to do with you?" Jay asked abruptly.

"He gave us money every month." Mary Jane reddened. "I didn't know it was from Mr. Van Fleet. Chris said it was a pension of some kind from getting hurt on a job when he was young."

"How much money?"

"Two hundred a month. When Chris married me, he was already getting it. And when I saw how hard it was for Chris to hold a job, I was thankful."

"Had he lived in Roggins before he married you?" Lynnette forgot her soup.

"He was born and raised here. His family moved away, but he was grown by then and stayed. Every month he'd trot over to Lawyer Henson's and come back with a check. He'd give me a hundred and fifty and drink the rest. The month old Mr. Clayborne died, Chris was off on one of his benders and so I dropped by John Henson's for the pension check."

She curled her lips and the tears flowed again. "Mr. Henson said there was no provision in the will to"—Mary Jane grabbed a handful of Kleenex—"to 'continue this milking of the Van Fleet estate' now that the old man was dead. He practically kicked me out."

"Hush money," Lynnette murmured. Jay's eyes warned her to be silent, but he couldn't quench the wonderful feeling that was replacing the depression.

"That was the first I knew the pension had anything

to do with the Van Fleets. I asked Chris about it when he came home, but he wouldn't talk about it. Just got mad and stomped over to Lawyer Henson's. Anyway, before Chris died he said something about getting what was coming to him."

"So why did he come up to the house? My uncle'd been dead three years."

"I don't know, mind you. But I figured at the time he was looking to steal something he could sell or even looking for money in the house. He was that desperate by then."

"To get what was coming to him," Lynnette said.

Jay stood up and rubbed the back of his neck. "I'll look into it, and maybe I can work out something for you when the estate's settled."

"But I don't want charity. I want to work for it."

He promised her he'd think of something and rushed her into her coat and out the door.

Jay Van Fleet looked gray with exhaustion when he took Lynnette home in the Oldsmobile. But she was bubbling over.

"Hush money, don't you see? Your uncle paid Chris Gunderson to keep quiet about your mother having his baby. It all fits."

"Does it?" he said without emotion as he pulled into the Olson farmyard.

"Yes! This is wonderful news. I'm not your sister, even you can—"

"Here, read this." Jay handed her a dirty half-torn sheet of paper and leaned back against the headrest, closing his eyes. "When Mrs. Benninghoff and Mary Jane cleaned out my—Nella's room—they stuffed some things in a box for me to check over before throwing out. I didn't get around to it until today when we were looking for things to start a fire. We tore paper, books, anything and threw them in a pile." He opened his eyes and looked at the paper in her hand. "By the time I saw what this was, it was too late to find the rest of it."

It was part of a letter written in a thick longhand.

. . . because I knew you'd come. I just did it to get back

at you, Olaf, I know you love me. I've always known. You with your prudish ways, your fat wife, your fat children. They don't know the Olaf I know, do they? And now I'm going to have a baby. It'll be the first real thing I've ever had. Clay thinks he can hush it up but he . . .

That was all there was to the letter although there was room for more on the page, as if the writer had been interrupted and never got back to it.

"That's my mother's handwriting," Jay whispered as if he were choking on the gravel in his throat. "I checked it with the photograph album."

Lynnette handed him the paper silently and opened the car door.

32

*R*everend Charles Birmingham removed heavy gloves to blow warm breath on frigid fingers. The soft beckoning call of a dove echoed somewhere near.

He felt for the flashlight in his overcoat pocket and for the Bible in the other. He was getting as bad as those silly old Catholics.

The Reverend had not come to exorcise a house, but himself.

Still, the feel of the book in his pocket was comforting. He had no other weapon.

He ducked behind a dead elm as lights went out in the gatehouse. Jay Van Fleet opened the door and stood on the porch to look up at the moon. Hymie Benninghoff and his mother joined him and the three walked to a dark car parked against a snowbank by the porch. Even their voices sounded chilled, brittle across the night. Hymie said something Birmingham didn't catch and Van Fleet's laughter crackled.

How could the poor boy laugh?

The engine of the car turned over again and again. Reverend Birmingham became impatient. He stamped numbed feet. He prayed that it would start and then chided himself for bothering God with such trivia. He would need Him for much more important matters this cold night.

But his prayer was answered as the motor caught and great billows steamed up behind the car.

Would they notice his car? No. He'd parked far away and in the opposite direction from where the headlights turned onto the highway. He'd walked forever across the fields and suffered the strain of a body still recovering from illness.

He'd heard that Jay was living with the Benninghoffs in the gatehouse, but he had planned to sneak by them.

Now that he didn't have to sneak, he felt very much alone under the cold light of the full moon.

Charles Birmingham turned to face the Van Fleet house . . . and himself.

The house stood in its own shadow, looking darkly evil amid snow cliffs aglitter in moonlight. He had the feeling that it had been expecting him.

He would try the front door. If it were locked, he'd try a window or the French doors at the back.

Branches of dead elms cast shadows that looked like black twisted fingers on skeleton hands against the moon-snow.

Did he feel a change in the frigid air as he approached? Did it grow as he came closer? He must not let his imagination beguile him now. He had come for truth.

His hand on the doorknob, Reverend Birmingham paused to pray.

The door was not locked. He watched the knob turn in his hand and realized he'd been wishing he could not gain entry so easily. A hanging stem of barren ivy brushed his hair, causing him to shiver as he passed.

The first thing his flashlight encountered was the painted grin of a broken alabaster cherub on the black marble floor.

He closed the door behind him and followed the gleam of his flashlight to the narrow corridor off the entry hall. His boots crunched on broken glass. What had happened to the place? It smelled of damp and dead fires.

Reverend Birmingham turned into the library, where he had faced his soul the last time he had come to this house. His flashlight flew out of his hand as he tripped over something soft and fell. Fear screamed inside his head.

The softness of upholstery met his fingers as he groped for the flashlight. *A chair. Just a chair.*

He stood and found a light switch on the wall inside the doorway. His flashlight lay not far from where he'd fallen against the overturned chair, and he knelt to retrieve it while his eyes surveyed the incredible shambles this charming room had become.

Everything but the fireplace had been toppled. Priceless antique lamps, books with costly bindings, furniture, lay in great heaps on the floor. A long, low pile of rubble, much of it charred and most of it paper, lay in the center of the room. What could have happened?

The lacy curtain nearest him billowed suddenly, exposing a window so shattered that even the wooden bars between the panes hung twisted.

The wind. Just the wind.

He paused again to pray. He'd come tonight in an act of penance. The word "penance" sounded Catholic too, but he couldn't find another to describe his feeling . . . need.

In this very library he'd come to believe in life after death. Astonishment came with the realization that after years of teaching just such a thing, he'd not really believed it. Shock had come from the fact that what he'd glimpsed here did not fit his learning, his conception of a God who ordered his heavens. His illness had given him much time to contemplate.

His own philosophy took for granted the good of God, the transitory evil of human beings. What he'd encountered here was an evil that was not human.

Charles Birmingham had come to prove a preconceived notion, to exorcise a ghost that had somehow gotten inside him. With the help of his Lord . . .

He took a step forward, and the light he had switched on in the library with his own hand switched off without it. Not pausing even to pray, he ran for the front door, his rubber boots crunching crisply on broken alabaster.

The narrow beam of the flashlight in his hand displayed a frenzied light dance on the walls and ceiling as he struggled with the knob, sensing danger behind him.

The door would not open.

He turned and swung shaking light into the darkness of the hall. Something swirled in the beam, something like the smoke from a cigarette, and approached along it. A faint but familiar smell hung on the cold . . . the cloying sweetness of decay.

Reverend Birmingham slid sideways and made for the staircase, bounding up it until his boots crunched on glass in the upstairs hall. He dimly registered a shattered mirror on the wall as his light swept past it. He turned into the master bedroom and flicked the lights on.

This room was in order, everything in place, but so cold he could see his breath as he ran toward the French doors.

The handles wouldn't turn.

He shook the doors, stood back and ran at them, butting them with his shoulder. Finally he broke a glass pane with his gloved fist and reached around to the handles outside. They wouldn't move.

Reverend Birmingham was still standing with his back to the room when he smelled again that odor, so faint it was almost a memory. A memory of Chris Gunderson.

He turned, feeling for the book in his pocket. He saw the room through a blur of tears and the steam of breath.

The mirror above the dresser snapped, and a long curved crack ran from a bottom corner to the opposite corner above. The glass below the crack hung for a moment then fell to the dresser with a crash.

The smoke-colored swirling appeared in what was left of the mirror. It formed a shape that could have been a distorted hand on an arm.

Reverend Birmingham didn't stay to watch. His Bible held in front of him, he made a blind dash for the door, panic tightening the muscles around his heart.

He was surprised to find himself alive in the hallway outside the master bedroom. But at the head of the stairs he bounced off something cold that didn't show in the flashlight beam.

He raced to the first bedroom door on the left because he knew those on the left had balcony doors. But it too refused to move. And so did the next and the next.

When a door did open finally, he fell across attic stairs, his bowels churning hot, demanding release. The flashlight was dimming as he made his way up the stairs to the attic where he knew he'd be trapped.

Could he find a place to hide? Was it even possible to hide from this monstrous thing? Trunks, boxes, pictures, furniture, dust . . . and then the flashlight flicked past an irregular place on the wall and came back to it.

The vague outline of a door in pine paneling. No hinges

that he could see in the shadows of the gables but what looked to be a metal handle of sorts.

A creak on the attic stairs . . . He slithered around an old birdcage on a trunk to the place on the wall where he thought he'd detected a door. But when he reached the wall, he couldn't find it.

Stuffing his flashlight, Bible and gloves into his coat pockets, he searched the wall with frantic fingers until he came to the cold metal of the handle. He pushed and pulled on it, sensing that his struggle was useless anyway, that he was no longer alone in the attic.

But he had been right. It was a door, a thick heavy one that pushed inward, a stiff one that had not seen much use. He was just able to squeeze through the opening his struggles had created. Once on the other side, he leaned against it hard to close the opening.

A hint of mothballs and the heavy scent of cedar hung on stagnant air. The flashlight, dim now, revealed a closet lined with cedar, a metal bar with turn-of-the-century coats, furs and dresses draped from hangers.

"Our Father who art in Heaven . . ." he intoned, his hand on the Bible in his pocket. "Hallowed be thy n—" he said just before the cold of the room entered his mouth, filled it, choked off his voice and reached for his lungs.

A sound, like air screaming past a racing car, grew and hissed into his ears, hurting them deep inside. . . .

33

The search for Reverend Birmingham extended even to the Olson farm, although his car had been found several miles away. Lynnette could see the search parties probing the snowdrifts with poles from the windows of the old farmhouse.

Wind and more snow had covered any tracks he might have left. Mrs. Birmingham had gone to bed thinking that he was working late with some committee at the church in Jewel. She had not reported him missing until the next morning. There had been no committee meeting that night in Jewel, and he had not been seen there at all. The mystery grew.

Hymie told her that Jay was making his own search, through the Van Fleet house, in case the minister had been foolhardy enough to enter it. But he did not find Birmingham and neither did the search parties.

The papers hinted at foul play, kidnapping, and the search widened as Reverend Birmingham was added to the missing-persons list. Two men from Minturn were picked up for questioning but released.

Roggins divided over the fate of the Reverend, some believing that he was murdered and his body transported to some distant place and others believing that he'd left the car of his own will and had frozen to death. He would turn up when the snows melted in the spring.

Lynnette saw very little of Jay Van Fleet for the next few months. Once a week she joined Hymie and Roger at the Jenson farmhouse for dinner. She was allowed to cook it, of course. But one night in late February, Jay showed up unexpectedly with Hymie.

She had little chance to speak to him alone and he acted unnecessarily cool toward her. Most of the discussion settled around the search for Birmingham and the strange way Nella had quieted down, stopped the nuisance tactics after the attempt to burn the house. Hymie thought she was waiting, perhaps building up to something unexpected.

At one point she passed Jay in the doorway of Myrtle's new kitchen and whispered, "I hate you, Jay Van Fleet."

"Good." And he treated her to that achingly beautiful smile.

Spring came early and suddenly. There were constant and ominous flood warnings as the packed snow melted in a rush, but there was no flooding and no Reverend Birmingham. The Olson farmyard was soon knee-deep in mud, the lane almost impassable.

Those afflicted with the Christmas flu returned to normal. Aunt Vera to her library, Lawyer Henson to his practice. Evelyn Birmingham moved to California to live with a married daughter when the new minister and his family moved into the parsonage.

Dorothy Tripp did not recover from her stroke and passed away in March.

After the harsh winter and before the strangling heat of summer, spring in Roggins seemed glorious. Soft breezes overflowed with the mating calls of returning birds, and the rains came softly, without thunder. They turned a world that had been covered with dirty white into the tender mint green of spring.

As Nella continued her good behavior, Jay moved back into the Van Fleet house, against Hymie's dire warnings. With the advent of planting season, Roger came out of his stupor over his mother's death. Bertha came out of her dirty cast and into a walker.

May dawned perversely hot and dry. The mud turned to ruts that couldn't be broken with an ax. Bertha looked at the sky and muttered something about a hot summer coming. As if that would be a surprise.

The day before Mother's Day Lynnette met Lawyer Henson in the library; he asked her to stop by his office that afternoon. When she arrived at his house, which was his office as well, the Bentley was parked in the street.

Jay rose to leave the minute she entered as if she had the plague. "Oh, I want to do something about the Gunderson family before I go." He looked through Lynnette. "But we'll discuss it some other time."

"Why? Jay, that family has bilked the estate long enough. Chris Gunderson was a scoundrel who—"

"Why was Clayborne paying Chris a pension anyway?" Lynnette broke in.

Lawyer Henson fussed with his tie and his papers. "That doesn't concern you, Lynnette. Please wait in the hall until Jay and I . . ."

Jay turned back from the doorway. "Yeah. What was he paying off for? Blackmail of some kind?"

"I don't think we should discuss this in front of an outsider. Who told the two of you?"

"His wife."

"I don't think you would want Lynnette to know about—"

"There's little else she doesn't know about me. Let's have it." Jay resumed his chair in front of the lawyer's desk and Lynnette sat beside him.

John Henson paced around his office, finally perching on the edge of his desk. "Remember, I warned you." He looked at Lynnette disapprovingly. "I suppose, Jay, you've heard rumors about your father."

"Yeah. Olaf Olson."

"Well, hardly. Although I think at one time or another every man in Roggins has been accused of siring you, myself included."

"You?"

"Well, I did step out with Nella occasionally—but that's not to the point. Chris Gunderson worked at the Van Fleet house . . . as far as I can remember for not even a year. He did odd jobs similar to what Hymie does now. He was about twenty-five at the time and unmarried. Nella was much older but restless. She had not wanted to return to Roggins, but your uncle cut off her allowance when her extravagances became too much."

"Are you trying to tell me Gunderson was my father?"

"That's exactly what I'm telling you. I didn't fully believe it myself until I saw the resemblance between you and Chris. You look a great deal like he did when he was younger and less dissipated. Have you ever taken a good look at the youngest Gunderson boy? Roddy? He resembles his father very much and you even more. I hadn't particularly wanted you to know that your father was an alcoholic and worse. Chris was a scoundrel from birth, a handsome scoundrel in his earlier years, but I don't see that that gives his widow the right—"

"I don't believe you. Lynnette and I know better. We share a father if not a mother."

"Jay, you would have been much happier with a man like Olaf Olson for a father, I know. Even under the circumstances. But it just isn't so. Olaf was almost as worried about Nella as Clay was. But she admitted, and in my presence, that Chris—"

"Read this." Jay drew a crumpled wad of paper from his pocket and handed it to his lawyer.

"You carry it with you?" Lynnette peered around into his face.

"Protection from little farm girls," Jay said dryly. And then to Henson, "I found it in one of Nella's books."

"Oh, dear," John Henson said when he'd read the partial letter. "It looks as though I'm going to have to go into the whole sordid story. I had so hoped it wouldn't be necessary."

"That's Nella's handwriting. I checked it and it does name an Olaf as my father."

"What this letter refers to is a meeting . . . I really would rather discuss this with you alone."

"Mr. Henson, it concerned my father and it concerns me. I've read that letter, too." Lynnette made designs in the dust on the arm of her chair. The lawyer's house was as dusty as he was. *Please prove it wasn't my father.*

Lawyer Henson finally settled behind his desk and related the story of Olaf, Chris and Nella. A simple story really. Olaf Olson and Nella had been childhood sweethearts. The lawyer guessed that Nella could not quite live with the idea that Olaf could give her up and lose himself in his wife and family, even though she had been absent from Roggins for years at a time. She'd been having an affair with the young handyman and one day talked him into meeting her in the abandoned schoolhouse

233

on the Olson farm. She left the Bentley in plain view in front of the schoolhouse.

Olaf had sometimes met her there, just to talk he claimed, and when he saw the Bentley, he walked in on Nella and her handyman, Chris Gunderson.

"He found them . . . he walked in at an embarrassing moment." Lawyer Henson told his story to the ceiling, pausing often to clear his throat. For an old gossip, he certainly didn't seem to relish telling Nella's juicy story. "Olaf was furious. I was in the library with Clay Van Fleet when Olaf stormed in and demanded that Clay do something about his sister. Nella came home a few minutes later, and Clay called her in and presented her with Olaf's accusations. She admitted everything freely and laughed at the three of us. Nella suggested that if her brother didn't like her conduct, he should send her away to Paris or Lisbon or someplace. Then she walked out laughing."

"The one-room schoolhouse . . ." Jay didn't look at Lynnette.

"Yes. Anyway, Clayborne had the Bentley put up on blocks in the garage. Gunderson was dismissed. And you were born nine months later. Clay let it be known that his sister was traveling in Europe. He dismissed the servants and kept Nella virtual prisoner in the house. It's not a pretty story. Such matters were not taken lightly in those days, and Clay was beside himself with anger.

"There were so many rumors connecting Nella with various men that when she claimed Chris as the father of her unborn child, I wondered if she could really know." He cleared his throat and began pacing again. "But as I've said the resemblance is there and it's quite distinct. Clay believed it because after his sister's death I was instructed to begin payment to Chris Gunderson. He picked up the money here so that Clay did not have to deal with him."

"What did it matter after she was dead?"

"Scandal. You'll have to remember, Jay, that very few people in Roggins knew of your existence until you were twenty-one. Why Clay chose to make you public than I don't know. He became very secretive in his later years, but there really was no other heir. I suspect he continued the payments after your visit that summer because he didn't want it known that a man like Chris Gunderson was the father of the Van Fleet heir."

Mr. Henson informed Lynnette that her mother could use her checking account and handed over some papers for Bertha to sign. "Perhaps she should go over these with Harold first. I'll be out next week to pick them up. Now, Jay, I hope to see you again before you leave. Roger Jenson has made a good offer on the land, but don't expect much from the sale of the house. You should be comfortable on your other assets for life. And do send me your address since there will be other matters for us to work out. You might begin looking for a reliable estate lawyer when you settle. I am not getting any younger and I'll have to retire soon."

All the while he was gently shepherding them toward the door. "And keep an eye open for good investments wherever you are. Check them out carefully, but remember to keep your money working for you." He closed the door on them and they stood on the front step still not looking at each other.

Lynnette turned her face up to the sun. "That kind of blows your protection, doesn't it?"

"Looks like it." He started down the sidewalk, his hands deep in his pockets.

"She was just goading my father."

"Yeah."

"Jay? Could I hitch a ride?"

He stopped but didn't turn. "Sure."

The top was down on the Bentley, the seats stinging hot. A funny little car. Thirty years ago it had sat in front of the schoolhouse . . . and again more recently in a November fog.

He pulled his sunglasses out of a case strapped to his belt and put them on. *More protection from little farm girls*, she thought and wanted to giggle. Jay Van Fleet was not used to ties. He would take some convincing.

The early heat made the smells of spring even sweeter, heavier, plowed earth, wild clover in pastures. For all its brutal moments, Iowa had a beauty very much its own.

Sweet wind swept about the Bentley and paused to tangle her hair. Ditches bright with dandelions swirled past them like whipped golden butter.

The Bentley halted abruptly at the one-room schoolhouse. Jay didn't turn into the drive but parked on the road and stared past her.

The schoolhouse stood peacefully in the sun, surrounded by the careful furrows of Roger Jenson's planter. No imaginary bygone sounds on the wind.

"Jay, it was just a coincidence," she said softly. But she couldn't ignore the eerie history-repeats-itself feeling.

He chewed on the knuckle of his index finger for a moment, then started the Bentley. He drove slowly to the Olson farmhouse, deep in thought behind his sunglasses.

"Sounds like the Van Fleet estate is settled and you're leaving," she said when they'd stopped.

"As soon as I can get out of here." He still didn't look at her.

"Jay?" She found she couldn't look at him either. "Take me with you."

"I'm . . . I'm going to have to think this out." The funny croaky whisper she hadn't learned to forget. "Okay?"

"Okay." Lynnette got out of the car and then leaned over the door. "Promise you won't go off without seeing me again?"

The sunglasses with her reflection in them nodded . . . didn't they? The Bentley crunched the edges of dried ruts as Jay Van Fleet ran.

It would take time.

Was there time?

34

The next day was Mother's Day and it began hot and sultry. Lynnette wore a secret smile to church. Bertha leaned heavily on her arm, using a cane with the other. This was definitely against the doctor's orders. But who had ever ordered Bertha Olson?

The new minister, young and polished, looked straight at Lynnette, or so it seemed. "Don't turn thy back on thy mother, for thou art but a seed that could not have flowered without her."

Oh, brother. Was that in the Bible? Birmingham's sermons used to be about the glories of motherhood and a mother's responsibilities. This one was aimed at the children.

Rachael Stewart sat composed as usual on the organ bench, but she seemed to have aged since her illness. No longer beautiful, just old. She didn't bother to accuse Lynnette with her glance.

On the way home Elaine apologized to Bertha because they were spending the rest of the day with Leroy's mother.

"Don't worry about that. I've got Lynnette. Harold and Margaret are coming tonight to take us out to supper."

"Looks like you've got company," Elaine said as she drove up to the gate.

The Oldsmobile sat in the middle of the farmyard. Elaine caught Lynnette grinning and winked at her. Their mother just grunted as they helped her out of the car.

"Well, where is he?" Bertha said when they stood alone at the gate. "Unless he's hiding in the trunk, he ain't in the car."

"Maybe he's in the house waiting for us to come home."

"Hadn't better be. Rich folks think they got the right to walk into other people's houses uninvited." She stopped at the back door. "I smell rain."

"Bertha, there isn't a cloud in the sky."

"There will be." Bertha took out the handkerchief she kept tucked inside her bosom and wiped her brow. "Good thing, too. We need it. Too hot, too early. I don't like it."

Jay Van Fleet was not in the house.

"Now, where do you suppose he got to?"

"Maybe he found us gone and decided to look around the farm. He'll show up." *And he didn't go off without seeing me.*

"Humph! Don't want no fancy good-for-nothing Van Fleet nosing around my farm."

"Afraid he'll find your buried treasure?" Lynnette giggled and bounced upstairs to change her clothes. She put on her nicest mint-green slacks.

They ate a light lunch and still no Jay. She'd made an extra sandwich just in case.

Bertha sat in a lawn chair on the back step while Lynnette pulled weeds from the flower bed along the house. "Those pants are going to get all dirty. But I suppose you have to look nice for Mr. High and Mighty."

Lynnette glanced sideways at the Oldsmobile. It looked lonely sitting out in the middle of the farmyard that way. Why hadn't he parked by the gate? Where was he?

"There! Told you so."

"What?" Lynnette jumped. "Jay?"

"No. The sky. Look."

A white puffy cloud was forming in an intensely blue sky somewhere in the direction of Roggins.

"Thunderhead." Bertha clicked her teeth back onto her gum. "Told you so." They watched the cloud form from nothing, almost double in size. Another began to form nearby. "I don't like it."

"Don't like what? You said we needed rain." Lynnette stooped again to the flowerbed. A trickle of sweat inched down her back.

"What did the weatherman say on the radio at breakfast?"

"Something about sunny skies and good weather predicted through Tuesday." Where was Jay Van Fleet?

"Punk fools. What do they know? Don't know enough to go out and look at the sky, feel the air. How can they tell anything?" Bertha stretched her neck and turned her head as if she were listening. She sniffed the air. "I don't like it."

"You've said that." Lynnette stood up impatiently. "It's too hot to weed." She laid her gardening gloves on the step and walked to the gate.

"Too hot for a walk too, Missy. That's right. Go look for him. Daughter of mine chasing a pair of pants. What's the world coming to?"

Lynnette closed the gate behind her and walked across the farmyard to the Oldsmobile.

Jay Van Fleet was not lying down on the seat. He wasn't in the machine shed or behind it either, or in the barn. When she came out of the barn, she was panting slightly. The air was thick. She searched the sky where another thunderhead was building itself into leaping heads of cauliflower and she had a premonition.

Lynnette walked slowly back to the Oldsmobile and opened the door. The key was in the ignition. Tucked under the gas pedal was a white envelope. She reached in and dislodged it.

It was filled with twenty-dollar bills. No letter with it. No writing on the envelope but she knew what it meant: Take the car and the money. Get on with your life . . . and get out of mine.

Without bothering to close the door, Lynnette turned toward the pasture, not even starting when Roger's boar lunged at the fence. She found the pasture a yellow carpet of dandelion heads. At the sight of her, the pregnant cow bellowed and followed her to the creek.

Lynnette sat on the bank and then realized that she still held the envelope in her hand. Her perspiring fingers had left smudgy marks on the white paper.

Jay Van Fleet was always calling himself a walking disaster area. For the first time she believed him. Something inside her felt destroyed.

She lay back, not caring what the tender grass blades and young dandelions would do to her favorite slacks.

Not a rustle from the normally chatty leaves of the

cottonwoods. She lay there a very long time, dry-eyed and empty. Eventually a chilly breeze stirred up the cottonwoods and then it was hushed and hot again. Bertha called but Lynnette didn't answer. A tractor started somewhere. The cauliflower clouds grew quickly, frothy and deep, their undersides beginning to darken until they looked like ever-growing piles of whipped cream on a thin layer of chocolate cake.

When the clouds covered the sky and blotted out the sun, Lynnette stood finally and crossed the pasture. The cow followed her, nuzzled her, almost knocked her over.

"All right, Bossy. I guess life must go on." She checked the water tank, filled the manger with hay and meal and blocked the door open so the cow could get in when it rained.

The Oldsmobile, its door still open, mocked her from the middle of the farmyard. She considered it a moment, biting her lip till it hurt, and then walked to it, removed the key, put it in the envelope and slammed the door. As she walked around it, she kicked the rear tire.

"Lynn, where have you been? Get in here, there's a storm coming." Bertha stood in her walker on the back step.

"Where are you going?" Bertha called as Lynnette avoided the houseyard and headed for the lane.

"To the Van Fleet house."

"But there's a storm coming, I say. Look at the sky."

"So I'll get wet. I won't be gone long." *Just long enough to stuff this envelope down Jay Van Fleet's throat.* Lynnette turned into the lane. The cow bellowed behind her. *I wouldn't use that car now to escape the devil.*

"Lynn. Look at the sky! For God's sake, Lynn—"

But she looked straight ahead, ignoring her mother, the sky and the flashes that lightened a prematurely dark countryside.

The air felt and tasted dirty.

Lynnette pictured Don Quixote approaching his final windmill. At least Jay Van Fleet would remember her in vivid color. If he hadn't already skipped the country.

Drops of rain, so heavy they hurt on contact, hit her just as she hit the road. Across the road Roger Jenson drove his tractor, with one hand, holding onto his hat with the other as the wind increased. He was getting in the last seed in the last field before the rain.

The rain was so sparse that the dust behind Roger's tractor hung in the air where he'd left it, as if that air were a charged magnet.

She clutched the envelope to her and lowered her head.

By the time Lynnette climbed the fence to the Van Fleet fields, she was puffing and drenched. The envelope was rubbery wet. Sheet lightning created an awesome blue-white world and she was cold and . . . afraid.

Too late to turn back.

The hail started, slanting from the south, before she could reach the fence that separated lawn and field.

It came hard. It pounded brutally at her body as she flattened herself to crawl under the fence to the lawn.

She forgot the envelope, lost somewhere in the field. She forgot Jay Van Fleet and Don Quixote and windmills. She screamed with a pain she'd never imagined possible as the demon-driven hail pummeled her back and head.

Crawling on her stomach across frozen lumps, she reached the partial protection of a tree on the lawn. She clawed herself along the rough bark to an upright position just as the hail, the rain and blue-white lightning ceased to be.

The dust in the air had turned to mud, as she started for the protection of the Van Fleet house.

Blood ran down one arm and dripped off her fingers to the ground.

35

Jay Van Fleet bent over one of the new suitcases on the bed in the mast r bedroom while great plops of rain splattered against the French doors and a faint uneasiness grew inside him.

He straightened and listened to the house. The doves were silent.

Did he sense a stirring? Did he feel her gathering somewhere? The whole place seemed to be charging. Was he becoming sensitized to Nella?

She'd been quiet for months.

Oh, hell, Van Fleet, get hold of yourself. The sooner he got out of this place, the sooner the whole nightmare would be over. All he needed was another hour . . .

He began throwing things into the suitcase. The neat stacks of clothes he'd taken from the dresser and assembled on the bed became jumbles.

Faster and faster he packed, thinking he could smell Chris Gunderson again, telling himself to quit imagining. And all the while a slow sinking feeling in his stomach.

And then Jay stopped, a sock dangling from his hand. From the corner of his eye, as he'd leaned over the bed, he thought he'd seen something move.

But when he turned his head to look, there was nothing.

Another day in this damn place and he'd lose his mind for sure. Lightning flooded suddenly through the French doors. Rain drove hard against the house.

A storm. Just a storm. He turned to see a suitcase lift from the bed.

It dumped his clothes on the floor and hurtled across the room to hit a chair and knock it over.

Another suitcase rose from the bed and spilled its contents. His shaving mug bounced across the covers, pirouetted in the air and landed at his feet.

The sickening smell that reminded him of Gunderson hung heavier now . . .

On the other side of the bed, a smoky mist gathered, writhed, seemed to evaporate, then returned, shaping, reshaping, swirling.

Oh God, no. Nella don't . . .

A hand and then another formed from the swirling mass, misshapen at first and then clearer on arms struggling to form.

"No! No!"

The hands reached out to him across the bed, palms upward, a slight beseeching curve to the fingers.

Lightning flared like fire across the floor, thunderous hail pounded at the balcony. Even through the racket he could hear glass crashing from windows throughout the house as a body gathered behind the arms . . . the beginnings of a head.

The crashing of the glass in the French doors drowned out the voice rising to his lips as he turned and ran blindly from the room.

"No! Nella . . ." He screamed her name without wanting to all the way down the staircase.

He tripped on the bottom step and sprawled across the polish of black marble.

The sound of the hail outside stopped short and the silence it left was filled with the sound of his breathing. Sweat, cold and briny, stung his eyes as he rolled over to face the woman who stood on the stairs above him.

Nella was no longer mist. She would have looked almost normal if she'd had any color. Instead she looked like a caricature of a fuzzy daguerreotype. Her lips moved without sound. Her eyes sunk in shadow . . .

A woman screamed from the direction of the sunroom and Nella's arms rose with a tortured slowness to reach out to him once again.

Jay stumbled to his feet. He ran down the narrow hallway with the yellow wallpaper, ignoring the hiss on the air behind him that sounded like a word: "Son" . . .

36

*L*ynnette stood on the patio pounding and kicking at a wall of toothlike holes, nothing but jagged shards left of the hundreds of windowpanes. A warm sticky trickle mixed with water from her dripping hair ran down the bridge of her nose.

Glass crunched under shoes as a dark figure opened the patio doors, causing more raggedy glass to tinkle from square frames. Jay Van Fleet almost fell out of the house, almost ran past her.

"Jay!" He stopped, turned to stare at her as if he didn't know her.

"You—you're all blood." His voice was hollow on the motionless air.

"Hurry—shelter—" The sense of Bertha's warning had finally punctured pain and weariness.

"What?"

"No time—hurry!" She reached out both hands to him to draw him into the house and he backed away, horror etching shadows on his face.

She must pull herself together, make him understand. She swallowed and tried again while he just stared at her, wide-eyed.

"Jay—have to get inside—dust on the air—" Her body shuddered, making her voice tremble. "Sheet lightning . . . hail. It's just starting. A tornado, Jay! Please!" Pain jabbed at her back and shoulders, the skin beneath her hair. "Hurry! We have to get inside." She turned toward the house, hoping he would follow, but he stepped in front of her, barring her way.

"Lynn. Nella's in there."

"Have to hurry! No time!"

"Jesus!" That vacant look was back in his eyes.

But she had already heard it. Licking her lips and tasting the salt of blood, Lynnette turned reluctantly.

The air was thick with solids. Giant hailstones streaked

with dirt stretched in melting drifts across the fields.

The funnel cloud was black.

Everything behind it was obscured in gritty gloom.

The funnel lifted, somewhere on the other side of the Olson farm, bounced back into a dirty sky as if it were a spring that had hit something to make it recoil.

They both stood transfixed.

The funnel hovered, distinct from the clouds that swirled rhythmically around it, as if it controlled all movement in the sky.

It slammed to earth again.

Dislodged farmland shot up in great billows around it. A jarring sound erupted like an explosion too loud to hear. The patio vibrated beneath them.

The tornado moved erratically and in slow motion. The obliterating end-of-the-world curtain that it brought with it obscured the Olson farm.

Bertha, Lynnette thought dully.

"Heading this way," Jay said with a fantasy-like lack of comprehension.

"Have to find shelter." It hurt the skin around her mouth to speak. What had the man on the television said to do last October? Get under a table? No . . . the basement. But Nella was there.

The gatehouse. That was it. If there was time.

Lynnette sensed she was already too late. A tortured keening approached across the fields. Then it wailed everywhere about them, its intensity growing.

Hymie stood in front of the toolshed, his mother beside him. Their mouths formed words she couldn't hear above the wail. They gestured toward the shed.

Hymie pushed Mrs. Benninghoff inside and followed her. Lynnette grabbed Jay's arm and, pulling him with her, raced toward the toolshed.

A head-splitting roar replaced the keening in the air and she let go of Jay to cover her ears.

Lynnette bounced off the corner of the shed and hit the ground in front of it. Colored lights danced inside her eyelids. Jay landed on top of her.

She felt his shoes scrape the abrasions on her back as he pulled himself off and began to drag her against the wind toward the door of the shed. It felt and sounded as if they were fighting the backwind of a thousand jet fighters taking off at one time from one place.

Hymie reached for them from a hole in the floor of the toolshed.

Lynnette was suddenly slathered in mud.

Hands tugged at her, slipping on the mud on her forearms, pulling her along the floor. The wind tried to tear her away. Her body lifted and then slammed against the wooden flooring. She couldn't breathe. The air was being sucked up out of her lungs.

Silence came suddenly . . . deadly.

Her legs were sucked skyward, the soggy shoes ripping from her feet.

And then she was in the hole, standing upright, crushed against another body. Air returned with the roaring, as the eye of the storm passed over. The chest against her own expanded, as hers did, to receive it.

The hole shuddered. The earth lurched. Lynnette was flung to the ground, someone else flung against her.

Total chaos bellowed above. All was pitch black below.

Hands felt along her body. A voice pleaded, "Lynn?" Arms gathered her in, held her cuddled like a baby.

The roar moved on.

Gradually a dusty twilight shone through the mud on her eyelashes. The light came from the hole above. She scraped her tongue along her upper teeth to remove the muck of mud.

"Lynn." It was Jay who held her. The only recognizable features were the vacant eyes staring from a face blackened with grime.

He looked so unbelievable she giggled until she laughed and laughed until Hymie slapped her.

"Stop it, Lynn! Let go of her, Van Fleet. She might be hurt." Hymie pried her from Jay and pulled her to her feet. "Anything broken?"

"I can't feel much. But I can stand."

"She was all cut by the hail . . . bleeding." Jay still sat on the floor.

"We'll have to wash the mud off so you don't infect.

Your shirt is in shreds." Mrs. Benninghoff moved from a corner.

"What comes next? Fallout?" There was a trace of wildness in Jay's laughter and more than that in his eyes.

"No." Hymie glanced at the hole above them as the dusty light grew brighter. "It's over now."

No one seemed too anxious to go up there.

"What is this place?" Jay picked up a handful of wood shavings.

A narrow table, cogs, wheels, small motors and pumps in various stages of dismantlement, oily cloths, tools . . .

"My hidey hole." Hymie looked sheepishly at his mother. "Watch out for glass, Lynn." He pointed to a broken oil lamp near her bare feet. "It's an old fruit cellar. They built the toolshed on top of it. Ma . . ."

"I know," his mother said with a tight-lipped smile. "I discovered it several years ago." She turned away and the curious smile vanished. "Let's go up and see what's happened. Don't walk around, Lynnette. There'll be glass and nails."

When they emerged, the sun shone normally on a depressing world.

Mrs. Benninghoff moaned softly behind her hand.

Hymie shook his head and tried to scratch at mud-stiffened hair.

Lynnette sat on the floor of a toolshed that was no longer there, Jay sitting close beside her, his arm pulling her against him.

Their feet hung over the foundation into a trench that once was a lawn.

The trench, a foot and a half deep, started somewhere in the fields and followed a demented path across the lawn past the toolshed. No tree was left as before.

Only a few jagged feet remained of the tree she had sought as protection from the hail. What if she'd stayed there?

Broken discarded tree limbs floated in a blackened swimming pool. Stalks of defoliated trees stood like ninepins.

A giant oak had toppled across the garage corner of the house, taking part of the wall, leaving silver-gray

247

patches of a dirt and leaf-spattered Bentley glinting back at the mocking sun.

White roots of the oak either dangled or pointed toward the sky, leaving a hole the size of a bomb crater in the earth. The topmost branches spread across the patio.

Lynnette looked back to somebody's stiff mud-coated cow lying on its side across the trench from her. Round wide eyes of black glass stared back, sightlessly. One leg dangled at the knee like the roots of the oak.

She'd read of the freaky things tornadoes do, had been a little girl in the fruit cellar when one took the old machine shed. But the reality violated all laws of reason, nature, and human belief.

The Van Fleet house stood.

The gatehouse was gone and most of the trees that had sheltered it. On the other side, the stand of trees around the tennis courts had split, their trunks broken in half, the top foliage lying over on the court.

But the Van Fleet house stood.

The oak had taken part of the garage wall, every windowpane was broken, one chimney tipped dangerously, some of the shingles were gone or scattered about the roof, a telephone pole with short wires dangling was wedged against the balustrade. The French doors of the sunroom hung broken from their hinges.

But the limestone blocks, torn from ancient barns long ago, had withstood the storm.

In its state of disrepair, rising defiantly above the debris of its lawns and the countryside, the Van Fleet house appeared stronger and somehow more sinister than it ever had before.

No bird, no insect, no breeze. Only a mortared stone fallen from the tilting chimney and sliding off the roof to break the stillness of aftermath . . .

And the whining of Roggins' civil defense siren sounding small and impotent across wasted farmland.

"The grain elevator is gone," Mrs. Benninghoff whispered behind Lynnette. "I think I can see the water tower though."

The haunting whine cried on and on like a child orphaned suddenly in a war zone.

"Lynnette, there's blood oozing through a crack where the mud has dried on your back."

"I'll see if I can start the generator in the basement." Hymie moved cautiously across the lawn slithering on the muck that coated everything. The storm's filth smelled vaguely of sewer stench.

"Don't go in there, Benninghoff." Jay straightened beside her.

"We have to get warm water to wash Lynnette, Mr. Van Fleet. That oozing on her back looks funny . . . pussy. The water from the well should be all right."

"But, Nella . . ."

"I don't think we have any choice," Mrs. Benninghoff said, too casually, and started after Hymie. "Better carry her. She doesn't have shoes."

"Can't we bring the water out here?"

She turned, her shoulders slumping, her expression dazed, dreamy. "There's no time. There's a shower—oh, look!" She pointed past them and they turned to see smoke shooting skyward over Roggins, a sickening, reddening glow at its base.

"I think Nella is the least of our worries right now, Mr. Van Fleet," she said reproachfully, turning back to the house. "There's a shower in one of the guest rooms. We'll hurry."

A breeze came to stir up the smell of sewer, to make a gauzy curtain, hanging outside a broken upstairs window, fly up and then flap down, as if the house winked at them.

Lynnette's mind and body were numb as Jay carried her across the lawn.

"I don't like this," he said grimly as they moved toward the Van Fleet house.

37

They had just cleared the snagging branches of the oak on the patio—Jay was trying to tell her something about Nella—when they heard the housekeeper scream.

Jay's shoes ground to a halt on glass shards and his arms jerked so sharply he almost dropped her.

Mrs. Benninghoff seemed to fly out of the dark hole left by the sagging French doors. She was jerked to a stop by a chest-high tree limb. Grabbing it with both hands, she closed her eyes and leaned over it to vomit onto the patio on the other side.

"What is it?" Jay tightened his hold on Lynnette and half turned, as if making ready to flee.

The housekeeper shook her head and pointed toward the dark hole behind her.

Jay moved to the entrance and peered inside.

Lynnette, with her arms around his neck, was looking up into his face when the mud cracked in long curving lines on his cheeks as he drew his lips back to pull a quick hiss of air through his mouth.

"Don't look!"

But she did. Automatically her eyes followed his to the floor of the sunroom.

One arm flung outward in a relaxed manner, his mouth open slightly, his body blackened, his face strangely clean and pale except for the stubby shadow of beard . . . his belt had caved into a funny dip in his torso.

Roger Jenson lay on his back, but the toes of his boots were sticking straight down into the carpet.

Hymie came along the narrow hall, a blanket over his arm. "You shouldn't of let her see this," he said as he covered his friend. Lynnette could hear Hymie swallow as she pressed her face against Jay. "I'll see about the generator now. You stay her till I give the word."

Something scraped on the floor. "Here, put her in this

chair," Mrs. Benninghoff said in a shaky voice. "I'll go find something for her cuts."

But Lynnette did not release her clinging hold. She kept her face against the rank folds of his shirt, and she felt Jay lower himself into the chair still holding her.

The rhythmic clopping of a helicopter sounded from somewhere outside.

The housekeeper's voice made them both start. "Hymie says it's working and to take her up. Here's a scissors to cut away her shirt."

"I can walk now, Jay."

"Wait till we get you some shoes. There's glass in here too," he said gruffly and lifted them both from the chair.

She didn't look at the blanket-covered form on the floor. She didn't need to.

They had to move around dislocated furniture to reach the hall. It looked as if the tornado had done its deviltry to the inside of the house without destroying the outside. But they all knew that this destruction had another source. The funnel could have lifted Roger from his tractor and flung him across the country and through the French doors, but it could not have scratched the little pieces of yellow-flowered wallpaper from the walls and littered the floor in the hall with them.

The grandfather clock lay over against the stairs, leaving just enough room to get by.

"I don't like this," Jay said again, almost to himself, as they started up the stairs slowly, carefully, his eyes darting everywhere. The housekeeper followed close behind.

Lynnette was finding it difficult to clear her mind enough to make her own decisions but . . . she didn't like it either.

They sounded like Bertha. Bertha had been "not liking it" all day long. . . .

"Bertha! I have to find her. Maybe—"

"We'll get the stinking muck out of those open wounds first. Then we'll find Bertha," he whispered. "Stop making so much noise, will ya?"

"There's a shower over the tub in the bathroom that connects the first and second rooms to the left."

251

"I know." Jay swung around at the head of the stairs and Mrs. Benninghoff turned into the master bedroom.

"I'll find clothes," she said.

The upstairs hall was long and dark. The door to Nella's room stood closed.

Lynnette didn't feel well.

A faraway scream of sirens wafted through broken French doors as they entered the bedroom.

Jay set her down in the bathroom.

"It's so quiet in here."

"Yeah, I know. That's what's worrying me." He turned on the shower and then started to cut away the rags of her shirt.

She leaned against the wall. Bullets of water hitting the tub and the strange buzzing in her ears lightened the silence of the house. "I have to find Bertha." She closed her eyes.

"Pretty soon." He cut through her bra and pulled it away. "Does it hurt?"

"Yes." She saw Bertha, a helpless cripple, standing in her walker on the back step and opened her eyes. The wall was lime green.

He stripped down her slacks and pants, and she shivered against the lime green. "You were going off without me. . . . I lost the money—I was going to make you eat it." She turned to see him pulling off his own clothes.

Jay held her up under the shower head. The water was lukewarm at first, but it grew hotter. And then Hymie was in the tub with them. She giggled at their nakedness and cried as Hymie rubbed soap into her back and hair. It stung her eyes as it ran down her face.

"Joey Stewart I could understand, Van Fleet. You I can't. But Lynn never did listen to me."

"Shut up and hurry. I want to get her out of here."

Lynnette felt the coldness of tile as she was stretched out on the floor and gently toweled. They smeared something on her back.

"Her skin's hot."

"Shit!"

And then the three of them stood naked in the bedroom before Mrs. Benninghoff. She looked too weary to blush

Lynnette remembered getting caught in just such a state with Roger and Hymie after a "community" swim when they were very young; that time Hymie's mother had not been too weary to blush. But the thought of Roger caused tears to form, and she felt feverish.

"I've found some overalls in the kitchen for Hymie that I'd been mending there. And a pair of pants for you, Mr. Van Fleet." Mrs. Benninghoff handed them out. "This is all I could find for Lynnette." She held up a lavender dress, filmy and fringed. "It seemed a little smaller than the others."

"Not that!" Jay grabbed the dress before Lynnette could reach for it. "It's—She can wear an old shirt of mine."

"All your clothes . . ." Mrs. Benninghoff sat heavily on the bed and folded her hands on her lap. "Your clothes have been torn . . . or cut up into . . . little pieces, Mr. Van Fleet. Even the suitcases have been slashed and your shoes . . . You'll have to wear the shoes you had. . . . There's not even a shirt for you. You should see the room."

"It's all right, Jay. It's beautiful." Lynnette slid the dress from between his stiff fingers and slipped it over her head. Her hands trembled. The darkness of her nipples showed through the filmy bodice. "Does it belong to one of your lady friends? It looks like something out of the twenties. Not a 1970's copy, but the real thing, complete with a mothball stink. It's—"

"It's Nella's."

"Oh." *Nella, always Nella.* "I hate Nella."

"She's not too fond of you either, remember? Let's go."

Hymie brought his own and Jay's shoes from the bathroom. "What about shoes for Lynn? Would Nella's fit?"

Lynnette had turned cold again, but Jay wiped sweat from his face. "Isn't there anything else? I've seen her shoes. They're no more sensible than that dress. We can carry her." He bent from the waist to tie his shoes. "Let's go."

"Carry her to Roggins?"

"They'll be getting doctors there first," Hymie said.

Jay looked almost wild. "The pickup?"

Lynnette whirled and watched the fringe fly.

"Gone."

"The Bentley looked okay. Can we get it out?"

Lynnette danced around the room, careful to avoid the glass by the French doors. "Wonderful dress, Jay."

"Roads'll be blocked." Hymie grabbed her in midswirl.

"Nella's clothes, the ones that are left, are mostly party clothes from her younger years. Mary Jane and I wondered when we cleaned the room. But we couldn't find the later ones. But . . . anything is better than barefoot on glass, nails—whatever we find out there."

Jay's face, clean and handsome now, looked tortured. "Okay, I'll go. You two stay with her."

"Maybe we should all stay together," Hymie said softly, and he and Jay stared at each other.

Jay gave in first. "Yeah, maybe so."

Lynnette sang as they left the room,

"Jay Van Fleet is a *bastard*, a *bastard*, a *bastard*.
He's afraid of his *mommy*, his *mommy*, his *mommy*."

She gave the fringe a tantalizing swing in the hallway and broke away from Hymie to dance alone toward Nella's room.

"Jay Van Fleet is *afraid* to love, *afraid* to love, *afraid*—"

"Lynn!"

She swirled herself and the oh-so-lovely lavender fringe around to laugh at them all as the attic door opened between them—and something fell past her face, fell out between them . . . something that grinned.

It wore an overcoat and one rubber boot.

Lynnette screamed and someone laughed wildly and the combined sounds echoed and crashed through the hall and Hymie and Jay stood stone still across the overcoat from her and Mrs. Benninghoff had her hand over her mouth again. . . .

But someone else was laughing . . . someone who wasn'

254

there. . . . Because Hymie and Jay had their mouths closed. Hymie's mother had hers clamped with her hand.

Was it the grin on the floor that laughed?

That must be it . . . a dried grin . . . the skin . . . brown, mummified away from clamped teeth. But no laughter in the sunken little raisin eyes . . . the whole face looked amazingly like . . .

"Birmingham," Hymie said as Lynnette backed away toward the door at the end of the hall.

38

*L*ynnette found herself alone in Nella's room, watching the door close in front of her.

She didn't remember opening it to enter but . . . She was feeling funny, dizzy. . . .

If Reverend Birmingham had been dead all this time, why wasn't he mushy or something . . . falling apart?

"What did I come in here for, anyway?" she asked no one. "Oh yes. Shoes . . . must find shoes. Must hurry."

The white dove lay very still on the bed, just a rim of red ringing a round black iris. Its head rested on the pillow like . . . *like a person's*. Lynnette giggled and turned to the wardrobe.

What goes with lavender? "Jay Van Fleet is a bastard, a bastard . . ."

A nauseous feeling made her grab the edge of the wardrobe.

This room smells bad. She moved the dresses aside to look down. Her neck felt stiff as if her glands had swollen.

Four rows of shoes in neat pairs . . . *lavender dress . . . lavender shoes*. There was at least half a row of lavender shoes. *Nella loves lavender. She loves Jay, too.*

"But I don't, I don't, I don't." She picked the only pair that really did justice to the filmy dress she wore and to the exotic fringe.

Lynnette turned with the lavender shoes in her hand, to find a woman sitting on the bed next to the dove.

The woman was smiling.

Lynnette closed her eyes and sat on the floor. When she opened them, the woman still smiled at her from the bed.

Perfect even teeth, like Jay's, but smaller . . . smooth pale skin with pencil lines for eyebrows . . . eyes, cat-green and mischievous . . .

Golden hair, curling and swooping around her shoulders to fade and disappear into the air at the ends.

She wore a lavender dress, too, with fringe on the bodice as well as the skirt, but hers had tiny straps over the shoulders. It was almost too colorful, too lavender, to believe.

"Fool." That one word rasped with a hollow echo about the room. But the smile didn't move. And Lynnette hadn't said the word.

"I love him, too," she croaked through the pain in her throat.

And the woman said, "He's mine." Didn't she?

Lynnette slipped the shoes on her feet and tried to stand but couldn't because the floor moved. She put her hands to her ears, but the buzzing in her head and the deafening pounding at the door behind her wouldn't stop. She realized vaguely that the pounding had been going on for some time . . . Jay was calling her name . . .

The woman laughed and rose from the bed. The fringe didn't sway with her movement.

She came to stand over Lynnette.

"Nella, you were forty when you died. You can't expect him to believe you look like that," Lynnette shouted over the racket. "You look younger than he does!" *I'm not really seeing her. It's because I'm sick.* But she reached out a hand to touch the fringe.

It met a cold substance that wasn't fringe.

Maybe I'm dying, maybe that's why I can see her. Maybe that's . . . why she's smiling.

"You see," she said to the long tapering fingers on either side of the lavender dress in front of her eyes, "he doesn't want someone to love. He can't handle it. So . . . Do you know you smell like Chris Gunderson?"

Wood splintered behind her. The door fell into the room with Jay and Hymie on top of it.

"Am I dead?" Lynnette asked them. "Is that why she's smiling?"

But they were looking at Nella and rising to their feet together, as if they were one man.

So they could see her, too.

Nella seemed to forget Lynnette, now that Jay was in the room.

And Jay didn't notice Lynnette on the floor, his eyes held by the cat-green eyes above her; the sandy hair on his chest and forearms shimmered. His mouth hung open but he didn't speak. His hair, still wet from the shower, curled and clung about his face, giving him a boyish look.

The two beautiful Van Fleets stood staring at each other forever, while Lynnette shivered at their feet, unnoticed.

Nella was lovelier than any of the pictures in the album had indicated, Lynnette thought savagely. But she had recognized her and knew the others had too.

Those two made Lynnette feel so ugly, sitting sick and soggy on the floor, with her hair still dripping on lavender shoulders, the dampness feeling cold and slimy to the hot prickly skin under the dress.

Lovely tapered hands lifted, ever so slowly, beguilingly toward Jay Van Fleet. He groaned but didn't move.

"Stay." Nella's voice behind unmoving lips, fingers curling slightly as if she longed to grasp him.

"She's no mother, Mr. Van Fleet!" The housekeeper's warning came from behind them and fell like ice on the room. "She's an illusion."

"I love you, Jay . . ." Nella said.

From the corner of her eye Lynnette could see Hymie inching toward them.

"Nella . . ." Jay whispered, his hands clenching and unclenching at his sides. Then they began to rise . . . but not toward Nella.

"You can't go back." Never taking his eyes from his mother, he stooped to lift Lynnette from the floor between them, his sweat dripping water onto her face as it had in the one-room schoolhouse.

Nella lowered her arms. Her eyes dropped to Lynnette and then moved back to Jay. The warped smile wavered finally. More of her hair disappeared into the air and some of the fringe. She began to back toward the bed.

The dove stirred.

"Come on!" Hymie was pushing Mrs. Benninghoff toward the French doors.

"Nella?" Jay pleaded.

Nella Van Fleet's dress had turned colorless. One arm resembled writhing smoke that drifted toward the dove.

Plaster fell from the ceiling. Hymie shook the doors. Even with the glass panes broken, he couldn't seem to open them.

"Nella! Can't you understand? Nella?"

Lynnette looked back to the bed to find Nella gone, but the dove seemed to be wrapped in a smoky haze. It shuddered and moved a wing. Despite the haze, Lynnette could see the black in the dove's eye constricting, the red rim growing inward.

It grunted, feet thrashing the air, and then, lifting its head forcefully and repeatedly from the pillow, it finally jerked its white body over onto its claws. White feathers ruffled and seemed to expand.

Hymie fell back from the French doors as the floor and even the walls lurched, and more plaster fell around them. The black credenza by the doorway crashed over on its front.

"Van Fleet!" Hymie pushed them toward the hall where there was no longer a door. Lynnette had never seen Hymie look panicked before. His eyes bulged and he was drooling.

The house quivered as a high-pitched keening, ugly yet plaintive, grew in the room.

I'm dreaming this. It's just because I'm sick. Oh God, I'm sick.

Jay leaped over the thing in the overcoat as the keening followed them into the hall. Lynnette gagged onto the lavender bodice as he stumbled with her toward the stairs.

The keening reverberated about them on the staircase. A fog of plaster dust lay heavy on the air, choking.

Mrs. Benninghoff fell on the stairs in front of them, Hymie pushed past them to pick her up and carry her across the black marble to the door.

The stairs swayed and, just as they reached the bottom, began to crumble beneath them. Jay fell.

Lynnette felt the jar of the fall as she hit the grandfather clock and slithered over it to the marble tile, ending up on her back. The ceiling and walls heaved in and out with the noise that filled the house. The ornate hanging light quivered and dropped to hang, swinging, from its black wires above her.

39

L anguidly Lynnette watched Jay hoist himself over the edge of the hole in the buckling marble, his face gone ugly with terror.

The floor lurched beneath her as if in an earthquake. Was Jay remembering the earthquake when a church had fallen on him?

He was on his hands and knees crawling toward her when a slab of dark paneling exploded from the wall and crashed across his naked back.

Nella will keep him with her, one way or the other.

But he was still coming. The grandfather clock tipped into the hole behind him and disappeared.

Jay reached for her arm, pulled her over onto her stomach, tugged at her shoulders until she was crawling beside him, the fringe ripping under her knees, the ceiling and the horrible crescendo of sound falling around them.

Hymie reached through the doorway and pulled her out, tearing the filmy dress under her arms.

Lynnette caught a glimpse of tender green ivy being crushed between crumbling limestone and of the doorway warping like Nella's smile.

Hymie carried her and Jay staggered beside them; they raced toward Mrs. Benninghoff and the foundation hole of the gatehouse.

It was peacefully quiet outside, Lynnette realized, after the raging noise inside. The Van Fleet house even seemed to fall in upon itself with remarkably little sound, except for the squawking terror of doves lifting from the roof to circle in panic above them.

Limestone walls suddenly pushed out as if the house had exploded from within covering the drive and the broken black stalks of dead elm.

The roof came down with a sigh and a rush of air that blew dust at them even where they stood. The far jagged corner of the front wall remained . . . swayed . . . and then stayed.

And that was all that was left of the Van Fleet house.

"Oh, no . . ." the housekeeper said, the shape of her mouth forming the "o" long after the sound of it was gone.

There was an angry red mark across Jay's back where the paneling had hit him. He started off without them and then turned. "Come on, fast!"

"What's the rush now?" Hymie's voice ached with exhaustion.

"Didn't you see it? One of the doves that flew off from the house? It was white."

Now they were all hurriedly picking their way over debris and trees, Hymie handing Lynnette to Jay and then helping his mother clear the obstacle, then taking Lynnette back so Jay could climb over.

"Are you sure, Van Fleet?"

"I'm not taking any chances, are you?"

Over Hymie's shoulder Lynnette saw dust still rising from the heap of broken house . . . and heard the mournful cooing of homeless doves.

"I lost the shoes," she said. "And after all we went through to get them."

"I don't think you're going to feel like walking anyway. Do you?" Hymie said.

"No . . . I guess not." She lay her head against his shoulder and closed her eyes.

"We've got to get help for her soon, Mr. Van Fleet. We don't have much time."

"We'll never make it walking." Jay kept looking over his shoulder as if he expected Nella to follow them. "What about Jenson's tractor?"

"That might do it. Wouldn't have to stick to the roads."

But they came to Roger's tractor lying upside down amid a pile of chicken feathers in the ditch.

Then they heard the sound of a helicopter again.

"It's coming this way!" Jay said, and he and Mrs. Benninghoff scrambled up onto the road grade, waving their arms.

The helicopter swooped low and hovered over them,

its thrashing blades drowning out their cries for help. A man leaned out with a camera pressed to his face and snapped pictures of them. Then he smiled and waved. The helicopter lifted and flew off, blowing dust from the road into their eyes.

"I don't believe it." Plaster dust from the Van Fleet house streaked the housekeeper's hair and made her look old and gray.

"Just like Vietnam," Jay muttered, squinting after it.

Hymie handed Lynnette to Jay. "Jenson windbreak is gone, but the buildings look okay. He had three tractors. I'll go see—" He took off running.

"We'll get you there, Lynnette, don't worry." Mrs. Benninghoff squeezed her hand. "You're burning up, poor thing."

"But Bertha . . ." Lynnette looked across the fields to see the Olson house, upright anyway. But no barn.

Jay tightened his hold on her and walked to the Jenson lane to wait for Hymie.

"There she is, your mother! I'll go tell her you're . . . alive. And stay with her till we can get her out."

Bertha crept down the Olson lane, leaning on her cane as the housekeeper ran toward her.

Lynnette sat on Hymie's lap as he drove Roger's tractor into Roggins. Jay clung to a fender, his feet on the axle. They roared, dipped and rose over ditches, downed power poles and fences. The tractor stalled at least once that she could remember.

A Jewel Fire Department truck sat helplessly on the edge of Main Street, its tires flattened by nails.

Main Street was leveled and still smoking.

Ollie Torgeson stood looking up at her. "Bad? There's an emergency station set up in the grade school. They're flying doctors and water in by helicopter." He patted her leg. "You're going to be all right, honey." Ollie seemed to choke on his tongue. "Not too many houses but all of Main Street. Haven't taken a death count . . ."

Lynnette sat on the gym floor in the grade school . . . where she'd played basketball as a girl. Someone

263

put a styrofoam cup filled with coffee in her hand. Someone else put a thermometer in her mouth so she couldn't drink it.

"This one goes out with the first 'copter," a solemn voice said from somewhere above her.

40

L ynnette spent a month in Minturn General Hospital, much of it lying on her stomach with her feet pointing down like Roger Jenson's. Much of it she would never remember.

Jay and Hymie and Nella visited her. And later she couldn't sort out who had come in a dream and who when she was awake.

Jay and Hymie had looked stricken and she'd wondered why. But Nella had laughed and her cat-green eyes sparkled.

And then Nella Van Fleet curled up into lavender smoke that whirled about Lynnette until it coalesced into a whirling lavender funnel that screamed in her ears. The Van Fleet house quivered and buckled and fell to the ground again and again. Jay pulled himself up out of a black hole . . . his hair curling wet about his face. And she had loved him.

And Nella and Jay, arms outstretched, walked toward each other looking beautiful . . . and Lynnette hated him. But the house crashed down again and she screamed for Bertha. Strangers came to hold her down.

But Bertha came, too. "I warned you," Bertha said. "I told you to stay away from him, Missy. You didn't listen to me, and look where it got you."

". . . we must know," a strange voice said. "You are a witness."

"A witness to what?"

"If the Reverend Charles Birmingham . . ."

"His eyes looked like raisins . . ."

"But you saw him *before* the tornado . . ."

"No, afterward when I went for shoes, he fell out of the attic . . ."

"If the tornado destroyed the house . . ."

"Nella destroyed the house. . . ."

It was not until Lynnette could sit up, until she had been walked up and down the hall by a jolly nurse, until she could read a newspaper, that she knew Jay Van Fleet was under suspicion in the death of Reverend Charles Birmingham. Under suspicion only because he'd made a point of the fact he'd found the body in the Van Fleet house after a tornado had supposedly destroyed it.

And then others discovered the body, officially. One of them was killed in a "mishap" while chopping through what was left of the house. The coroner stated at the inquest that the body showed no signs of "foul play," that if it had been in the house, which was neither heated nor lived in during the last particularly severe winter, it could have dried in the sub-zero temperature instead of decaying as would ordinarily be expected. By spring the odor would be gone. The verdict was cardiac arrest. The newspaper implied that the authorities were not satisfied but had no evidence to hold Jay Clayborne Van Fleet. A bizarre account of the Van Fleet history and Jay's life followed.

And following that, a host of visitors for Lynnette.

First doctors, explaining how lucky she was to be alive. She endured.

Mrs. Benninghoff to report that she and Hymie were living with Lawyer Henson. He had needed a housekeeper for so long. Lynnette was glad for them.

Bertha to hold onto her and cry. "I thought you was dead, the hail came and I couldn't see you no more. And afterward I had to go looking for you . . . even if all I found was you dead. Do you know, Lynn, they had me up here twice while you was so sick? To help calm you down. . . . You was calling for *me* . . ."

Aunt Vera, looking older since her illness but able to laugh again, to tell her of the proposal to rebuild Main Street with the help of government funds. One side of it to be businesses and the other a row of town houses, the homeless and elderly getting first chance at the town houses.

Elaine to tell her that the funnel had lifted before it had taken Joey's house and that house had been saved from the fire. "But the Gunderson house went. Mary Jane told me that Jay Van Fleet has bought them a house in Minturn. It's nice of him . . . but why would he do that?"

Eight people had died, six in Roggins and two on farms, one of them Roger Jenson. Reverend Birmingham didn't count. The dead and injured were mostly elderly people who had no basements or couldn't reach them in time.

And then Hymie came to look at her and shake his head. "Thought you'd bought this one for sure."

"Where's Jay?"

"He was up here. . . . You told him you hated him and started screaming for Bertha."

"Why hasn't he been back since? I was too sick to know what I said."

"He's had a bad time, the earthquake, Nella, the tornado and then the inquest. He's about gone crazy with it all. . . ."

"Hymie?"

"He left town, Lynn, after the inquest. Said he'd been a haunted man even before he came."

"Left town? Didn't he leave a note for me or—"

"Said he was no good for you. He might have left the country by now. Lynn . . . maybe he's right. Maybe you'll find another Joey someday. . . ."

After that Lynnette didn't care who visited her.

When she was released from the hospital, she joined Bertha at Elaine's. Her hair was still uneven because patches of it had had to be shaved. There would be scars on her back . . . and in her mind.

The first day at Elaine's, she had her nephew drive her to the Olson farmhouse, where she gathered up a few of her things. The next day Harold and Margaret arrived for a visit and Lynnette walked into Elaine's kitchen wearing a backpack and hiking boots.

"Going into the library again, Lynn?" Her brother smiled affectionately. "Hope you'll let me give you a ride this time."

"No. I'm going to the bus depot in Minturn to catch a bus for Colorado."

Harold put the car keys back into his pocket. "I thought that tornado would have knocked some sense into your head."

"Lynn, can't you stay awhile, till we think of something?" Elaine pleaded.

"Sure she can. Because I'm not taking her anywhere and Dennis and Leroy have the car and the pickup. So—"

"So I'll walk. Walk me to the road, Ber—Mother?"

She and Bertha spent a long time looking at each other across Elaine's kitchen. Then Bertha sighed and reached for her cane.

"Mom, you shouldn't walk so much without the walker and . . ."

"Oh shut up, Harold." Bertha picked up her purse from the counter and started for the door.

"Lynn, I forbid this. How can you even think of leaving your mother at a time like this?"

"Shut up, Harold." Lynnette followed Bertha out of the house.

"Now, you let me know the minute you get there. Call collect. And don't get in any cars with strange men on the way to Minturn. And don't talk to any on the bus." Bertha walked slowly, leaning heavily on the cane, watching her feet move. "You sure you feel good enough to walk to Minturn? Maybe I can talk Harold into . . ."

"I don't really want to listen to Harold all the way to the bus depot."

When they reached the road, Bertha opened her purse. "You'll need money . . ."

"Hymie gave me some."

"Now you have more." Bertha stuffed a wad of bills into her hand.

"Will you at least look into the town houses in Roggins? Please?"

"Won't promise nothing, but I might look into them." A spasm crossed the big face.

"It isn't . . . that I don't love you . . ."

"I know, child, I know. You always was a wild little thing . . . never took to taming. I don't like it, but I understand it." Bertha reached into the front of her dress for her hanky. "You write to me every week hear?"

"Okay." Lynnette started down the road.

"Lynn?"

Lynnette stopped but didn't turn. "What?"

"You'll come back . . . just for a visit sometimes?"

"Of course I will. Just for a visit." She turned then and almost lost her resolve at the sight of the sagging figure. "And maybe you could come out on the bus sometime."

"Maybe . . . well . . . good-bye."

Lynnette walked on, gritting her teeth against the sob trying to fight its way up her throat. She turned again after a long stretch of road. The lonely figure was very small in the distance. But it still stood beside the road. . . .

And it waved a hand good-bye.

Epilogue

By the time Lynnette came to the crossroads at the corner of the Van Fleet estate, her tears had dried. On the outside at least. She stopped and adjusted the straps on her shoulders. She felt tired already.

Jay had run, but he would never really get away from the nightmare he'd known here. He'd carry his ghost with him wherever he went. And so would she. Whenever she closed her eyes, she'd see a solitary figure waving goodbye from the side of the road.

Lynnette crossed the highway and turned left to start the long trek to Minturn. A hint of still uncollected animal carcass haunted the hot summer breeze that rumpled her hair.

She stopped again, this time to stare across the fields to the jagged corner of the Van Fleet house. Without the dead elms even the ruins looked like another place in another time.

Two lower window holes were left in the remaining corner, peering over debris-strewn lawns. They looked like gaping sockets in a backless skull, their dark stone outlining the misty humid-blue of sky pieces behind them.

"Well, Nella, it was a good fight," Lynnette whispered. "But it doesn't look like either of us won much, does it?"

Was this the end of Nella? Somehow, Lynnette couldn't believe it was.

She turned to face the road and stepped onto the new patch in the paving where repairs had tried to wipe out all trace of swirling destruction. She had a few traces to wipe out herself. And it was a long way to Minturn. She wondered if she could make it.

Tires screamed at the stop sign behind her. She could hear a car gun onto the highway.

Harold. Coming to talk sense into her. She shouldn't

have walked so slowly. But she was surprisingly weak still.

Lynnette clamped her teeth tightly as the car came up behind her, braked beside her. It wasn't Harold's Cadillac.

It was a strange car, and brand new. Nella's son slid across to roll down the window on the passenger's side and squint up at her, a tired little smile on his lips.

"I thought you had left," she said when she could find her voice and the air to speak.

"I did." Jay Van Fleet shrugged. "But . . . I didn't get very far."

"When did you get back?"

"Yesterday." He opened the door and stepped out of the car. "I tried to call you, but they said you wouldn't talk to me."

"Figures." She ran damp fingers through her ill-conceived hairdo. "No one told me you'd called."

"I've just been to your sister's place. They were all standing out by the road trying to get your mother to go into the house." He stuck his hands in his pockets and kicked a stone with the toe of his shoe.

They both watched it tumble into the ditch.

"Bertha said you were gone and never wanted to see me again. But your brother said you were hiking into Minturn to catch a bus."

"So?"

He looked down the road, and at the sky, and into the ditch. But he didn't look at Lynnette. "Was Bertha right?"

"What do you care? You tried to run out on me twice."

"Yeah." He finally met her eyes. "But I didn't make it."

Lynnette used her sleeve to wipe the sweat from her forehead.

"You look beat."

She straightened sore shoulders. "I'll make it."

"Lynn . . . get in the car. Please?"

"I've got a bus to catch." She turned and forced shaking legs to walk away from him.

The gravel on the roadside crunched under her hiking boots and then under his shoes as he came up behind her.

"Look, I've been in the hospital for a month, I'm too tired to argue, Jay. Just . . ." His hands stopped her as

271

they reached around to unfasten the waist cinch on her pack. "Jay . . ." The pack lifted from her shoulders and he turned her to face him.

That empty, haunted stare . . . *Has Nella left him anything for me? Has she?*

Jay opened his mouth to speak and then closed it as she swayed. He led her to the car, threw her pack into the back seat next to his suitcase and lifted her in, closing the door. She leaned against the headrest. It felt so good to be off her feet but . . .

Jay had slumped against the front of the car, looking toward what was left of the house, one hand rubbing the back of his neck. Lynnette sighed and closed her eyes. No, this wasn't the end of Nella Van Fleet.

"Where are we going?" she said through a haze of fatigue when he sat beside her.

"Well . . . I can tell you where we aren't going." The old flashy smile brightened the car. "We aren't going to the bus depot in Minturn." The smile faded as he reached for the ignition. "We both need a good rest. Let's head West. Take a vacation." The engine roared. "Then we can decide . . . where we're going. Okay?"

"Okay."

Neither of them looked back as the car moved forward.

Wind sighed around the battered corner of the Van Fleet house and moaned through the window holes. A white dove perched on the highest jagged limestone block, cooing softly to itself, red eyes watching the car on the highway.

The dove grew silent as the sound of the car's engine came across the fields. Even the wind hushed. The dove watched the car gain speed as it passed the entrance to the lane, watched it disappear finally at the hazy point where the road seemed to touch the sky.

The remaining blocks of the Van Fleet house crumbled, shattered, fell to join the rubble while the dove glided around and around to come to rest near a broken shaving mug on the edge of the ruin, to spread a wing and preen a tapered pearl-white feather . . . and to settle itself to wait. . . .

272